Imperfect Memories

Vivian James

Half Past Three
Publishing

Half Past Three Publishing

Book and Cover design by SB Designs
ISBN: 978-0-9948167-2-6

First Edition: July 2016

10 9 8 7 6 5 4 3 2 1

DEDICATION

This one's for you, Mom ~ never would have gotten hooked on romance if not for your reading stash!

ACKNOWLEDGMENTS

This story began as a short submission
to a steampunk anthology.
I knew two things after the first thousands words:
it wasn't steampunk, and it wasn't a short story.
Thanks, Patricia M. Bryce!

1 The Asylum

"PLEASE BE SEATED, Miss, er," Dr. Sheldon began, gesturing towards the utilitarian metal chair across from his desk. "I hope you've had a chance to read over those pamphlets I gave you. However, before we discuss treatment options, there is a small matter..." He sat down, laced his fingers together and rested them on his desk blotter. "Do you suppose there's any possibility that what happened to you was not an accident?"

His question was quite unexpected and for a brief moment I wasn't sure I'd heard correctly. I'd been found wandering in a daze in the streets of Dorset, Maine. They say I was black from head to toe, with red raw burns and cuts on my arms, blood on my face, my clothing in smouldering rags. I was barefoot, bare-headed, and unable to talk. I have no memory of that; my memory begins with

1

waking up on a bed in a room with bars on the window and a lock on the outside.

My wounds had been cleaned, my cuts stitched, and I was swathed in cotton gauze. Dr. Sheldon, the director of the Penobscot County Asylum for the Insane, was called when I could give no account of myself, neither name nor whence I came. He suggested I voluntarily admit myself as a patient under the state's care until such time as my memory returned. Having no other choice, I did, though with misgiving.

That had been three weeks ago, and while my physical injuries had mostly healed, my memory remained elusive. I had no inkling of what had befallen me.

"You believe someone deliberately tried to, to hurt me?" My gaze moved involuntarily to my forearms, which were still tender and pink with new skin and would be forever scarred. It was quite disconcerting to think someone had deliberately caused whatever unhappy accident had left me thus.

"No need to panic," he said, reading my emotion exactly. "But there have been some suspicious people asking after my amnesiac patient. All the measures designed to keep dangerous patients in will also keep you safe, but," he paused, "I should exercise caution if you venture out into the gardens again."

I glanced toward the window. It was mid March and the winter snow had yet to vanish entirely. The gardens were but slightly frosted hillocks surrounding a rough terrace that gave view of the river below. I found visiting the terrace an attractive alternative to my prison-like room or the cold common room where other inmates—pardon, patients—would ramble and shout as whim directed. I had no proper clothes for going outside this time of year—no proper clothes at all, in fact—but a blanket wrapped around me as I sat in a wheelchair allowed me a welcome bit of solitude that felt almost like freedom.

The measures he spoke of did not entirely reassure me. I had a room to myself, which I knew was a luxury, though it contained only a bed and a wash stand. The window bars would effectively keep someone out as in, but the door could not be locked from the inside and I wondered how difficult it would be to find the keys.

Unable to remember who I was had so far been a manageable, if troubling condition, exacerbated by the draughty, under-heated asylum and the poor food. But the idea that someone might actively wish me harm—and to have no idea who it might be! I swallowed the lump of fear in my throat. "Thank you for the warning," I managed to say calmly. "Though I trust you're wrong."

"I hope so. However, I think it would be best if we were to try more radical methods of stimulating your memory—the sooner you recover it, the better, don't you agree?"

Suspicion immediately replaced my fear. The pamphlets he had given me for these radical treatments he wanted to try were couched in terms like "the latest in scientific advancement" but they also claimed to cure a long list of mental illnesses, amnesia not among them. He had been urging me to submit to them for the past week or so, while I hoped my memories would return before I had to decide. The sudden appearance of "suspicious people" now seemed very fortuitous, for him, so anxious he was to try these new therapies.

"I realize the longer I stay, the greater burden I am on the asylum," I said meekly, "And if someone is trying to harm me, then staying here puts all the patients and staff in danger..."

"Oh well, I don't know that they're all that dangerous," he said, caution in his voice.

"Give me a few days to think about it," I said, though he'd given me more than that already. "It may be in everyone's best interest to have me sent elsewhere."

"I'm sure that won't be necessary, Miss, er, but please give me an answer by the end of the week."

His inability to decide how he should address me, after three weeks, was still amusing, but not enough to prolong this interview. I stood up, and he rose hastily to his feet. "Thank you, Dr. Sheldon. Good day."

I spent the next few days watching without expectation for these mysterious persons and to my surprise, the doctor was not lying. The rush of fear that followed on that realization rapidly transformed into curiosity as the two people I noted did not seem all that threatening. There was a woman, too beautiful, too well-dressed, too obviously furtive to go unnoticed, and a gentleman, also more handsome than a man ought to be, though he strode with determination as if he belonged, making him a slightly more difficult to detect.

There was little doubt it was me they were interested in, and it amused me how they would pretend to be visiting other patients whenever a nurse walked by. Nor, I must confess, was my curiosity the only instrument involved in overcoming my fear of these strangers. I did some skulking about of my own to view the treatment rooms where Dr. Sheldon was so eager to place me and what I saw made me far more fearful than a mere man and woman who seemed only interested in staring at me. I wondered if I were a person of note or fame, but dismissed it—surely if I were, someone would have come looking for me sooner.

I devised a plan to confront the woman and determine what they wanted of me—it could not be as bad as what Dr. Sheldon wanted! I inveigled a nurse to indulge my desire to sit outside. It seemed a relatively secluded spot for a confrontation, given the doors of the asylum would remain shut to retain what little heat it could manufacture. The nurse brought a wheeled chair, which I did not protest—without shoes or proper clothing, an actual walk around the gardens in this weather was not even a little desirable. A thin wool blanket was wrapped behind and over my feet and lap, while an equally thin shawl covered my shoulders and the nurse pushed me to edge of the terrace, near a flower bed where spring bulbs were just beginning to poke through the soil.

The exterior of the asylum presented as a grand old home. Madness, they said, was caused by the stress of modern living, therefore the cure was to live more simply in the country. The fact that very few inmates—I mean to say patients—ever left the asylum did not seem to alter anyone's belief that it was effective.

Beyond the narrow flower bed bordering the terrace was a brown lawn which gave way to a steep meadow leading down to the river. This was my fourth time outside, and I had the nurse bring me to the edge of the flowerbed since I'd discovered how difficult it was for me to wheel myself across the uneven stones.

The river was a muddy grey and majestic chunks of dirty ice flowed sluggishly by. I shivered, thinking again how odd it was that I knew what it was like to be warm, but I couldn't remember being warm. Behind me, I heard the door open and another wheelchair emerge. I turned to my right and saw one of the wealthier patients, relegated to the brisk air, but with a quilted bed jacket and warm blankets - her own, of course. She was muttering to herself as the nurse tucked her blankets in and promised to return shortly.

I forced the chair around just as the mysterious woman, accompanied by a tall, dark haired man I had not seen before, stepped into the garden. She stopped as she saw me looking at her, looked over her shoulder at the closed doors to the interior of the asylum, and then marched toward me, the tall man in tow on her arm. "Miss Bayfield, if you please," he said, his voice deep and annoyed, which for some reason brought a smile to my mouth. His hat was askew over unruly dark curls, he wore dark cinder-glasses, as if it were a bright sunny day, and his ascot was off-center. I had an irrational urge to straighten his ascot and hat.

"It's she," she said in a soft urgent voice, and knelt by my chair. "Hello," she said, this time addressing me, and adjusting her tone to match the gentle expression on her heart-shaped face. "Do you know who I am?"

"The woman who's been sneaking about spying on me," I said, trying to contain my amusement, but gratified by the tall man's stifled snicker. I studied her as I could without staring. Her beauty at this close of a view was not perfect, which for some reason was reassuring. "I have a better question: do you know who I am?"

"Of course!"

I waited a moment for her to elaborate, but when she didn't, I prompted: "Would you object very much to telling me?"

The tall man coughed out a laugh, before clearing his throat. If they intended me harm, they were awfully amiable about it. I decided impulsively to go with them, not tempted at all by the fact that they looked warm and well fed and unlikely to strap me to a medieval torture device rigged with electricity.

"Charlotte Backus," she said. "You are Charlotte Backus. I'm Elizabeth Bayfield, and tall, dark and surly here is Gideon Lyons."

The names meant nothing to me. Charlotte? I would have thought I'd be prettier, with a name like Charlotte. "And your other companion?"

Miss Bayfield's pretty face creased in confusion. "My other-?"

"This gentleman, Mr. Lyons, he is not the one who normally accompanies you to spy on me."

Again, Mr. Lyons snickered, glancing my way impersonally. The dark glass spectacles gave him a sinister look, the sort I imagined a dime novel villain might have. "Mr. Westham does like to boast about his skill in skullduggery," he said dryly.

"He's inside, looking for the key to your room," she said, softly.

"So you do mean me harm, as Dr. Sheldon suggested?"

Miss Bayfield rose swiftly to her full height. "He said that? In so many words?"

Mr. Lyons looked as affronted as she. "Of course we mean you no harm!"

"I'll explain later, Charlotte, but for now, just trust me. We're going to get you out of here." She glanced at the door. "Mr. Lyons, when I yell go, you must grab Charlotte's chair and go down to the river. That's straight down hill from here. You'll find a path that runs alongside the river. Turn right and wait for us at the bridge."

He sighed and adjusted his spectacles. "You know how dangerous that is, for both of us?"

"I'm not going to leave Charlotte in this awful place. You were the one who helped me convince Westham that we should not leave her here."

He sighed again. "No, I agree. I am only pointing out..."

I wasn't certain if they were kidnapping me or rescuing me. I certainly didn't feel either was warranted, although the idea of someone pushing me down that hill was mildly alarming, as was Mr. Lyons' mention of danger. Uncertain if I should be amused or concerned, I chose concern as they dragged my chair over to a break in the flower beds where in warmer days one might wander, I imagined, to the river bank. "I pray you mean me no harm."

"Please, Miss Backus—trust us," murmured the man from behind me. Trust was asking a bit much of me, but I decided to forgo crying out when I realized that I was feeling anticipation, excitement. If nothing else, I might get some proper clothes, a warm bed and please some food that had flavor!

Out of the corner of my eye, I saw Miss Bayfield kneel beside my fellow patient and murmur to her, before rising and heading towards the asylum. "Nurse!" she called, "I need a hot water bottle!" Her voice dropped to barely more than a whisper as she added, "Now! Go! and hurry!"

2 THE RESCUE

GIDEON LYONS DID not hesitate but pushed my chair with considerable force through the flower bed and across the grass until gravity asserted itself. We gained momentum, rolling ever faster down the hill toward the river. He was running now, and I grabbed frantically at the arms of the chair to keep from bouncing out. My shawl caught in the breeze, fluttering away and I dared not grab for it. "I pray you mean not to drown me!"

"That is most definitely not my desire," he called back, and my arms locked automatically fighting my body's inertia as he tried to slow the chair. The wheels hit some hump of dead grass and bounced to the right, so hard I nearly fell out. The blanket, finally free, slipped off my lap and caught in the wheels. I released my grasp on the chair's arms enough to try to reach for it—too late.

The chair jerked to a halt so abruptly, I made rapid acquaintance with the coarse stalks of last summer's grass. The chair bounced over me, and onward to the river as Mr. Lyons fell with a thud and rolled over me. He groaned and pushed himself to a sitting position, asking with a grunt, "Are you injured, Charlotte?"

I was still drawing air in panting gasps, but did not fail to notice the familiar address. I could at that moment neither speak nor move, and my vision was limited to the dry straw before me and the dark fabric of his trousers beside me.

"Charlotte?" His voice held an urgency I did not understand and I struggled to draw breath enough to speak.

"Just winded, Mr. Lyons." I could feel the sting of scrapes on my chin, my right elbow, and across my left forearm, which was still tender from the burns sustained in my accident. My ribs and knees would no doubt ache tomorrow, and the thin flannel of the hospital gown and dressing robe would not serve past this day, but I was otherwise unscathed. I righted myself to a seated position, noticing that Mr. Lyons had not risen to his feet. "I seem to be no worse for the tumble. What of you, sir?"

He reached up to adjust his spectacles and patted his head, not so much as looking my way. I wondered if it bothered him to see the scars on my face that would be with me forever, a reminder of the accident I couldn't remember—there was irony in that. "Only my pride, which at least serves to demonstrate I still have some," he said dryly, rising to his feet with surprising grace. He offered his hand to me, or in my general direction, and I accepted. He pulled me to a stand with ease. He ran his fingers through his already unruly hair with a sigh. "I apologize, I seem to have lost my hat."

His comment, so out of place in our situation and in light of my own state of undress, was almost laughable, and I couldn't refrain from smiling. I could not see his hat, nor my shawl. The blanket had gone to the river with the chair, leaving only scraps of frayed wool behind as mute evidence it had existed at all. I pulled my dressing gown close against the chill air, and hoped whatever came next would come quickly.

He mouth twisted. "I'm afraid I've become a bit turned around in our tumble, my dear Miss Backus—would you be so kind as to orient me?"

"Orient you...?" My brow furrowed, unable to see the reason for his request.

"Ah, yes." He slid his spectacles down his nose, allowing me to see his eyes—or where his eyes should have been. "Perhaps you see now the folly in having me run down what proved to be a rather steep hill with you."

I don't believe I actually flinched, but it was a shocking surprise. His face had the elegant symmetry of a Greek statue, sculpted cheekbones and a strong chin; his eyebrows were thick and dark but his eyelids were flat, fallen shut against the emptiness behind them. He had some small scars of his own, the most obvious across his nose, but I had not seen it because of his spectacles. He pushed the cinder glasses back into place. "Oh," I said. "I beg your pardon, sir, I didn't realize." I touched his arm lightly. "This way. Do you need any assistance?"

"I shouldn't object to being led. I do think it was a very poor plan that sent me with you. If we hadn't hit... whatever it was we hit, we might both have ended up in the river."

I glanced at the river as we both stumbled towards it. Large brown and grey chunks of ice were jammed on the river banks, creating an ominous tangle into which the wheel chair had vanished. If we hadn't broken our skulls on the ice, we would have surely died in the frigid water. "Poor planning? I'd say it was insane."

Silence before he uttered a short laugh. "I've always appreciated your sense of humor, dear Charlotte."

Again, the very informal address. I shivered again, but with my hand on his arm, I couldn't keep hugging myself for warmth. We came to a well-worn path along the riverside and I set us in the right direction. "May I ask why you and your friends felt the need to, er, rescue me?"

"I was told the asylum wouldn't release you without a ransom."

I blinked in surprise. "A ransom?"

"It seems the doctor in charge, recognizing your name, decided he would not release you without receiving a rather substantial amount of money, first."

Given the asylum's many deficiencies, I found it easy to believe Dr. Sheldon would ask more than my stay had cost. But did he ask because he thought I—or maybe we—could afford it, or because he thought I couldn't? A shiver chased down my spine that had little do with the cold hard ground and chill air.

Mr. Lyons could not know the reasoning behind the doctor's demand, but he could answer one question: "What is our relationship, Mr. Lyons?" His familiar use of my name suggested a very close one, indeed.

He sighed. "Complicated, my dear. Complicated."

It wasn't a useful reply, but before I could press him on it, the path abruptly angled upward towards the bridge. My paper slippers had shredded some time ago, but even had they not, I doubt they would have spared my feet as the path changed from flat packed dirt to rough gravel. Cold as my feet were, I felt every stone, and flinched almost every step.

The path grew steeper, my toes were numb and I stumbled just as a horse clattered onto the bridge with a carriage, obscuring the curse word that came easily and automatically to my lips. I fell back, unable to regain my footing with such cold feet, right into Mr. Lyons. His arm went around me to steady us both and the sudden warmth set me to shivering violently. "Good heavens, my dear, you're practically naked! Why did they allow you outside like this?"

"The resources of the asylum are few, and I am a charity case," I stammered through chattering teeth. I hadn't realized how extremely cold I was until I felt his warmth. "I-I had a shawl, but it was lost when we careened down the hillside. I, the, the bridge is ahead." I knew I should be mortified to be in public in this state, never mind in male company, but I had been three weeks at the asylum in nothing more, and now my modesty was lost to the cold.

"Yes, I heard the carriage," he said. "I'm sorry about your shawl; the others should be here soon. Would you have my jacket?"

"No, no, we need not both take a chill," I said reluctant for some reason to take his aid. I expected him to release his hold on me. Had I been properly attired and married to this man, such an embrace would be frowned upon; in my current state it was indecent. Instead, he pulled me aside only long enough to unbutton his coat and tried to stuff me inside like a stray kitten.

"This should keep you warm enough, but when the steam car arrives you will take my coat for propriety."

His casual familiarity left me quite speechless. He'd said our relationship was complicated, but this—! Even were we married such familiarity would only be suitable in the privacy of our bedchamber. I opened my mouth to protest, but he was so very warm and we were not, strictly speaking, in public view. Still, I had to ask however hesitantly, "W-wha-what manner of woman am I that this is acceptable?"

He snorted and replied very dryly, "A cold one, wearing far too little clothing for decency."

I could not argue, but I was at a loss as to where to put my arms. I had no room to hug myself, and hugging him was out of the question, though such a thought had my face warming a bit too much. Instead I pulled my forearms up tight against me and pressed my hands to opposite shoulders. I took a steadying breath and asked, "May I ask why it took so long to find me? I was not... missed?"

His grasp on me tightened briefly, and I held my breath, startled by my reaction. "You were missed, Charlotte," he said, his voice tight. "But we looked in hospitals and asked around all the private practices within a hundred miles. We didn't think to check the insane asylum."

That made perfectly reasonable sense. They would have no way of knowing that I'd forgotten everything. "And do you know what happened to me?"

He sighed again, his deep breath another vivid reminder of how inappropriately close we were. "It's a story that can wait until we're safe and comfortable. I'm sure the others would prefer to know exactly what you're told." His voice turned mocking, but I was unable to tell if it was directed at me.

"You are not my family." I was hoping to be correct, given my reaction to his proximity, so I made it a statement, not a question.

"No. You were an an only child, Miss Backus, and your parents are... dead. If you have any other relatives, I've never heard of them. I-I used to work for your father. You and I, we have lived under the same roof since you were fifteen."

I tried to imagine what circumstances would warrant such an arrangement. "You were... his apprentice?"

He exhaled sharply, and coughed and I wondered if he had stifled a laugh or if I'd inadvertently insulted him. "Something like. Your father died in the accident that took my eyes. You graciously allowed me to continue to live in the house, though Miss Elizabeth Bayfield insisted on moving in as well, to protect your virtue."

I frowned. If I had virtue to protect, then why was I tucked, half naked, against him? I pondered his words, considering what they answered, and the hundreds of other questions they inspired. "And Miss Bayfield is to me...?"

"You and she were close friends when I met you, I cannot say how the friendship began."

His clipped words led me to believe he had opinions on Miss Bayfield that were not altogether complimentary, but I was uncertain how to frame further questions on the matter.

Uncomfortable with every aspect of my situation, I was unsure what next to say or do. The chuffing of a steam engine, rapidly approaching the bridge, gave me something else to focus on. At the sound, Mr. Lyons nudged me out of the shelter of his arms and shrugged off his coat. "My dear, for your modesty."

I pulled it around me without protest. After the shelter of his embrace, the air felt even colder while his coat carried his warmth and a faint scent I already associated with him. It occurred to me that if I'd taken his offer of his coat at first, I might have avoided the indiscretion of being forced into such an intimate embrace.

His coat had taken the worst of his tumble, so he appeared, but for his missing hat and the sad state of his ascot, quite dapper. He reached up automatically as if to adjust the hat he'd lost, and motioned vaguely in my direction. "This way," I said softly, pushing through the branches until we met the steam car. The woman, Miss Bayfield, was driving. She remained behind the wheel as her companion—Mr. Westham, I presumed—came to assist us.

He was overtly handsome; there was no other way to describe him. His clothes were immaculate, his grooming impeccable. He had a moustache so perfect it might have been made of wax. Mr. Lyons' classic features seemed to fade next to Mr. Westham. He studied me, in the same way he'd studied my window, making no comment on my scratches, my attire, or my wearing of Mr. Lyons' coat, but noticing, "Your feet, my dear—you have no shoes! Come, we must get you home." He lifted me unceremoniously into the carriage's rear seat. "Come, Lyons, don't dilly-dally. Charlotte is freezing!"

Mr. Lyons exhibited astonishing facility getting into the car and settling beside me as Mr. Westham took his place beside Miss Bayfield. When the elegant vehicle jerked into motion, he said crossly, "Westham, what possessed you to suggest I run off with Miss Charlotte? The hill was considerably steeper than you led me to believe —I nearly put us both into the river! At least we would have frozen to death before we drowned."

"Nonsense!" the other man called cheerily. "Once hypothermia made you lose consciousness, you'd drown, then you'd freeze to death."

"I'm sorry I didn't realize your feet were unshod," Mr. Lyons said, speaking loudly to be heard over the engine.

I glanced down at my feet, well covered in dirt. They felt like two lumps of ice at the end of my legs, the mild throbbing of the toe I'd stubbed notwithstanding. "No matter." The rear seat was raised high enough that my knee might hit the head of the handsome gent who seemed so cheerfully callous. I wondered if he'd meant to be witty.

As if sensing my regard, he turned. "Lyons isn't exactly observant." He smiled, which did nothing to dissipate the unkindness of the comment, then added, "Don't worry, we'll be home soon, dear Charlotte."

I smiled tentatively in return, unaccountably nervous of yet another strange man making familiar use of my name, even if I wasn't quite used to it being mine, yet.

The car puffed along the gravel road quite speedily away from town, until we came to a narrow lane. The woman, Miss Bayfield, she slowed the conveyance before we turned down the smoothly graveled lane towards the river.

The lane gave way to a garage that hid what looked like a large garden before turning into a looping drive between the river and a modest two story red brick house. The house was trimmed in crisp white, giving it a formal look. A porch ran across the front and around one side, and a glass conservatory came into view as we rounded the drive. The drive curved down in front of the house around a covered well with a pump and I wondered just whose home I'd been taken to.

The handsome gentleman jumped out and rounded to assist me, saying, "Take care of the car, will you, Lyons? I must get Charlotte inside."

Instead of setting me on my feet, he carried me into the house, which under other circumstances I might have protested. I did wonder how Mr. Lyons would take care of the car, given his impairment. "Take her right upstairs," the woman said, "She needs a bath and clean clothes."

"I'm not an invalid," I remarked, annoyed at being treated so. I might well have not spoken for all the difference it made.

Mr. Westham deposited me at the top of the stairs and Miss Bayfield took charge of me, ushering me into a small room with a steaming tub. I needed no urging to get in, though my feet were so cold the water felt as if it were boiling. The hot water was exquisite and warmed a chill out of my bones that I'd had as long as I'd been at the asylum. I took my time washing off the dirt accumulated on my dramatic rescue and, upon spying a jar of English hair soap, I pulled the pins from my hair and washed it, too. Clean and warm, I left the bath before the water began to cool too much. The towels I dried myself with were so delightfully thick and absorbent.

Clean undergarments were laid out for me, including a corset. It was already laced with an open busk. I put it on cautiously. I found that even though it was somewhat loose, I didn't doubt it was mine. It surprised me not at all that I'd lost weight at the asylum. I thought that these people who claimed to be my friends could be the most wicked of criminals and I would happily cast my lot with them for these luxuries.

In the adjoining bedroom—my bedroom, I deduced though I recognized nothing—Miss Bayfield hurried me to the dressing table and began the tedious task of combing out my hair. "You shouldn't have washed it, there's not time to dry it; what will the men say."

"Mr. Lyons won't know if you don't tell him," I said slyly. "And I imagine that under the circumstances, Mr. Westham can forgive me." As she continued to fuss, pulling my hair into a loose braid that she then began to coil this way and that, I asked in exasperation, "Am I the sort of person who likes to be fussed over like this?"

She stopped immediately, putting one last pin in my hair. "No, of course not. But you were missing for weeks and I—. After seeing the conditions at the asylum, I suppose I feel somewhat guilty for not checking there. Though," she added, "we never dreamed there might be something wrong in your head. Uh...well, you're home now." Her smile in the mirror was strained.

I frowned, but hastily replaced it with a smile lest she think I agreed that they should have looked at the asylum sooner. I imagine it would not have occurred to me, either, if I was looking for someone with physical injuries.

At this moment, I would have much preferred to be left alone, to explore this room and try to discover more about who I was, and find out who these people were later, but they were here in what I gathered was my house, and I needed to sort that out first. "Who is this Mr. Westham," I asked hesitantly. "That he calls me so familiarly?"

She smiled tightly; I could see her face in the mirror, though she was looking at my hair and not meeting my eyes. She was all the beauty I was not, and even that unnatural smile looked lovely on her. "Maurice Westham. Isn't he just too handsome to be true? He is your fiance."

My fiance? That certainly explained his familiar behaviour, but I found myself gripping the chair arms in alarm. "We are to be married?" I was glad he was not in the room to hear the dismay in my voice.

"You haven't set a date, if you're worried you might have to wed before your memory returns," she said soothingly. "It must be quite frightening to realize you're engaged to marry a stranger. I assume Mr. Lyons introduced himself?" Her voice carried more than casual curiosity.

"Yes," I replied, her not so subtle change of subject working beautifully. Mr. Westham's familiarity made me feel uneasy, and thinking that we were to marry was as much alarming as puzzling, but Mr. Lyons... he intrigued me. However, I wasn't sure I wanted to—or even should—talk about that. "I'm sorry, Miss Bayfield, that I do not remember you or Mr. Lyons or my... fiance."

"What about this house? You grew up here." She gestured broadly.

I took another quick look around the room before shaking my head in the negative. It was strange to think of it as my house. It did have a certain feeling of comfort as I imagined a stranger's house would not, but it gave no feeling of recognition. "Even my name, it is like hearing the name of a stranger. The doctor said my memories should return on their own." I decided not to mention his more frightening suggestions.

She patted my shoulder, bringing my attention again to the disparity of beauty in our faces. My countenance looked somewhat ferocious beside hers, one broad scar running just ahead of my ear across the bottom of my cheek to nearly my chin, the second largest on the other side, bisecting my eyebrow, before cutting into my cheek and angling towards the bottom of my ear. There were a few smaller ones, that were expected to disappear when the healing was complete, but these two would be forever part of me, and very likely the first thing anyone would notice of me hereafter.

I rather liked them. The face I could picture without them was unremarkable, neither ugly nor pretty, lacking any memorable characteristic. I was certainly no prettier for the scars, but perhaps remarkable. Miss Bayfield in contrast was a portrait of feminine beauty. Her features were too delicate for me to count her the female counterpart to Mr. Westham's beauty, but the two of them would have made a more likely match, appearance-wise, than he and I. I wasn't sure why I thought that would matter.

I started to ask if Miss Bayfield knew the supposedly complicated relationship I had with Mr. Lyons, but she said, "If the doctor says your memories will return, then we mustn't worry, Charlotte. Come; let's meet your fiance properly, shall we?" I put the question out of my mind until later.

3 Home

BELOW IN THE parlor, both gentlemen had changed into less formal house wear. Mr. Lyons had donned a lovely brocade banyan—perhaps a little too informal—and his wrinkled shirt, unruly hair and dark cinder-glasses put me in mind of a rogue who'd slept late and had consumed too much alcohol to happily bear the light of day. His slouch and the cynical line of his mouth enhanced the impression.

Mr. Westham by comparison was so perfectly turned out, he appeared still too formal for this casual meeting in the parlor. His rich brown hair was carefully combed and his clothes permitted no wrinkle or speck of lint, from the crisp shirt and elegantly patterned waistcoat to his open jacket and sharply pressed trousers.

I was secretly impressed that a woman of such modest physical assets as my own had attracted a man of such broad shoulders and fine features. I was wearing a house dress that Miss Bayfield had laid out for me, and the dark blue on darker blue print was pretty enough, but far from the height of fashion represented by Mr. Westham. Again, we seemed oddly matched - would he not want a fashionable, pretty wife? Perhaps I was wealthy, or a sparkling conversationalist.

For now, I crossed the room to him and said, "Miss Bayfield tells me we are affianced, Mr. Westham. I hope you are not offended I do not remember."

He clasped my hands in his, stared deeply into my eyes, and said, "I cannot tell you how happy I was when Miss Bayfield found you were still alive, my dear, dear Charlotte." I blushed at the intensity of his words and pulled my hands free. He was immediately apologetic. "Forgive me, I forget that I am as a stranger to you."

I was embarrassed at the depth of his feeling for me, when I remembered nothing—felt nothing—regarding him. For some reason, in my initial assessment of him, it had never occurred to me that he might wish to marry me for reasons of affection. I twined my fingers nervously together and, unable to meet his eyes, I murmured, "I am as a stranger to myself."

"Please, my dear - shall we sit?" He gestured me to the settee where Miss Bayfield had already settled herself alertly.

Once seated, I found them all—aside from Mr. Lyons of course—looking at me most curiously. It was more than a little unnerving, and I clasped my hands around my knee, until I saw Miss Bayfield frown at me. I hastily replaced my hands in a more ladylike fold on my lap.

"The silence leads me to suspect we're not quite sure where to begin, Miss Backus," Mr. Lyons said, pushing himself from the chair and walking to the sideboard with consummate grace, as if he could see.

"Whiskey, while you're pouring, Mr. Lyons," said Mr. Westham, not taking his eyes off me.

"Your usual, Miss Backus?"

I gave him a startled look, saw the curve of his mouth even as Miss Bayfield assured me, "He's teasing you, Charlotte." She sent him a withering glance to which he was happily oblivious. "Though he is correct, it's difficult to know where to begin.You must have so many questions—perhaps you should simply ask us what you want you want to know."

I wanted to know everything about me! With so many questions, it was as difficult for me to know where to start as for them. I decided to begin with the obvious: "What happened?"

Mr. Lyons carried two drinks in crystal glasses to Mr. Westham's general direction and held out one, which Westham rose slightly to accept without comment. "Short answer," he said, settling himself into the wingback chair, "You were at the lab when a boiler exploded. Your body was never recovered, leaving us unable to know if you were dead or alive. If you want to know what caused the explosion, the insurance company is still investigating."

I frowned at him. "Lab? As in laboratory? What lab?"

"Your father's research lab," Mr. Westham interjected, garnering a look from Miss Bayfield and a snort of possible derision from Mr. Lyons.

"Mr. Lyons told me my parents are dead, that I have no family."

There was a brief pause, which Miss Bayfield filled. "Your mother passed when you were very young. You and I, we've been friends since we were but seven years of age, and she was already gone when I met you. Your father, Theodore Backus, was an engineer, first and foremost, but also an inventor and scientist. He... well, it's a strange coincidence now that I think of it, but he died in an accident very like the one that happened to you."

Dr. Sheldon's dire warning suddenly recalled itself to my mind. It did seem a strange coincidence that both father and daughter should experience similar accidents. Boilers did explode, from faulty valves, or weak rivets, or poorly welded seams (and how did I know that?) but surely a laboratory would have higher quality equipment?

Still, I could not believe that these three were behind any such thing. It would have been a very simple matter to send me into the river, had they wished me dead. Mr. Lyons could have simply let go the chair when it was far too late for me to have escaped. Well, had he been able to see where that moment would be. It would have been better to have Miss Bayfield take my chair in that case... I dragged my thoughts from contemplating ways in which they might have killed me. "When," I cleared my throat, "when was my father's accident?"

"Three years ago," Mr. Lyons said, his voice clipped.

"It was the sad occasion of your father's death that caused us to meet, Miss Charlotte."

I gave Mr. Westham a small smile. "Indeed. I should like to hear more of that."

His expression remained serious. "You were very fond of your father—"

"We were all fond of him," Mr. Lyons said, almost inaudibly. Then he added louder, "Your father was an admirable man."

"He was." Miss Bayfield agreed quietly.

"And I was sent by Mr. Edward Walton—your father's attorney—to see to his will and the finer legal points of his business. You were inconsolable, my dear, and with Mr. Lyons receiving treatment and therapy in New York, it was I who was responsible for keeping Backus Engineering steady, and bringing it back into production. However," he added in a gentler tone, "I came to appreciate your," he hesitated every so briefly, "unique qualities. I waited, of course, for your mourning to be over before asking if I might court you."

Mr. Lyons slouched lower, and Miss Bayfield studied her hands, neatly folded in her lap. Neither said anything, so I could not tell exactly what part of Mr. Westham's speech was affecting them, or if each might not be reacting to different parts. "And how long have we actually been engaged, then, Mr. Westham?"

"Just a few weeks over a year." He frowned briefly, looking away from me, then returned his gaze to me. "As a junior partner, I am required to do much of the footwork for the firm, so I was unable to court you as ardently as I might have liked. You took some convincing," he added with a sly grin. "However, one thing or another has always come up when we tried to set a date, otherwise we would be married already, and we would not be having this conversation."

I inclined my head slowly as understanding of his words came to me. Were we wed, I would have been safely and properly at home, rather than in any sort of laboratory. The idea did not seem as comforting as it should have and for a fleeting moment, a shadow of memory was nearly mine. Then it was gone, like smoke. "I expect I mourned for my father for longer than was merely social," I offered, a logical explanation to why I might not have wished to marry precipitously.

"Quite," he allowed with a polite inclination of his head.

I studied the two men, as they were opposite me and I could do so relatively discreetly. Mr. Lyons had told me he lived here, which explained his change of clothes, but what of Mr. Westham? I chose to frame my question in the general, hoping Mr. Lyons didn't assume I doubted him. "What is the nature of our living arrangements, might I ask?"

Mr. Lyons sat slightly straight and raised his half empty glass in my direction, repeating his earlier words with slight elaboration: "I have lived in the downstairs servants quarters since your father brought me here from Boston. After his untimely death, you were gracious enough to allow me to continue living here." He seemed about to say more, but his mouth tightened and he sipped again at his drink.

"It was then that I moved in, for propriety's sake," MIss Bayfield said, touching my arm lightly.

This much Mr. Lyons had already told me, and I wondered what he'd been about to add. There was much, I felt, that remained unsaid. I looked at Mr. Westham, who started in surprise. "Oh, yes. Well, after Miss Bayfield so fortunately discovered your whereabouts and we decided to bring you home with or without the asylum's permission, I did some research and discovered a paper that suggested amnesiacs more often recall their memories when surrounded by their, er, loved ones. So I asked permission of Miss Bayfield to take up the guest room." He smiled charmingly. "I'm afraid I can only remain a week before my duties again require me to locate to my far more accessible apartments in Bangor."

That his occupancy was temporary was a relief. As handsome and charming as he was, it was awkward to think of myself as affianced to him, and some distance between us as we—I, actually—became reacquainted with him would be a relief.

I nodded in acknowledgement of his words. Dorset was a small town that existed solely because of the lumber industry. Frustrating how I could remember so much as long as it was not directly associated with me. I guessed we would live in Bangor after we married, and I wondered what would become of the house. Those concerns were for a private conversation, in a few days, when I was more used to the idea. For now, I turned to Miss Bayfield and asked, "How exactly did you find me?"

She hesitated, then began slowly. "We didn't know what had happened, initially. I mean, the shop is close by—if not for the trees behind the house, you could see it. The telephone in the study rang, and I only answered it when you did not. I, we, didn't know at the time that you were there, you see."

I opened my mouth to ask why I was there, and closed it. If they hadn't known I was there in the first place, my reason would also be unknown. I gestured for her to continue.

"I was under the impression that Mr. Lyons was working that evening, so I didn't think to advise him of the telephone call, only ran up the stairs calling your name." She hesitated, sending a subtle glance in Mr. Lyons' direction that I couldn't interpret. He was still slouched, but he did not look relaxed. "I checked every room on both floors, then ran down to the cellar—you get some strange ideas sometimes and the dumbwaiter cable has been catching... regardless as I came down the stairs calling your name, Mr. Lyons emerged from his rooms wondering what I was fussing about. He went to the shop to see if there was anything he could do, while I looked for you in the barn. It wasn't until the fire was put out and shreds of your clothing were retrieved that we even suspected you'd been at the lab."

I understood "we" in that sense to mean she and Mr. Lyons.

"Once we understood that, we called around to Mr. Westham in the city to advise him that you were... well, we just didn't know. The fire fighters said a few people had been taken out with minor injuries—nothing worth even calling a physician for—but no one remembered seeing you."

"We checked every hospital and doctor's office from here to Bangor and halfway to Portland," Mr. Westham added. "We contacted the police in both cities..."

"As the days passed and turned into a week, we even checked the morgues," Miss Bayfield continued. "We had no choice but to start believing you were dead, else you would have made some effort to communicate with us. None of us wanted to be the first to suggest it... Mr. Lyon proposed filing a missing persons report...."

"That was my idea," Mr. Westham corrected, drawing a grunt

from Mr. Lyons, who otherwise added nothing to the tale.

Miss Bayfield gave Mr. Westham a look that said it was irrelevant whose idea it was and continued: "It was only a routine trip into town with Hannah—the cook—to buy some essentials for the pantry that I happened to see the poster." She frowned, making even that expression look pretty and delicate. "It was quite poorly drawn, and I couldn't be sure it was you, but the date you were found seemed to coincide with your disappearance and I simply had to check. Dr. Sheldon would not permit me to see you on a mere suspicion, so I enlisted Mr. Westham's help, he being a lawyer, you understand."

"And that was when Dr. Sheldon asked you for the," I looked to Mr. Lyons for confirmation, forgetful he could not see me. "Ransom, I believe Mr. Lyons put it?"

She snorted. "Ransom is a superb description. Yes. When Mr. Westham told us the amount the good doctor asked for—I rather think the good doctor wanted to keep you, Charlotte. It was simply unconscionable! Chagrined, we debated on what to do. Mr. Westham suggested we leave you there as the doctors would be best able to help you, but Mr. Lyons and I disagreed and we managed to convince him you would be better here at home. We started, erm, investigating the conditions of your situation... and Mr. Westham devised the plan to rescue you."

"Brilliant," muttered Mr. Lyons.

"It worked, did it not?" Mr. Westham returned with arrogance in his tone and sending an ineffective glare towards Mr. Lyons.

"Oh!" said Miss Bayfield abruptly. "I must get supper on the table, I'm sure you're hungry, Charlotte—would you care to help me? Mr. Lyons, will you be joining us for supper tonight?" Her tone made her question sound more like an order, and Mr. Lyons' mouth curved cynically.

"My pleasure," he said.

I could not imagine what I would say to the two gentlemen,

one of whom I was supposed to be engaged to, so I willingly followed Miss Bayfield to the kitchen. Of course, I didn't know what to say to her, either, so I just sorted through the food in the ice box and helped put together four plates of cold meat, cheese, bread, and pickles. It seemed a task I was familiar with, considering the ease I felt performing it. "I thought you said we have a cook?"

"She's part time. She makes sure we have food for supper and she does the dishes in the morning. So... what do you think of your fiance?" She sounded genuinely curious.

"He's very handsome," I replied neutrally. It felt so strange—these people behaved as if they knew me, yet I had only just met them, at least I only remembered just meeting them. I wanted to respond to them as if we were strangers, and they kept reacting to me as if we were intimates.

"He is that," she agreed with a short sigh and called the gentlemen to the table. The meal was awkward, as if I were a guest in a stranger's house, with no knowledge of my hosts even to make small talk. When the food was eaten and Mr. Lyons offered to clear the table—an operation I should have liked to witness under other circumstances—I made my excuses. "I should like to go to my room now, if you'll excuse me. I need some time to think on, on everything."

I must confess, I concerned myself more with the coal stove in my room, and the heavy cotton nightgown and thick wool blankets. Warm and well fed for the first time since I'd awoken without my memories, I slept the deep sleep of one who has gone too many nights cold and hungry.

4 Discovery

IN THE MORNING, I attended my toilette, relishing the comfort anew. The house had been modernized to include hot and cold running water, gas lighting, and coal stoves tucked into the fireplaces. I assumed that, had my father lived, he would have eventually installed steam radiators to replace the coal stoves—he did seem to love the luxuries afforded by technology... and money. Yet our cook was only part time.

My wardrobe was also not one of a wealthy woman, in spite of the house's luxurious appointments. The contents ran full spectrum from several plain, sturdy dresses such as a housemaid or laundress might wear to more pretty but subdued tea gowns and business like skirts and blouses, to two exquisitely beautiful ball gowns.

I could not imagine what my life was, that I would wear both the sturdy work dress and the elegant ball gown. I pulled out one of the tea gowns and found myself wishing for something a little more cheerful. I imagined the sombre colors were due to still feeling grief at my father's death. I felt some degree of guilt for not being able to remember, to feel it; to look at those clothes and wish for brighter colors.

I had progressed no further than donning my corset, still staring in confused wonder at the contents of my wardrobe, when Miss Bayfield knocked and called out. "Come in," I invited.

She smiled broadly to see me still in deshabille. "Well, some things haven't changed." Her hair was combed into a smooth chignon, glossy as polished mahogany. Mine, while also of a shade known as brown, looked dull and curled rebelliously. I sighed silently. While at the asylum, I had noted I was no particular beauty, but the direct comparison was disheartening. She looked at the dress I had finally chosen and said, "That one looks so lovely on you."

She helped me into it, then pulled the pins from my hair and restyled it, while I frowned into the mirror. "I really didn't think it was that bad." I did think it was that bad, but it irritated me to have her help.

"Mr. Westham will be at breakfast. You want to look your best for him, don't you?"

"I only met him yesterday," I said crossly, and knew immediately I was being unreasonable. I smiled to take the sting from my tone and tried again: "If he and I are to wed, shouldn't he be already aware of my inexpert hairstyling?"

"I know to hear him say he's courted you for a year and you've been engaged for another year after that seems a great deal of time, but you have not really been that much in each other's company," she said lightly. "Time enough for him to appreciate the real you after you're married."

There was an undercurrent to her words, as if she were being oblique about something and I ought to understand. Perhaps I was imagining things in the discomfort of the situation. Her use of the word married was giving me an entirely different anxiety, again of a nameless sort. I was glad I was not already married to Mr. Westham and in this state of amnesia. I could not imagine having the expectation of marital intimacy with someone who was a stranger to me.

Breakfast, I learned, was served promptly at six-thirty, six days a week, by a cheerful cook named Hannah. She also prepared delicious dinners for which the three of us would return to the house to enjoy, though I wasn't entirely sure where we returned from. Mr. Lyons from the shop, I guessed, thought it was still shut down. Before leaving for the day, Hannah would arrange simple-to-prepare ingredients in the ice box for us to make our own supper. We were left to our own devices on Sundays. This particular morning, breakfast consisted of sausages, eggs, fresh bread, oatmeal, and preserved peaches—sheer heaven after the thin gruel offered at the asylum.

Through the course of conversation, I discovered that Miss Bayfield ran a finishing school in Dorset, but had taken a leave of absence to be with me during my recovery. As a result several students came to the house to be tutored. This she apologized for, explaining that she had done similar after my father's death, and that as much as she loved me, she needed to maintain both her reputation and her living. I was impressed that Dorset could support a finishing school, and I could see no inconvenience to me. "But of course I don't mind—I've no need of the parlor during the day."

Mr. Westham looked disapprovingly at me, then at her, but he said nothing against the idea, only expressed a hope that such an activity might not disturb him whilst he was at work across the hall in the study.

33

"My students are respectful and well-behaved young ladies and gentlemen," she said primly.

The study, Mr. Westham reminded me, had the luxury of a telephone. My father had needed such a device that he might be in constant contact with both the shop and his clients, but I suspected it was as much his personal indulgence as a necessity. Mr. Westham would be using the den and the telephone to manage both my affairs and his, so he assured me.

Mr. Lyons did not confess his plans for the day, instead eating his meal in the same quiet concentration he'd demonstrated the previous evening, responding to Mr. Westham's accusation of "not holding up your conversational obligation" with a derisive grunt.

"Have you decided what you shall do today, Charlotte?" Miss Bayfield asked.

"I want to explore my room. I believe—I hope!—that some personal item will trigger a return of my memory. If nothing else I might have a journal." I smiled and shrugged.

"I've never known you to keep a journal," she replied dubiously, "but..." she stole a glance at Mr. Westham, which he did not notice, and did not finish her thought. "I wish you luck with it! Shall I see everyone at dinner? Mr. Lyons?"

He said, "Hannah has a special menu planned for Miss Charlotte's safe return. I would not miss it."

The windows of my room provided a wonderful view of the back gardens, which this early in the year consisted of little more than the evergreen boxwood hedges, some brave green spikes that I guessed to be crocus or jonquil, and a tangle of thorns that promised roses in June. The hedges formed a maze on either side of a peculiar staircase leading to a small roofed pavilion. The staircase was perforated with an arched passageway granting access from one side to the other within the maze, without needing to circumnavigate the stairs. Beside the passageway, curving away from the staircase on either side, were walls, the tops of which curved as if an arc of a circle, bisected by the staircase at the low point in the middle, the sides arcing up to just below the pavilion.

The structure had a certain kind of familiar beauty that I just could not pin down. From my vantage point on the second floor, the pavilion was almost straight across the garden. I was startled to realize that someone was there, and let the curtain fall.

Frustrated, I turned to examine the portraits on the mantel over the converted fireplace. The first showed a man and woman, and the tinting told me her dress had been pink. She held flowers and I guessed this be a wedding portrait of my parents.

My father was a handsome man. If male beauty could be scaled, then I would put him between Mr. Lyons and Mr. Westham in appearance. My mother, on the other hand, was every inch as plain as I. If a handsome man like Father could marry a woman like Mother, then perhaps it was not so odd after all that Mr. Westham desired me for a wife.

The second was a family portrait, my parents and an awkward girl-child astride a toy horse—me, I presumed. The house in the background I didn't recognize. The third was my father and myself, at perhaps ten years of age, in front of this house. As I studied the portrait, I remembered how my mother had died—in the process of attempting to deliver me a sibling. I frowned, for though it was more progress than all the three weeks at the asylum, the memory carried no emotion; it was a fact recalled. I put the portrait back abruptly.

Miss Bayfield was correct about my lack of journal. I searched every conceivable place in the room and a few inconceivable ones, to no avail.

I cautiously explored the other rooms on this floor. My chamber on the back of the house had an adjoining dressing room with its own slipper-shaped bath. Across the hall at the front of the house was Miss Bayfield's room, a flushing water closet, and a bathroom with another lovely slipper tub and a coal stove to keep it warm. At the end of the hall was a discreet stairway originally meant for the servants. Mr. Lyons said he lived in the servants' quarters, and I knew Hannah the cook returned to her own home each afternoon. I would later learn that I also employed a housekeeper who came in twice a week to do the heaviest cleaning while I and my boarders saw to the day-to-day matters.

The main staircase bisected the upper floor and Mr. Westham was temporarily installed in the front guest room, which was beside a smaller room that might have originally been a nursery and now contained various small tables and stools, and a chest of old clothing, including a pink dress and the enormous bustle needed to shape it properly. My mother's wedding dress. I sat on the floor holding that dress for some time, feeling a sad sort of nostalgia that wasn't quite real emotion or memory, but a regret.

A fourth bedroom faced the back, as mine did, and contained nothing that meant anything to me. The bell rang for dinner just as I concluded that I should go to the lab, the scene of my accident, and see if that would restore my memories. The notion filled me with a peculiar sense of dread. I thought I should do so alone, but since I did not know where the lab was, I needed to ask help. The midday meal proved timely indeed.

I went downstairs, past the closed doors of the parlor and study and into the dining room. Miss Bayfield came in behind me as Mr. Lyons came in from the kitchen. The table was already set and the smell of the food from the covered serving dishes was delicious. Mr. Westham soon arrived, a sheaf of papers in hand. He smiled at me and held my chair as I sat. "My dear Charlotte. Were your endeavors successful?"

"I remembered how my mother died," I said, and it was only the sudden silence that called belatedly to mind that such a blunt statement might not be appropriate at the table. I didn't apologize, however. It was my house, and if these three were the closest I had to family, then surely they should be used to my occasional bluntness. But I did clarify into the silence, "Not the actual event, but being told of it. You were right about the journal, Miss Bayfield, sadly. I should go to the lab this afternoon."

"Charlotte, you should not go near there!" Miss Bayfield declared. "It's dangerous, and dirty. I can't imagine seeing such a thing would help!"

Mr. Westham was equally appalled. "It was no fit place for a lady before it was partially destroyed, Charlotte, it's certainly no place you need to be now!"

Their vehemence was unexpected, and annoying. "I understand your concern," I said, even though I did not, "But I think it's necessary."

"I am too busy to accompany you, Charlotte and I forbid you go alone!"

I stared at Mr. Westham. He forbade me?

Mr. Lyons snickered and consternation crossed Westham's face. "I only mean that I would worry too much, Charlotte. Don't go, for my sake."

I continued to stare at him, not entirely convinced. Then I waved my hand as if dismissing the entire concept. "I will speak no more of it," I said and he nodded, as if I'd agreed to his demand.

Hannah, a woman who looked to be perhaps ten years older than me and Miss Bayfield, came into the room with her hands clasped. "Ma'am, sorry to intrude. I made your favorite dinner, in hopes it helps you remember. I, um..." she looked down as if at a loss for words.

"Thank you, Hannah," I said, touched by her generosity. "That's very thoughtful, thank you."

She smiled and bobbed slightly before returning to the kitchen. With the matter of my visit to the lab resolved to the satisfaction of my companions, I decided to see if Hannah's cooking would remind me of anything. There was tender chicken in a flavorful gravy, but it was the steamed winter vegetables that raised a ghost of memory, too elusive to grasp.

"Anything?" Miss Bayfield's voice startled me out of my frustration.

I shook my head. "No." It was pointless to report an almost memory. I helped clear the table, thanking Hannah again for the wonderful meal while noting that Mr. Lyons took the stairs down to his rooms. I started up those same stairs, heading for my room when an idea occurred to me.

Miss Bayfield claimed that Mr. Lyons and I at best tolerated each other, for the sake of the business, and his behavior towards me, after my initial rescue, had been distant to say the least. If he did not worry for me, then perhaps he would not care if I went to the lab. I reversed my course and went down the stairs, past the kitchen and raised my hand to Mr. Lyons' door. He could only say no, as the others had. I rapped my knuckles across the door.

"What," he growled, throwing open the door so suddenly, he must have been passing by it the moment I knocked.

His hair was more unruly than ever, his shirt a wrinkled contrast to the crisp brocade of his banyan. He was not wearing his cinder glasses and I drew in a breath of surprise to see his flat eyelids. His mouth twisted at my small gasp. "I, forgive me for disturbing you, Mr. Lyons..."

His expression grew less ferocious. "Miss Backus." He bowed, an exaggerated gesture and motioned me inside.

Mindful of the impropriety, I nevertheless replied, "Thank you," and stepped in, as if in response to his unspoken dare.

To his credit, he left the door open. He crossed his arms across his chest. "To what do I owe the pleasure of your notice?"

The sarcasm of his tone stung, as I knew of nothing I'd done to deserve it. "I had thought to ask a favor of you, but it seems I've already imposed too much. Good afternoon, Mr. Lyons," I said, taking a step towards the open door.

As if he could see, his arm flashed outwards to the jamb,

barring my way. "What manner of favor?"

Although he was no longer mocking me, I nearly refused him a response. But I was still certain that I must go to the lab so my voice was stiff with reluctance and wounded pride when I said, "I still wish to go to the lab."

His arm dropped and his brow creased. "So go. You need not ask my permission."

I raised my eyes heavenward, shaking my head. "I am not asking your permission, it's my lab isn't it? It's only..." I hesitated, irked to have to state the obvious. "I don't remember where it is."

His mouth twitched and he cleared his throat before saying, in a much kinder tone, "Of course, how foolish of me. Give me a moment, please."

"You need not come with me, just tell me the way."

He shrugged off the banyan and walked with measured steps to a chair where his jacket was draped. "Oh I think not, my dear. The last time you went to the lab alone—" he snapped his mouth shut abruptly and pulled his jacket on. He slid his hand along the tabletop to find his cinder glasses and put them on, then with facility found his hat and put it on at an angle to match his careless hair.

I didn't protest—I no longer liked the idea of going alone. "Perhaps on the way, you can tell me the cause of the enmity between us."

He gestured me ahead of him, grabbed a walking cane, and said as we exited the house, "I have a much better idea. I shall forget our enmity as you have, and we can remake our acquaintance as if for the first time."

5 Return to the Scene

ALTHOUGH WE COULD have gone up the drive and along the road, Mr. Lyons informed me, he led me through the gardens, behind the barn, to a well-worn path through the woodlot. "It's quicker this way," he said, beating the path before him with his walking stick. "I've never walked it with a companion on my arm," he explained, "so I may not be so nimble."

"I could follow behind."

"And how should we converse that way," he said, making it a statement.

I smiled and kept hold of the crook of his elbow. "Perhaps you could tell me about my father, and the work you and he did."

He hesitated a moment. "Do you know who Nikola Tesla is?"

I hesitated in my turn, surprised by my answer. "Yes, actually

I do. I seem to remember everything I knew before, unless it relates to me on a personal or emotional level."

He seemed to take that in before saying, "Your father was... well not a friend, but an acquaintance of his. Mr. Tesla is a fount of brilliant ideas, with not enough time—or money," he added as a quiet aside, as if sharing gossip, "to develop them all. He is normally very protective of his ideas, however, he seemed to take a liking to your father, and offered to share. Specifically his ideas relating to energy sources and transmission. Existing energy," he added for emphasis.

How intriguing! "But... we have been unable to puzzle out what Tesla conceived?"

"Not exactly. One of the reasons your father recruited me was that he thought I'd be able to help him reach Tesla's level of genius, our two heads might equal one Tesla," he said with a wry chuckle. "The problem is, I think we did figure it out, only... I hate to say it, but the concept is flawed." He slowed his steps and added, "We should be almost there."

"The idea... doesn't work?" I found that a little difficult to believe, but I was pleased to see the return of the kindly, talkative man I'd initially met.

Evidently, however, I'd expressed my disbelief prior to losing my memory because Mr. Lyons chuckled again and said, "You've already checked and double-checked our work. The problem, we believe, is either that the aether is composed of a substance that fails to transmit as Tesla said it would or it may not exist at all. The most logical conclusions of our years of experimentation is that, if the aether existed, then Tesla's concept would work magnificently. But it doesn't. Your father was trying to figure out a way to advise Tesla of our results without causing insult when the accident happened."

I repeated his words in my head—had he said I checked their work? I must surely have misheard. The door to the lab—this was surely not the main one—looked perfectly normal. And locked. "Do you have the key?"

He patted his pockets and sighed. "Check under the largest rock below the hinge. There should be a spare there. All three of us were wont to forget our keys. Sign of a brilliant mind, your father always said."

"So if you two were so busy trying to tease out the secrets of Tesla's concept, who did the actual work here?" There was a key under the rock. I unlocked the door and we stepped inside.

"That would be you, my dear."

I turned to stare at him, certain he was teasing, but there was no curve to his lips, as there had been when he'd ask after my usual drink. "Me?"

"Your father or I would assist, simply because we had more experience. I handled most of the practical matters of business while you were in Paris."

"But... I'm a woman!"

"Yes," he replied softly. "Yes, you are." In a different tone of voice he said, "The boiler in the lab is separate from the ones we use for, as you say, actual work, and on the opposite side of the building."

The building and the business within were both much larger than I expected from the way he and Mr. Westham had spoken of it.

"After... after your father's death, you reorganized the shop so that I might continue to work here. We employ over two dozen men just on the floor, so it wasn't as if you were doing everything single handed."

"That's strangely gratifying." There was no one present now. Until the insurance company had finished their investigations, Backus Engineering was shut down. "I wonder why Mr. Westham seems to think I'm a shrinking violet."

"Probably because you deliberately let him think so?" Mr.

Lyons' voice had taken on some of the sarcasm it had held in the parlor.

I ignored his comment, pausing by a large open doorway.

"That's the primary machine room," he said, noting my pause.

"How do you know?"

He smiled. "I know where every room is, by the number of steps. I don't even need to count them any longer, it's automatic."

I nodded, impressed, before realizing he couldn't see the nod of my head. "May we go in?"

"As you wish," he said, leading me through the broad opening.

The smells of this room were so familiar! If I tried I could pick out machine oil, and the rancid stench of the grease used to lubricate the larger machines. The recognition of these scents told me Mr. Lyons was not exaggerating or teasing about my role here. I dropped his arm to pick up a heavy mallet and hung it on the wall. It was for pounding out - or in - dents in sheet metal and I knew where it belonged! Yet I couldn't remember! "Damn," I swore softly, unthinking.

Mr. Lyons chuckled, and I blushed.

"I-my apologies, Mr. Lyons."

"Unnecessary, my dear. I am well used to your more colorful turns of phrase. I use plenty myself, here. What is the cause of your dismay?"

I explained my frustration, and he said sympathetically, "You mustn't force it, Charlotte. Maybe... maybe there are some things it's better to have forgotten."

"I haven't forgotten *some things*, Mr. Lyons," I said sharply. "I've forgotten everything that matters!"

He inclined his head, touching the brim of his hat in acknowledgement, then he asked: "Is there more in here you wish to see?"

I took his arm rather than reply, and he walked with practiced ease back through the door and into the hall. The crunch of glass beneath our feet announced our approach to the scene of the accident.

The glass was from a window in the lab door, which had been blown outward by the force of the explosion. I must have been outside the door at the time. I let go Mr. Lyons' arm and held my arms up to my face as if to ward off the debris, and decided that was how it was the scars on my face were to either side, and my forearms had been so burnt. The door itself bulged toward us, but had held. "It was here. I was standing right here," I said, my voice sounding staccato to my own ears. "I can't go in, I can't go in!"

"But why?" His voice was gentle and his hands fumbled to rest on my shoulders. "There's nothing in there...?"

His light touch calmed me a little, but I could feel the dread rising inside me just the same. He let go of me and walked towards the door, every crunch of glass under his shoes loud and grating. He grabbed the door and started to pull it open, screeching across the floor and panic leapt up inside me. "Gideon! No! Gideon!"

I think I blacked out for a moment, for I don't remember how he got to my side so quickly, arm around me, hurrying me away from the sight of that awful door as I sobbed uncontrollably.

6 COMPLICATIONS

BY THE TIME we reached the barn, I felt nearly my usual self, but Mr. Lyons sat me down on bale of hay and knelt before me, taking my hands in his. "What is it, Charlotte? What did you remember?"

"I don't know," I said. "I just don't remember." I pulled my hands free to hug myself, though my sense of distress was rapidly fading.

"Perhaps the others were right, you should not have gone there," he said darkly. "This is my fault."

"Your fault?" That was nearly as bad as Mr. Westham's attempt to forbid me from going in the first place! "I would have found out how to get there from the cook and gone alone, had you not been so kind. Then who would you blame? The cook for giving me directions? Am I a witless child to be absolved of all responsibility?"

He rose to his feet, a wry smile on his face. "Quite right," he said, holding out a hand to help me to my feet.

I considered asking him to keep our adventure between us, but I couldn't imagine he'd risk the censure of both Miss Bayfield and Mr. Westham, so I merely accepted his hand and then led the way to the house. He needed no guidance from my hand on this path.

Mr. Lyons joined us for supper that evening, and as predicted he said nothing of our visit to the lab. I, too, was quiet, allowing Miss Bayfield and Mr. Westham to regale us with tales of their day. I helped Miss Bayfield clear the table and we scraped the plates and left them neatly stacked for Hannah in the morning.

We joined the gentlemen in the parlor, where Mr. Lyons was already setting out crystal glasses. "Brandy? Sherry?"

"Whiskey," Mr. Westham replied, pushing an ottoman aside with his knee as he walked to the door to meet me.

As he took my hands, I said, "I would like some brandy, I think?"

"Me, too," chimed in Miss Bayfield.

Mr. Westham frowned but said nothing, leading me around the ottoman to sit beside him on the settee. "I realize I shall have to court you all over again," he said kindly, "though not for another whole year I trust!" He laughed jovially, as Miss Bayfield and I smiled. "I so long for our wedding day, dear Charlotte, but now see, I'm being too forward."

"Your brandy, Miss Elizabeth," Mr. Lyons said, and she rose to accept it from him, nearly tripping over the ottoman. Something was bothering me... was it that Maine was a dry state, but the sideboard was well-stocked with liquor?

"Charlotte," Mr. Westham said, trying to get my attention. "Charlotte?"

"Mr. Westham—oh!" My exclamation was for the sudden

shower of whiskey and brandy as Mr. Lyons tripped on the ottoman. That was it! The house was as ordered as the shop, for Mr. Lyons' sake; move one item of furniture and the room was suddenly unfamiliar and dangerous for him.

"Lyons, you clumsy fool! You've doused us quite thoroughly!"

"My, my apologies," Mr. Lyons muttered, his jaw clenched. He'd not fallen, nor dropped the glasses, but he now looked quite disoriented.

"It's quite all right, Mr. Westham," I said aiming for a conciliatory tone. "He had no way of knowing you'd moved the ottoman, or where."

"I? I didn't move it!"

I wiped the liquor from my face with my sleeve, wondering if he really did not remember. I'm sure at his own home, he never thought twice about moving furniture and would he really have planned to have himself splashed with liquor?

"I should have noticed," Miss Bayfield said. "I nearly tripped over the silly thing myself, and I can see!"

Mr. Lyons head angled down, his brows creased, but still not moving. I jumped to my feet and touched his elbow. He flinched away from my touch. "I think I should like to retire, Miss Backus," he said tersely.

"Of course, Mr. Lyons. It's been an eventful day. May I walk with you to the door?"

Miss Bayfield was on her feet. "Let me take those glasses, Mr. Lyons."

A stiff inclination of his head was his only acknowledgement.

"I'm sure Mr. Lyons is quite capable of finding the door, Charlotte, do sit down," Mr. Westham said, an edge on his voice, and Mr. Lyons shrugged off my hand as if in agreement.

"One eighty and straight," I whispered to Mr. Lyons as Miss Bayfield put the dirty glasses on the sideboard.

Watching him hesitate toward the door pained me. Such a

thing should not have happened, not under my roof. It, it was a breach of hospitality, or, or something. Once he touched the door frame, his confidence returned and he strode out of sight. Mr. Westham was looking quite unhappy, as I picked up my skirts with my thumb and forefinger, saying, "I too shall bid you goodnight, as my clothes are... in need of laundering."

Mr. Westham rose belatedly to his feet and bowed briefly. "Of course, my dear. Perhaps after breakfast tomorrow we can renew our courtship?"

I smiled tentatively, and Miss Bayfield came to my side. "We should both say our goodnights, Mr. Westham. Sleep well, and please turn off the gas before you go upstairs."

We climbed the stairs in silence and without asking, Miss Bayfield followed me into my room. "We have our laundry done in town," she said as I lit an oil lamp, "except for such unmentionables as we wash ourselves downstairs on the back porch."

I nodded, not overly worried about my dress. I pulled the curtain aside and looked out. It was not yet full dark and a bright half moon shone over the garden. "Is that Mr. Lyons, do you suppose? In the pavilion?"

Miss Elizabeth came over to look. "Lyons has always been partial to that folly of your father's. He's up there at least once a day, since I've lived here."

A knock on the open door startled me and I dropped the curtain. "Forgive the intrusion, ladies," Mr. Westham said from the hall. "I wished to apologize for disrupting our evening, however accidentally."

"Perhaps it's Mr. Lyons you should apologize to," Miss Elizabeth said dryly, and his gaze shifted momentarily to the window.

"Perhaps," he agreed stiffly, and inclined his head. "Sleep well, Miss Charlotte, Miss Bayfield."

After he left, I turned back toward the window and lifted the curtain again. "Father's folly," I murmured.

"Thing is going to fall down one of these days."

Something about the shape seemed so familiar. The gathering twilight obscured the garden, leaving only the curves silhouetted against a rapidly darkening sky and it was suddenly obvious. "It's a sundial! Oh my goodness, it's a giant sundial!" I let the curtain fall and grinned at Miss Bayfield. "My father built a giant sundial."

She smiled back at me. "You remember?"

I shook my head. "But I very much like what I'm learning about my father. I wish I—" could meet him, I'd been about to say. I felt a pang inside, like a distant echo of somewhat similar to what I'd felt at the lab with Mr. Lyons. My hand went to my heart, and I asked, "Was I... at the lab when my father...?"

"No," she replied, her head titled in puzzlement. "You were in Bangor, overseeing some final installation or something. I met you at the train station in Dorset... and..." She twisted her hands, clearly still affected by the event, and I felt guilty for remembering nothing.

I quickly changed the subject. "Mr. Lyons mentioned that I was in Paris at some point?"

She looked up at me, frowning. "You and Mr. Lyons seemed to have had quite the extensive conversation whilst he was rescuing you."

Chagrined, I confessed. "I talked him into taking me to the lab this afternoon. He was telling me about my father and he said I'd been to Paris."

"The lab." She shook her head, frowning, but said only, "Your father determined you should be educated by the best minds in the field. There were closer schools, but none would accept a female student. I accompanied you, though of course, my studies were more to the arts, and literature." Her smile was somehow sad and wistful at the same time. "Those ball gowns in your wardrobe? You acquired those in Paris. Your father insisted."

I was getting a picture of my father that I very much liked.

***

At breakfast, Mr. Westham was all conciliatory smiles, perhaps because of Mr. Lyons' absence. He invited me to sit with him on the front porch. The front of the house faced the river, the same river that ran Dorset's lumber mill and flowed in front of the asylum. I imagined in the summer it was very beautiful, but for now it was chilly and I had a warm wool shawl wrapped securely around me. I appreciated he wanted to avoid the parlor so soon after last night's fiasco. I also appreciated that he brought out a small kerosene heater to warm our feet.

I tried to put Mr. Westham's less than favorable words and actions out of my head. If he had a personal quarrel with Mr. Lyons, it wasn't fair to judge Mr. Westham's entire character on that basis. "My dear, I've heard you've been spending your free time with those suffragettes," he said, his mouth forming a moue of distaste that his mustache struggled with. "Now, I know a woman of substance such as yourself must find ways to occupy her time, but wouldn't it be more suitable to your station if you were to give your time to supporting the arts or historical preservation?"

Suffragettes? I wondered in what capacity. "Mr. Westham —"

"Maurice."

"Maurice," I repeated reluctantly. "I only recall meeting you a short while ago, and before we speak of improving my behavior, might I ask you an indulgence of you?"

"Anything, my dear," he said with a smile.

"Would you mind terribly to call me to mind all the things we have in common that led us to agree to marry?" I needed a concise summary, if I had a hope of feeling comfortable with this engagement and by extension the marriage to follow.

His smile faltered, faded, and reasserted itself. "But of course."

He proceeded to tell me in detail of how we met and how brave he'd thought I was for going to work at the office after my father's death—something different from what Mr. Lyons had told me. That discrepancy troubled me, and reminded me that Mr. Lyons had accused me of deliberately allowing Mr. Westham to believe I was more of a, a traditional sort of woman.

Apart from my personal strength and "bravery" I could not tell what else he saw, though clearly he considered my lack of beauty to be akin to a disability that my other fine qualities compensated for. Not that he said so directly, but the words he chose and his grimaces left me little doubt. He again glossed over our courtship, dismissing an entire year with just a few sentences about my initial reluctance and how his charm inevitably won me over. I'd have thought in almost a year of being engaged, we might have had at least one outing worth mentioning. A theater performance, a concert, something special for my birthday, whenever that might be.

"When we are married, you'll be able to lay down the burden you've carried for so long, leaving your father's business in the hands of those more capable. I haven't been the most social of men," he admitted, "But of course as I gain seniority within the firm, that will change." He stopped, studying my face, a furrow between his brows. "Well, we'll worry about that later."

Tension was settling in my jaw at the implications of his words. He seemed to have no substantial reason for marrying me, nor could I yet see anything attractive in him past his handsome face. But I kept my misgivings to myself and followed his change of subject from the past to the future. "What of the house, Mr. West-Maurice? I assume we'll be living in Bangor after we're married?"

"My dear Charlotte, I could never part you from your family

home. Of course we'll keep it as a second residence, a country retreat. As I gain more seniority in the firm, I will be able to take more time off, and we can one day spend entire summers here."

His smile and tone were bright, but something didn't feel right. I knew I was frowning, but I could not help it. "And children, have we spoken of children?"

His brow furrowed and he frowned at me in return. "Children are often a consequence of marriage, I trust I need not explain where they come from?"

I blushed and looked away. All our interactions, the ones I remembered from my awakening, involved nothing more intimate than a kiss on my hand upon parting. I suddenly wondered if we'd had passionate moments, a heated exchange of kisses, a fumbling of clothing and reminded ourselves to wait for that happy wedded day. Perhaps our original connection was based more on passion than affection?

I lowered my lashes and studied him in silence, a silence he seemed to welcome as well. He was so very carefully groomed, it was difficult to imagine him with a hair out of place or a wrinkle in his clothing, such as might happen during passionate kissing. Indeed, I could scarce imagine him simply waking up from a night's sleep with less than perfect hair. My observations struck me as humorous and in my anxiety, I nearly laughed aloud. I ducked my head demurely, choked on my laughter and cleared my throat. No, passion seemed even less likely than honest affection.

As the silence threatened to turn awkward, he began to talk about local politics, and I was pleased to discover I could carry on a discussion in this area, until he again raised the subject of women's suffrage. I found I had very strong feelings about it, perhaps because of my involvement with Backus Engineering. If women were to work and pay taxes, then should we not have a say in our governance? But Mr. Westham clearly believed that governing was too complex for the female brain to fully grasp, therefore women could not make an informed vote. I did not argue with him, though I seemed to have many arguments to hand, and his earlier comment about how I ought to spend my free time began to have some context.

The conversation faded into several awkward silences and I began to believe we had absolutely nothing in common. I had a dim understanding of my personal wealth. The house was luxuriously appointed, but my wardrobe was modest, and I had only two part time servants. I did not know how profitable the company was, so perhaps I was an unassuming heiress, more interested in masculine pursuits? It was a great relief when Hannah rang the bell for dinner.

Mr. Lyons did not join us at the table, and I almost envied him the ability to absent himself from Mr. Westham's company, but when Mr. Westham announced he would spend the afternoon in the study, working, my smile was genuine. I was eager to explore my father's giant sundial. I found a short, heavy wool coat, and carried it down the servant's stair to the kitchen, that I might not disturb Miss Bayfield at her tutoring, or Mr. Westham at whatever tasks he was performing.

I was surprised to see Mr. Lyons, taking his now empty plate over to the sink where the cook was nearly done washing up. "Oh! I was just going out to admire my father's sundial."

Mr. Lyons turned toward the sound of my voice, smiling without any hint of animosity. "You discovered that, hmm? Be careful if you climb the stairs, it's been neglected since your father's death, and more than a few boards are loose. I'm afraid carpentry isn't one of my talents."

"Is it one of mine?"

"You mean to undertake repairs?"

I shrugged. "I love that my father built that thing, it would be a shame to let it fall to ruin. Besides, I could use a project to keep busy."

His smile turned to a grin. "I'd be willing to assist, if you like?"

I gave the proposition serious thought. "I would like," I said, most curious as to how he would help.

"I think we'll need a few things," Mr. Lyons said, and he ducked into the pantry.

I heard the creak of stairs and surmised he'd gone to the cellar. He returned with a hand saw, a hammer, a measure and some marking pencils, which he dumped on the table with a clatter, drawing a dismayed look from Hannah, though she held her tongue. "You have a coat?"

I nodded, remembered he could not see me, and said, "Yes."

"I believe there are nails in the barn," he said, ducking into the back hall for a well worn brown wool coat.

I smiled as we collected our toys to go out and play, for that was precisely how it felt.

The damage to the staircase gnomon was obvious on close view, but Mr. Lyons confidently led the way up the stairs, advising me to watch where he stepped. The stairs were weathered grey, with worn, sometimes crumbled edges. Some had split, but were otherwise strong enough, while others looked like they might give way at any second. It was a little unnerving to watch him step so surely. "This one," he said,demonstrating by pushing at the stair with his foot. "See? This is the worst."

The board was spongy, like wood should not be, and sagged in the center. "This is not a task we can complete in an afternoon," I remarked. He sat down on the third step up from this one and I examined it from a few stairs below. I needed to ascertain how they were constructed in order to figure out how to repair them.

"Until the insurance company clears us for business, we've not really anything else to do," he said, sounding rather cheerful.

That was true. I wasn't sure what else I could actively do to encourage the return of my memory, until Mr. Westham should leave the grounds. For some reason I hesitated to search the study while he was nearby. It was my study, and at least some of the business he claimed to attend within was also mine, yet for some reason I did not want him to know I was in there. I poked the soft board with the hammer. "I think we need a pry bar."

That afternoon, we pried and measured and cut some half dozen treads, quite inexpertly, and with lots of walking back and forth from the gnomon to the barn. Carpentry, it seemed, was not one of my talents, either. We had replaced several boards and were in the barn to cut more, in the correct length this time, when I noticed how long the shadows had become. "I think we should quit for the day, Mr. Lyons."

"I will not argue," he said. "I swear, we do not work this hard in the lab."

I smiled, certain he was exaggerating. My smile faded as I took in our appearance—our coats were flecked with hay, we had sawdust in our hair and my skirt and Mr. Lyons' trousers were covered in dust and dirt and slivers of wood. "I do believe, Mr. Lyons, that we did not dress appropriately for this."

He leaned back against a pole worn smooth by animals kept by the previous owners and laughed. "I believe you are correct, Miss Backus."

He offered his arm and I took it, walking back to the house in companionable silence.

The agreeableness of the afternoon vanished as Miss Bayfield was in the kitchen when we came in. She scolded us both quite thoroughly and sent me up to change as if I were a child. "What would Mr. Westham say!"

I was fairly certain what Mr. Westham would say, but wasn't so certain that I particularly cared.

7 THE GNOMON

I WAS PLEASANTLY surprised when the previous night Mr. Westham, instead of retiring to the parlor with us, made his excuses: "I must go into the city tonight, for a meeting first thing in the morning, my dear. I shall return for dinner!" He bade me farewell, kissed my hand, and departed in a smart two-wheeled cabriolet pulled by a sleek black horse.

I told Mr. Lyons I would be delayed helping with the gnomon repairs while I searched the study for something that might assist me in recovering my memories. The room contained a wall of built in bookshelves, with titles that were familiar to me and stories I knew, though I didn't remember reading them. In front of that was a large desk facing the window, the curtains drawn back to let in the light. A table held a lovely brass orrery, and a variety of charts were pinned to the pale gold wall paper. While the objects in the room helped fill in the personality of my father, I was disappointed that not even an elusive whisper of memory skittered in the shadows of my mind.

That is not to say I learned nothing of value. Mr. Westham had indeed been working on my behalf and diligently. The accounts were in good order and showed that I had a modest settlement from my father, and the business continued to earn profit. I was relieved to discover that Mr. Westham was not taking advantage of me, nor had he after my father's death. I was forced to conclude that he must genuinely care for me, in his own way. I must have returned it, to some degree, for surely I wouldn't marry a man solely because of his feelings without regard for mine?

I found a bound folder with what appeared to be a copy of father's will in a bottom drawer and set it on the desk. I would have read it immediately but I recalled my promise to Mr. Lyons and realized I had already tarried far longer than I'd planned. I didn't bother to hide that I'd been in there, but I took the folio to my room for later reading, changed into one of the sturdy work dresses in my wardrobe and hurried down the back stairs.

I guessed Mr. Lyons to be in the barn, but when I pushed through the door, the work area we'd set up yesterday was deserted. "Mr. Lyons?"

"Up here, Miss Backus."

I looked up. What was he doing in the hayloft? I astonished myself by climbing the ladder nailed to the wall without hesitation. At the top I looked around in surprise. The loft had been cleared of hay and now contained two workbenches that sparked a familiarity as my father's study had not. The back wall was lined with precision tools and on the free standing work bench was an array of small brass parts. "Have I been here before?"

"I don't believe so. Your father helped me set it up initially for my personal projects. I..." he gestured at the table. "I like to play with clockwork."

Before him was a collection of gears and sprockets, assembled into something about half the size of the palm of my hand. The brass pieces on the table had been hammered into short, thin strips. "What is it?"

"Nothing important," he said, shaking out a cloth cover. "I thought perhaps you'd regained your memories; it's nearly time for the mid-day meal."

I couldn't see the connection between those two thoughts, but I shook my head. "I am not excessively wealthy," I said, unable to hide my puzzlement.

He chuckled and strode to the ladder. "You aren't on the Vanderbilt's guest list, to be sure, but you must have gleaned that much before?" He gestured me to go down first, and I felt a sudden urge to jump from the loft, into the hay below. I shook my head and went down the ladder.

When he joined me, he picked up several boards that he'd cut while I'd been inside. "Grab the nails, would you? The hammer and pry bar are already at the gnomon."

We had started at the top, and were working our way down, prying up one step at a time so we still had some place to kneel or stand as we replaced. I stood on the bottom most of our newly installed treads and helped him find the right place to insert the pry bar to the step below. He was on the step below that, making us almost the same height. "What made you think you had more than moderate wealth?" he asked, leveraging the bar.

"Why am I engaged to Maurice Westham and not you?" I blurted without thinking, hitting upon one of the more pressing baffling things in my life, but my wording implied things I hadn't meant. "I mean," I added hastily, "If I should be engaged to anyone, it would make more sense that it should be you; you at least seem to know me better."

His silence was long, his brow creased as he concentrated on the board, tearing it out with a screech of nail. Given the enmity between us that I couldn't remember, he was probably appalled at the idea of marrying me. "I confess to a similar confusion," he finally said.

I opened my mouth and closed it. Confusion as to why I was engaged to Westham? Or not engaged to him? The ease I'd felt with him til now was filled with awkwardness and I said, "I just thought he wanted to marry to me because I had money. After all, I'm not pretty, especially with these scars and..." I stopped, wishing I'd never raised the subject.

"Scars?"

I appreciated his ignoring most of my embarrassing ramble. "From the accident."

He set the pry bar aside and tossed the broken stair over the side. "May I see?"

"P-pardon?"

He held up his hands, fingers splayed. "My eyes, now. How do you think I manage to work with gears and such?"

"Oh." Of course, I had noticed how he used his hands to measure in spans and found the right placement for the nails by feeling both boards, but I hadn't thought it fully through. He wanted to touch my face, to see my scars. The idea was a bit unsettling, but I saw no logical reason to deny him. "Um, yes?" I said hesitantly, guiding one of his hands to where the larger scar bisected my eyebrow, and closing my eyes.

It felt very strange, his fingers moving gently across my face, then his other hand began tracing across the other side of my face, my forehead, my eyebrows, lightly brushing across my closed lids, and finding the scars, one across my cheek, the other along the line of my jaw. "You were lucky," he said softly, tracing the largest scar up and across the eye that was mercifully spared.

I nodded ever so slightly, and this time I knew he could see it. His fingers brushed lightly past my ears, as if drawing the shape of my face, then the corners of my mouth. He gently brush my lower lip with his thumb and before I could react, his lips touched mine in a light kiss. My eyes flew open, and I would have returned it, when he drew away and let go my face.

"Forgive me, Charlotte," he said, his voice husky. "I forget myself."

I had no time to say anything before he was all but running down the stairs. "Wait..." I wasn't sure what I wanted to say or do, but as my weight shifted forward to follow, the board beneath my feet flipped, and sent me tumbling after him.

It seemed to last forever, every impact of my body against the stair seemed painfully distinct, yet it was also nearly instantaneous and I barely remember falling into Mr. Lyons, taking him with me to the bottom of the stairs. I truly believe had he not been there to slow my fall, I should have broken my neck. As it was, I lay at the bottom of the gnomon, half on Mr. Lyons's unmoving form, unable to move myself. "Mr. Lyons?"

He did not respond. I forced myself to breathe, then slowly moved each arm and leg. I felt quite bruised and battered, but nothing seemed to be broken. I pushed up with difficulty and looked at Mr. Lyons. His spectacles had partially slipped off and his breathing seemed shallow. "Mr. Lyons? Gideon?"

He groaned and then sucked in a great breath of air. Relief filled me and my head sagged as a tension I hadn't realized was within released. He shoved himself into a sitting position, rubbing his head and fumbling with the cinder glasses. "Charlotte? Are you all right? What happened?"

"I feel like I fell down a flight of stairs," I said, "But nothing's broken. I-the stair I was standing on gave way. Are you, did you break anything?"

He got stiffly to his feet. "It seems the only thing I broke was your fall." He held out a hand and I grasped it, needing his strength to stand up. He frowned. "I thought you were standing on the last board we repaired?"

"I was."

"But we nailed those down."

He was right. "I, I must have stepped down one."

He turned toward the gnomon, still frowning, as if he could see it. I must have taken a step before the board flipped on me, there was no other explanation, and right now I didn't much care. It felt like every part of my body had hit some part of those stairs on my rapid descent and I wanted to go inside and have a bath and feel a little sorry for myself and forget that kiss.

As if reading my mind, at least on the first part, he tucked my hand into his elbow and we hobbled across the garden to the back porch. "You're limping," I pointed out.

"So are you. We should call the doctor."

"I'm fine."

He smiled. "As am I, my stubborn Miss Backus."

I smiled in spite of my bruises, until we entered the kitchen. Hannah exclaimed over our appearance and vanished into the dining room. I sighed and sat heavily at the kitchen table as Mr. Westham and Miss Bayfield came in, wearing expressions of mixed relief and disapproval.

"What have you two been up to now," Miss Bayfield exclaimed.

"Miss Backus had a slight tumble on the gnomon stairs," Mr. Lyons said quietly

Mr. Westham's disapproval dissolved into horror. "Oh my dear Charlotte! What were you doing on that rickety thing! If it were up to me, I'd have torn that thing down!"

"My father built it," I said in soft voice, hoping he understood.

"Are you hurt? You could have been killed!"

I would have felt more confident in his concern had he reinforced his words with a gesture, something as simple as an arm around me, though I should have very much liked a hug. A gentle hug, I thought with an internal wince. Was his sense of propriety so strong he could not spare me the slightest of physical comfort?

Mr. Lyons disappeared after another thorough scold from Miss Bayfield, without ever revealing that he, too, had fallen part of the way down those stairs with me, and I was finally given leave to change for dinner. I schooled my face against the pain and walked without limping to the backstairs, the quickest way to my room. I stifled a gasp of pain and dragged myself up the stairs, changing out of the sturdy work gown with difficulty.

I found a handkerchief and blew my nose and wiped my eyes with my sleeve. Self-pity would have to wait. By the time I was ready for the dining room, Miss Bayfield and Mr. Westham looked put upon for having to wait for their food. "You need not have waited," I said quietly. "It was entirely my fault for falling down some stairs."

Miss Bayfield actually had the wherewithal to look hurt, while Mr. Westham immediately smoothed his features to a more sympathetic expression. "You really should tear it down, before someone else gets hurt. You could have been killed," he reiterated, and his distress appeared quite genuine.

"I rather like it, Mr, Westham. There can't be many sundials in all the world of this size. It is simply in need of repair."

"I suppose you're right." He smiled. "I am biased against it, for the harm it caused you. Are you certain you don't want me to fetch a doctor?"

"Quite." I tried a smile back and slowly ate. The meal did make me feel better and afterwards, Mr. Westham asked me if I was up to a walk in the gardens. I considered. "Yes, I think it would keep me from stiffening up, if we walk slowly." I would have begged off, but I needed to talk to him.

As we walked slowly through the gardens, I allowed myself to be distracted by the bright green spikes in the flower beds. It was most satisfying to see the signs of spring beginning to take over. I hesitated over what I was about to say, but without my memories to guide me, I had to be honest. "Mr... Maurice. I am wondering if... that is to say..."

"Just say what's on your mind, Charlotte," he said, his voice gently encouraging in a way that made me feel even more doubtful.

I took a deep breath and let go his arm, studying the boxwood before me with great intensity. "Very well, I hope you'll forgive my bluntness. It's only that... since I've been home, while I have not remembered anything of substance, I... feel things."

He gently pulled my far shoulder so that I was forced to face him, and I hid a wince. "Feel things?" His tone held a note of indulgence, that I could not help but read as condescending.

"Yes. For example, Miss Elizabeth claims a friendship since childhood, and I recall none of it, yet when we are together, I feel... a connection, a comfortableness that I ought not to feel with one of such short acquaintance." I struggled to put into words something I'd never experienced before.

"Some sense of the history you share?"

That wasn't quite what I meant, but it seemed close enough. I nodded. "And... I don't feel that with you. Is it..." I paused, taking a deep breath before plunging on, "Is it possible that I might have deceived you, with regards to my feelings for you?"

His mouth tightened in what might be anger—I did seem intent on reading every negative connotation out of his expressions—before resuming kindly gentleness once more. "I can't pretend we have a great and mutual passion," he said. "But we do have a mutual admiration and respect, and I do care for you, Charlotte."

I believed him. The concern he'd shown had been genuine and the lack of a hug had indeed cued me that this was not a love match. "So we agreed to marry on that basis?"

"You've never had suitors lining up for a chance at your hand, Charlotte. Most men are too, too shallow to see past your face. And now, with the scars...." He trailed off and spread his arms wide in a gesture that suggested everything was now evident.

That was a bit more honesty than I was quite prepared for. Mirrors at the asylum had informed me I had never been a beauty, but neither had I been the kind of homely that makes one look twice in disbelief. I was simply plain. I imagined that as a young girl if my interests were in physics and manual labor, he was very likely accurate about the number of suitors in the Backus parlor. Now my dull but inoffensive face had been scarred, pushing me all the way to ugly, at least in my fiance's opinion. I touched the scars with both hands, more than self-conscious of them for the first time since they'd begun to heal. "Perhaps in light of circumstances, we should reconsider the wisdom of our union."

He rolled his eyes and sighed. "Please, my dear, don't be ridiculous." His expression changed yet again and he asked, "What of Mr. Lyons? Do you have feelings about him?"

I was hoping he wouldn't notice that I'd not mentioned Mr. Lyons. "I must be honest, what I feel towards Mr. Lyons is... confusing. I do feel some connection with him." That so brief kiss was suddenly vivid in my memory. Given that I had met Mr. Lyons but a short time ago, I ought to have been shocked at the very least by the liberty he'd taken. Instead, my first instinct had been to kiss him back, and a surge of emotion had risen within me. I'd almost forgotten in the shock and pain of the fall immediately after, but now I felt guilty.

I could tell my answer wasn't what he expected. He drew back in affront, his eyebrows drawing together in a downward angry glare. "Gideon Lyons? You favor that surly cripple over me? That accident clearly affected more than your memory! Maybe you should go back to the asylum after all!" Before I could be more than stunned at his words, he dropped to one knee and held his hands up to me in an imploring gesture, "Charlotte forgive me! I was so upset by the idea of losing you... I've never liked Mr. Lyons, I can't deny that, but the asylum is the last place I want you to be! My darling, please forgive my harsh words!"

His abrupt change left me more in doubt, not less. "Of course," I said, offering the socially correct response with some effort.

He stood up, clasping my hands tightly in his. "You've known Miss Elizabeth since the two of you were but children, and Mr. Lyons since you were what? Sixteen? Of course you'd feel a deeper sense of connection with them, and drawn to Mr. Lyons as one who knew your father. You must know you never got along with him, so long as I've known you? And of course, you and I have only known each other three years, two if you count the fact that you grieved so for your father, you probably didn't even notice me! Give it some time, Charlotte. Don't ruin both our lives because of your *feelings*!"

His imploring speech should have warmed my heart, but all I heard was a rather contemptuous emphasis on feelings. Afraid that I was subconsciously judging him in the worst possible light, in order to justify what I felt, or thought I felt, I reluctantly agreed to give our relationship more time before coming to any conclusions.

8 News

I DID NOT go down to breakfast the next day, and when Miss Bayfield came to find out why, she seemed surprised to see the bruises on my arms. "I fell down the gnomon stairs," I reminded her.

"I didn't realize how serious it was. How did Mr. Lyons find you?"

"I ran into him on the way down. Like dominoes."

She started at me and sputtered a laugh. "I'm sorry, Charlotte, but that's... quite the image you created. Look," she said patting my arm gently, "I'll go get you a plate. I can see why you wouldn't want to face that table this morning."

I wasn't sure she did, but I was grateful. The tray she brought me held three sticky buns and two cups of tea. "The oatmeal congealed, but the buns are delicious," she said setting out napkins with great care. "When we were small, we always said we'd eat sticky buns for breakfast."

Wary at this change of demeanor, I asked, "You aren't going to go on about how I shouldn't have been on the sundial?"

She grinned. "Charlotte, I might as well try to stop the sun from rising and setting as to stop you from getting dirty. Even with the shop closed, I figured there was little chance you wouldn't find something dirty to play with. What were you doing up there?"

"Repairing it. Mr. Lyons was helping me. Neither of us, it seems, is that skilled at carpentry, as it was one of our replaced boards that sent me flying," I said, doubting my words as I said them. Mr. Lyons was correct, we had nailed all our replacements down, not without some colorful language, as he put it.

She sighed. "Lyons again."

I wasn't sure I wanted to talk about Gideon Lyons just yet. "Why am I engaged to Maurice Westham?" I broke a bun in half and nibbled delicately for perhaps two full seconds before taking a big, satisfying bite that left sugar on my face. Miss Bayfield smiled and took an even larger bite.

When we were both sugar-faced, she said, "You don't like him?"

I made a face at her and slurped my tea. "I'm trying." I toyed with the handle of my teacup, before I decided to be honest. "No, I don't like him. I know he's handsome and a good prospect and I should be flattered..."

She tipped her teacup back, wetting the sugar on her top lip so it looked a sad brown mustache, and I snickered.

"I'm not all that sure you should be flattered," she said.

"So if I wished to break my engagement...?"

My words wiped the smile from her face and she looked at me in deadly seriousness. "Charlotte, I can't deny the idea of you sundering your relationship with Mr. Westham is a pleasant one. You've surely noticed that he isn't the kindest of men."

"Was he always like that?"

"I imagine so, though with him staying here, we're certainly being treated to some of his worst. I may not care over-much for Mr. Lyons, but he doesn't deserve to be so cruelly treated."

"Then why have you been nagging after me to be more ladylike and mindful of what Mr. Westham thinks?"

She picked up her cup and swirled the contents. "I know you don't remember, but you made me promise to remind you to act proper for Mr. Westham. You emphasized how important this match was to you."

"But I didn't tell you why?"

"No. And believe me, it's been as baffling to me as it is now to you. But you are an intelligent woman and I trusted you to know what you were about." Her brows came together and her lower pouted a bit. "So I admit I feel a little worried, too. If you break this engagement, might you not afterwards remember why you wanted it so, and...." she shrugged helplessly.

I split the remaining bun and passed half to her, which she accepted without comment. I contemplated the sticky mess for a moment before trying to stuff it all in my mouth at once, causing Miss Elizabeth to giggle.

When I could talk again, I said, "Maurice has asked I give him more time to make his case, so perhaps in that time I can discover at least one very good reason to either marry him," I made a face, "or cease our association." And I thought of Mr. Lyons again and shifted uncomfortably.

***

While Mr. Westham worked his Monday afternoon away in the study, Miss Elizabeth and I occupied the parlor. She was in the window with a sketchpad and a box of charcoal stubs, while I tried to lose myself in a dime novel romance. I wasn't exactly avoiding Mr. Lyons. I just needed to let my bruises heal a little before facing the gnomon again, or so I told myself.

The knock at the door startled me, and I looked up to see Mr. Lyons holding a board. "Hello? Ladies? Anyone in here?"

"We're here, Mr. Lyons," Elizabeth said, "Miss Backus and I both."

He stepped into the room and paused.

"The furniture is where it ought to be," I said just loud enough to be heard, and Elizabeth nodded, perhaps in approval.

He still walked cautiously, towards the sound of my voice and knelt before my chair, holding up the board. "This is the board that caused your accident. I cannot find any nail holes in it. Did you perhaps place a board that we forgot to nail?"

I frowned, setting aside my book for the board. It was cut as badly as our work, but there was not a single nail hole in it. "We placed them one at a time, we even remarked on our inefficiency. Is it possible you placed it yesterday morning when I was in the study?"

He stood up and held out his hands for the board, which I carefully gave him. "No."

"That does seem unlikely, Charlotte. Mr. Lyons has shown himself to be extremely methodical. Perhaps someone else saw the work you'd done and decided to help?"

He seemed surprised at her support but reminded: "There aren't a lot of someone else's about, Miss Bayfield."

"There's Hannah's husband Carson, who keeps the grass cut, and,um, Mr. Westham," she said dubiously.

"I can't imagine Mr. Westham helping, he might... wrinkle something," I said, and covered my mouth with my hand. I hadn't meant that to sound so sarcastic.

A grin appeared and disappeared so swiftly on Mr. Lyons face, I wasn't entirely sure I'd seen it and Miss Elizabeth snickered.

Mr. Lyons asked when I might be ready to help him finish the gnomon. He behaved as if the kiss had never happened, so I pretended likewise. "I think after lunch I should like to try. I won't pretend I'm without nerves, but the sooner it's repaired the sooner we may use it to enjoy the gardens."

"I don't know the state of the gardens, Miss Charlotte, but your father wasn't a gardener nor did he think he should employ one, so he hired a landscaper to created the entire garden of plants and flowers that bloom each year without much in the way of maintenance."

"It's too early to tell yet," I said.

"It's overgrown," Miss Elizabeth said, "but in a very pleasant way. I personally was never fond of the precise, clipped English gardens my mother so adores." She put a finger to the side of her nose and gave me a look I failed to interpret, saying, "We should install a statue or two, don't you think, Charlotte?"

Mr. Westham appeared in the doorway before I could respond, bearing a grin that faltered somewhat upon seeing Mr. Lyons. "Charlotte! I have good news! The insurance company has completed their investigations—Backus Engineering is free to return to business!"

"Oh, that is good news," I said. "We must inform the employees. How soon can we be back in production?"

Mr. Westham's cheer faded a little more. "Well... you, that is, the company needs to replace the boiler, of course. I'm sure if you say something at the church next Sunday, the news will travel fast enough."

Church, of course. We had not attended yesterday, and that had gone unremarked in the household. That, at least, was one thing I did not feel guilty for. It would be my first social event since I'd awakened in the asylum. "You're right, of course, Mr. Westham."

"Maurice," he corrected with an encouraging smile.

I nodded forcing a returning smile. "Maurice." I turned to Mr. Lyons, remembering to address him as he couldn't see my movement. "Mr. Lyons, we make boilers, do we not?"

"We do."

"How swiftly might we have such a thing?"

He relaxed for the first time since Westham had spoken; a slight smile played across his face. "We should be able to put together a working boiler in three or four days, Miss Backus."

Maurice Westham had said he could only stay at the house a week, and now I was actively looking forward to the day he left. And I felt guilty about it, because he was, overall, kind to me. But unless my memory loss had turned me into a different person—and from my interactions with Miss Bayfield and Mr. Lyons, I didn't think it had—he didn't desire to marry me, but rather the woman he believed me to be.

I'd like to report that in the course of the following days, my memory returned in full and all mysteries were solved and that is the end of my story. But instead, I finished repairing the gnomon with Mr. Lyons, who then took me back to the shop. I asked to see the inventory he kept, and he produced it with a flourish, smirking. "Not the official inventory, of course," he said, "but very complete."

I sighed and passed the papers—embossed with countless raised dots—back to him. "Very amusing, Mr. Lyons."

"We have the sheet metal and all the necessary rivets, valves, pipes and connectors," he said, still smiling. "Given sufficient man power, we can have a new boiler in three days, but we will need to bring back some employees. It is an impossible job for just the two of us."

"What makes you think I want any part in building this thing."

"That is one thing about you I am very sure of, Charlotte," he said with a confident smile.

He was correct, of course.

I forced myself to return to the lab, but the broken glass and deformed door were gone, in fact the entire wall was gone and within was an open floor exposing pipes and ventilation ducts.

New pipes lay in the corner awaiting installation, and a stack of lumber was all ready to replace the floor. Outside, a wagon of new bricks was being unloaded. The new boiler would be installed before the wall was constructed. With no trace of the original lab left, I felt no hint of anxiety, only anticipation.

At home, Mr. Lyons kept to himself, leaving Mr. Westham free to court me without further displays of malice. Miss Bayfield's presence kept it from being too awkward a process, but often he was content to let she and I converse, while he indulged himself with my liquor.

I was having difficulty reconciling the fact that time spent with Gideon Lyons was, well, pleasant. Enjoyable, I might say. For hours we could work and talk, and I almost—almost—forgot about that kiss. I felt a connection to him and I confess I found him very agreeable to look at. Yet we supposedly had a long-standing enmity between us.

Time spent with Maurice Westham was, in spite of his handsome appearance and his unfailing kindness (to me, at least) was on the other hand awkward, if not outright dull. We had so little to discuss, so when he did talk it was of the changes he wished to make to the house and grounds, and he did not ask me what I thought or seek my consensus, he was merely informing me. He occasionally included some less than kind references to the departure of Mr. Lyons and Miss Bayfield. None of his plans really seemed to include me, except incidentally.

In fact, the more Maurice Westham courted me, the more certain I was that I would not be at all happy to be married to him. It did not even make sense from a business perspective, that is to say, as an economic or business related relationship, as far as I had been able to determine.

I must be missing something!

9 THE BOILER

MR. LYONS USED the telephone to call Strudwick's Mercantile in Dorset. This was an exceedingly swift way to spread the news that we were reopening and needed a few men in the morning. Perhaps my father's fondness for the latest gadgets was useful after all. Half a dozen or so men stood apart from the construction crews when we arrived at the shop Thursday morning.

As much as I wanted to watch them work, I had other tasks the seemed more pressing. I found myself in the main offices, a tidy little complex of rooms fronted by a reception desk. Behind was a large office that looked very official and clean, perhaps for meeting customers. Another room seemed devoted to accounting and employee records, and a third room was decorated with a long table, chairs, and a big chalk board—a planning room, I guessed.

Since we had asked for labor to get that boiler built and weren't officially open for business, there was no one else in this part of the building. I was in the large, formal office with an assortment of files, trying to get a sense of precisely where the business had been before we were shut down. And that's where I was when a man, dressed in a brown suit and matching derby hat, knocked on the open door. His waistcoat was black and white check, and the chain of his pocket watch was large enough to stand out on such a field. His face was dominated by a pair of imposing sideburns.

"Miss Backus, congratulations on returning to business!"

"Thank you," I said in quiet reserve. "I must ask your pardon, sir, but... who are you?"

He stepped in through the door, pulling his hands from his pockets. "So it's true, you have lost your memory. John Macklemore."

He stared at my face, not offering me the courtesy of his hand. I did not know if that was his usual way or an oversight caused by the two dramatic scars on either side of my face. "And do you work for me, Mr. Macklemore?"

He managed to meet my eyes and laughed. "Ah no. I work on behalf of your employees."

"Ah! You're from the union." I still had no idea why he was here but invited him to, "Please, have a seat and tell me what brings you by."

"Um, well..." He settled into the chair opposite the desk on which I was perched. "As you know, the union has several on-going issues with your floor..."

"Actually, no. I don't know that."

An expression resembling a smile flashed across his mouth, nearly hidden by his mustache. "Ah yes, well, we can talk about those another day, I suppose, but what brings me here today is the matter of worker safety."

"That is, I'm sure, a matter I take quite seriously."

He gave another quick smile. "Indeed. Two boiler explosions within a five year period doesn't sound all that safe to me. And I understand you are building the replacement boiler as we speak?"

"Two explosions that resulted in one death and two injuries," I said stiffly. "Rather impressive in terms of worker safety, I would say, certainly in comparison to other shops."

"It was only sheer luck that the explosions didn't kill or injure more people," he insisted. "I assume you are constructing this new boiler to more exacting standards?"

"I would hardly call the death of my father lucky."

He nodded his head, contrite. "I didn't mean to imply otherwise, Miss Backus. But the problem remains."

"We will, of course, have the insurance company thoroughly inspect and test it, but if you would like to supervise the construction process...?" Insurance for boilers was a special commodity, one that had proved its usefulness repeatedly. It could not be had without the issuing company making regular inspections of the boilers to ensure they were safely constructed and maintained. But if Mr. Macklemore thought he could tell the difference between a well constructed boiler and one made of rubber and tin, he was welcome to inspect the work.

He stared hard at me and I touched my scars self-consciously. Then he said, "Maybe I should take a look, talk to the men working on it."

I stood up and he jumped to his feet. "Allow me to show you where they're working."

"Oh, um, well... now?"

"Now is when they're building it, later will be too late," I said dryly.

"Of course," he said, a flush coming to his cheeks. "Lead the way."

On the floor, I found Gideon Lyons, his shirt sleeves rolled up to his elbows, his face flushed and a sheen of sweat on his brow. His cinder glasses were on a work bench, his waistcoat and jacket draped over the back of a chair. Strangely, in spite of his flat eyelids, he looked more ordinary without his spectacles. I thought his spectacles gave him a certain character, rather as I thought the same about my scars. And then I remembered that kiss and dropped my gaze to the floor.

I hastily placed Mr. Macklemore in his care, and gave an envious glance at the two men welding the large seam down the length of the boiler. The shooting star of sparks and distinct smell tickled something in my memory, fleeting and insubstantial. I was certain I knew how to do what they were doing.

* * *

When all was quiet but for the creak and rattle that was natural for the building, I walked down the darkened hall to the shop floor. Most of the lights had been turned out, but I could see the boiler had already been moved forward to the smaller of the two pressure testing rooms. This was accessed from the main shop by a pair of bay doors, closed now, with a normal human sized door that was open. If it was in there then the fire box and fire tubes had already been installed, and the first tests had either been performed or would be tomorrow. I crossed the floor, eager to see what had been done.

I pushed the switch to the light. We used our own generated electricity for most of the lighting here as gas was too volatile, but even still we did little work after dark. The click sounded loud in the room, and revealed Mr. Lyons crouched beside the cylinder, running his fingers over the newly welded rivets. He rose to his feet, bringing a spanner with him. "Who's there?"

"It's only me."

He relaxed visibly. "I should have known. Care to grab a

grease pencil? I know Jackson did a thorough visual check of the welds, but there are some that I don't like the feel of."

The cylinder was on its side on rails that raised it some three feet off the floor. It was long enough that it took up nearly the full width of the room, and the rails had actually had to be raised on this end to lift it over the work bench along the wall. It was now on the other side, where another set of large doors were closed. It would be rolled down, through those doors, onto a cart, then put into the new boiler room behind the reconstructed lab. Clay blocks kept it from rolling off the rails, though in the dim light I couldn't see them.

"Rather funny that the first thing we manufacture after re-opening is a boiler for ourselves." I said, following him as he pointed out one or two welds he considered less than perfect, and circling them with the grease pencil.

"Had it not come so close to killing you," he said gravely, his voice muffled as he ducked beneath the rails, "I would almost call it serendipitous since we needed a larger boiler anyway."

"Do you suppose the men will be offended when you ask them to redo these welds?" I asked innocently.

"I'm sure since everyone's safety is at stake they won't mind — oh. You want to redo them yourself to spare their feelings?"

I couldn't see his face, but I could hear the humor in his voice. I kept my voice mild and reasonable as I said, "In the interests of having happy employees, you understand."

"Perfectly. Lets check the other side," he said, and I eased between the wall and the end of the cylinder. It was a very tight fit. Normally smaller boilers were tested in this room, but this boiler was just too small to be safe in the larger testing room, so it was squeezed in here. Mr. Lyons sidled between the wall and cylinder, using his fingers to check the welds and rivets that were holding in the fire tubes, while I tried to decide if I should duck under the rail and collect dirt on my skirts or go closer to the large doors to step over the rails at their lowest point. I glanced at Mr. Lyons. He wouldn't see if I hiked up my skirts to step over the rails, but I still couldn't bring myself to do it. Stifling a sigh for the constraints of dress, I chose to cross the rails near the doors.

Shadows were deeper on this side, much of the light blocked by the boiler. Mr. Lyons, his back against the wall, his face a study in concentration, stretched to run his fingers over the seam across the top of the cylinder. I glanced at the doors. They opened onto the yard where the wagons would come to collect items for shipment. We didn't just build boilers, we also manufactured all manner of parts to repair steam engines as well as running the research lab where we tried to continually increase efficiency and output.

A groaning crunch had me turning curiously towards Mr. Lyons even as he called, "Charlotte?"

I had no time to answer—the blocks had given way and the cylinder was rolling at me in nightmarish speed. Unbelieving, I could only stare for too many seconds, realizing the doors were my only chance, if I could run fast enough. I hit the doors hard, but my panicked fingers couldn't work the bolt.

"Charlotte!"

I dropped to the floor, making myself as flat as possible and squeezed my eyes shut. My heart beat rapidly in terror as the cylinder thudded into the door, pressing down on me. It took a further minute for me to realize I was still alive. The curve of the boiler left me just enough space between doors and floors to keep breathing.

"Charlotte! Christ, Charlotte! Where are you? Charlotte?!"

I was aware of Mr. Lyons yelling, but I could not draw enough breath to call out. I sucked in air, trying to move, but I couldn't. "H-here," I managed to gasp out, not certain he would hear me.

I saw his legs as he squeezed himself into the small space between the boiler and the wall. "Here where?"

"Under the boiler."

"How can you be under the boiler and alive?" His voice held a mixture of relief and frustration.

"Geometry."

He growled a few very colorful words as he eased behind the boiler and knelt down, sticking an arm into the space created by a curved object resting on a right angle. I grabbed his hand with my one free arm, the other was trapped at my side. "Can you move?" Worry had replaced relief in his words.

"No, I'm... wedged tight. Can barely... breathe."

"What about your toes? You're just—nothing's crushed?"

I wiggled my toes and discovered with relief that not only did they all seem to work, I could actually move my legs a little, at least from the knees down. "Nothing's crushed." His hand let go of mine and vanished. "Gideon?" Panicked, I didn't notice my use of his name.

"It's all right. I need to figure out how to get you out of there. One of the rails cracked, so rolling the boiler back up is out of the question, even assuming I could do it by myself. There's not enough room for me to just pull you out." His voice had taken on a distance that I recognized, the vagueness of speech that comes when one is busy thinking. After a silence that seemed very long to me, he asked, "Do you think you could push with your feet, if you had something to push against?"

I flexed my ankles. "Maybe. I can bend my knees... perhaps an inch..."

"I'll be right back—don't move," he added sternly.

"Droll, Mr. Lyons."

While he was gone, I tried again to see if I had any wiggle room, but my shoulders and hips seemed very well compacted into the small space. With nothing to occupy my mind, it seemed a very long time before I heard scraping on the floor. "This is a series of blocks, since whole lengths of wood wouldn't fit. Let me know when you feel resistance."

Resistance, yes, think of it as a physics experiment. I let him keep going until my knees had no where else to go. "That's good, let me try."

I sucked in a breath, realized that full lungs take up more space than empty ones, and exhaled as deeply as possible, pushing as hard against the wood as I could. I moved perhaps an inch, a very painful inch as my right shoulder caught a rivet. I pushed again, teeth clenched and eyes squeezed shut. I relaxed, panting. "I moved...a little...give me a minute..."

"As much time as you need."

My knees slammed into the boiler as he pushed another block in. "Enough!" I repeated what I'd done before, only this time to no avail. Where, I asked myself, where is the resistance? I pushed again on the wood, trying to feel what precisely was stuck. I released the tension and tried to laugh while gasping for another breath. "This isn't going to work—my skirt is under the boiler."

There was a brief silence. "Well can't you wiggle out of it? This is hardly the time to worry about modesty!"

Wiggle out of it? Did he think I was so fat as to have no waist? "My waist is actually... smaller than my hips," I said dryly. "I have one arm trapped at my side," pause for breath, "but it's to the front of my hips, I can't...unfasten my skirt."

Another silence. "Let me get a rope."

"What for?"

But there was no answer and I couldn't even hit something in frustration. Then he was back and pushing a rope at my free arm. "Take this. I'm going to climb on top of the boiler and try to pull you, while you push. Maybe we can simply... rip your skirt off."

"Rip my skirt...?"

I heard his sigh and he replied with irritation, "Would you rather stay there until tomorrow?"

I didn't have to think about that one. "No. Tell me when to

push off."

He pulled until I thought my arm would come off, while I pushed with everything I could muster. The waistband of my skirt dug painfully into my stomach and side, but I kept pushing as he pulled until my legs gave out. I whimpered and the pressure on my arm ceased instantly. "Charlotte?"

My eyes filled with tears and I tried to choke down a sob. I could barely breath as it was, I didn't need to try it while sobbing.

"Charlotte?"

"I-I'm fine."

"Hmpf. Last idea. I don't like it because it's dangerous, for both of us, but it might be the only way to get you out of there."

Dangerous? "I'm wedged under a boiler."

"Ever the optimist. Listen to me, my dear. I can't move this damned thing by myself, but I might able to lift this end, for a few seconds or so. I'll pretty much have to hang myself to do it, and once its up, you must roll into the middle of the room as fast as you can, for I don't think I'll be able to hold it long. Do you think you can do that? Because if you're not fast enough... I might end up crushing you to death. And I should be very upset about that."

I would be rather upset as well. I didn't much care for the plan, but I was certainly motivated to roll quickly. "Be careful, Gideon."

I heard the scrape of the chain he used to harness the boiler tried to guess when I should be ready to roll. Finally the boiler budged, barely a foot, but I rolled hard into the middle of the room, just as the boiler clattered back to the floor. A chain clattered and Gideon Lyons fell to the floor beside me. "Charlotte?"

"I am uncrushed," I said, my breath still restricted by fear.

I was startled to be hauled into an embrace nearly as suffocating as being jammed beneath the boiler. Only, this was considerably more pleasant. "Charlotte, you scared the hell out of me," he said. I was trembling, more frightened of what didn't happen, as people are wont to be, but frightened all the same.

His hands stroking my hair, which had lost most of its pins some hours ago, were a sorely needed comfort. Then he was kissing my face, as if to reassure himself I was still alive, and when his kisses landed on my mouth, I kissed him back, to reassure myself I was still alive.

And as we sat on the filthy floor, both dirty from the day's events, those kisses evolved. Kisses of panicked desperation gave way to tender affection, and then became longer, more intense, and my lips parted under his. My heart began to beat faster again, for a different reason and he pulled his mouth from mine, with a sigh I couldn't interpret.

My cheeks burned with embarrassment. I may have known him for all the years he claimed, but I only remembered meeting him less than two weeks ago. What manner of woman was I? He stroked my cheek and smiled. "So. That is what a blush feels like."

"Tell me about this part of our relationship," I said, my voice little more than a whisper.

He chuckled without humor. "This," he paused, "is not part of our relationship."

I wasn't ready to believe I was the sort of woman who would do what we'd just done on such short acquaintance, but the relationship between us seemed complicated indeed. "Because, because of our enmity?"

"Our enmity," he repeated, his voice taking on a bitter tinge I hadn't heard since he'd decided to forget our enmity and start anew. "Also the small matter of you being engaged to another man."

"Oh. That." The heat in my cheeks had started to fade, but now returned.

"That."

I struggled to my feet, not waiting for him to rise first and assist me. I was engaged to marry another man, one whom I was supposedly trying to give the benefit of the doubt. I smoothed the front of my dress and touch the sad remains of my chignon. "I should go," I said quietly. "I bid you good night, Mr. Lyons."

"I suppose that's best," he said stiffly, and walked unhesitatingly toward the workbench.

I wondered how it was he hadn't lost his orientation whilst we... after he rescued me from beneath the boiler. "How did you know just which direction to walk, if I may ask?"

He picked up his spectacles and replaced them to his face and gave me a tired smile. "The direction of the floorboards." He bowed mockingly in my direction. "Until tomorrow, Miss Backus."

As I walked back to the house, deeply shaken by both the accident, and my subsequent indecent behavior. The accident was not an impossible thing, but something about it bothered me. It was the second to befall me in as many weeks, and seemed like an attempt at Divine punishment... for being such a shamelessly awful person.

I didn't know much about myself, but most of the time I seemed to be a very logical, rational woman. And yet I seemed to give a great deal of weight to my feelings. Maurice Westham, of all people, had suggested I not be too dependent on feelings, and that did little to reassure me.

As if thinking of him invoked his presence, he was waiting for me when I came inside the house. "Charlotte... oh my goodness, what happened to you?"

It took me a minute to realize I was filthy from rolling about the dirty floor, my blouse ripped at the shoulder. "Oh, just a little problem in the shop. Mr. Lyons was checking the welds on the boiler and asked my assistance as I was the only one still about. The blocks holding the boiler in place gave way and I had to...dive out of the way."

The expressions chasing across his face filled me with guilt:

shock, horror, disbelief. He clearly cared for me in his own way. "You could have been hurt!"

"No, no," I assured him, touching his arm lightly. As before, his expression of worry was unaccompanied by an embrace, which would have gone far in convincing me he cared about me in ways he found difficult to otherwise express. Mr. Lyons, on the other hand... but no, I mustn't think of his embrace, I dared not, not now. "Just give me a few moments to change, Maurice, then I'll join you in the parlor."

"You missed supper, I'll get Miss Bayfield to fetch you something."

And those words very tidily represented for me my misgivings regarding Maurice Westham. They were spoken with concern, but rather than get me something himself, he meant to have Miss Elizabeth do so, as if she were a servant. His natural underlying arrogance—something he might not even notice, himself—was one of the primary reasons his suit put me off. I could perhaps accept his cruelty to Mr. Lyons as personal dislike, and be dismayed at the level of unkindness but concede a generally kind demeanor, if only his arrogance were tempered with something resembling empathy.

I entered the parlor only moments before Miss Elizabeth came in with a tray. I gestured her to join us, unhappy to see her falling into the role Maurice Westham saw her in. She had, I noticed with a smile, included a glass of wine for herself.

"Two accidents since you've returned to us, Charlotte," she said without preamble, "I find that a little difficult to credit to coincidence." Maurice must have told her what happened.

"Don't be ridiculous, Miss Bayfield." Maurice was scornfully dismissive, helping himself to the whiskey at the sideboard. "Who would want to harm our Charlotte?"

"I have to agree with Maurice, Elizabeth. I'm..." I shrugged, my hands spread wide, thinking of reasons why one might be murdered and failing to find myself fulfilling any of them. "I'm not famous, nor possessed of fantastic wealth. I've nothing to inspire jealousy, nor any great secrets to topple nations...." I paused. "No secrets that I can recall," I added, an attempt at levity that failed utterly.

Maurice pulled the ottoman, the one he'd moved before, across the room to sit before me. "My dear," he said indulgently, "If you knew any great secret, so would Miss Bayfield know it, and myself, and who knows how many people you would have told?"

When I did nothing save look down to hide my irritation at his assumption of my inability to keep a secret, he added, "Isn't that right, Miss Bayfield? You are her dearest friend, she'd have told you."

"I suppose she would have," Elizabeth agreed.

Something in her voice made me look at her, but her attention was directed at Westham. Had I kept other secrets from her besides my reason for marrying Maurice? I cursed silently my lost memories. If only I could remember, things would be so much simpler! "I was speaking in jest. These accidents are just an unfortunate coincidence. Honestly, Elizabeth - the boiler is heavy. Faulty blocks are infrequent, but hardly unheard of." By making light of it, was that more deceit or justifiably saving them from worry when I was just fine? "I'm more worried about the boiler," I added, in for a pound.

The relief on Maurice's face again filled me with guilt, but Elizabeth still looked troubled. "If you say so. But it does seem strange."

Sharing his patronizing indulgence with Elizabeth, he said, "You read too many dime novels, Miss Bayfield. I ask again, who would benefit from harming Charlotte?"

It irked me to find myself in agreement with him, once more.

10 More Complications

I WAITED IN my room until I saw Mr. Lyons walking briskly through the back yard on his way to the shop. This made me late for breakfast, but since I had no desire to spend a great deal of time with Maurice Westham either, it worked to my advantage. "I don't think you should go today, Charlotte," Maurice said after I joined him and Elizabeth, who had already started clearing the table. "It's dangerous."

"Hardly dangerous," I demurred. "It isn't like I spend hours at a time in the shop."

"With those muscular men," Elizabeth said. "I should so like to paint them." Maurice sent her a glare and she gave him an innocent look in return. "In Paris all the models were so... clean. Do you remember, Charlotte?"

I struggled to hide a smile. "No."

"That is a shame. But look now, your fiance is as handsome as any of those boys, isn't he? Would you pose for me, Mr. Westham?"

"Wh-what? You mean like a portrait?"

Her brow creased. "Oh. Well I suppose. I was rather thinking something more... pastoral."

His face reddened and I coughed. "I should like to continue sorting through the piles of paperwork, Maurice, there's so much I've forgotten."

He sighed. "You'll be giving that all up when we get married. And didn't you hire some fellow to be your replacement nearly seven months ago?"

I put my bread down in annoyance. "I don't remember," I said, more acerbically than I intended. Since it turned out I wasn't a secretary, it seemed rather unlikely I'd hired someone to replace me. Had I outright lied to him? I already felt like I was deceiving him because I couldn't find it in me to return the affection he seemed to feel, but I had told him that. It didn't lessen my feelings of guilt because he chose not to believe me. I did not seem to be a woman of very strong moral or ethical fiber. At some point I was going to have reconcile myself with that.

"My apologies," he said, ignoring my tone. "Very well. I need to drop off some boxes there anyway, you can ride with me."

"Um. Thank you. That's very kind."

"I cannot extend my stay here much longer, so it will be nice to spend the extra time with you, my dear. Once I return to my apartment in Bangor, I'll come out to pay court on you as often as I can, but..." He picked up his napkin and patted his mouth, careful to ensure no crumbs lingered in his mustache. "I think you should start thinking about flowers and a dress and whatever other sorts of things women think about when they get married."

"That feels very hasty to me, you know I only remember

meeting you two weeks ago."

"I do understand, my dear, but two weeks to you, over two years for me. It's been well over a month since the accident and no sign of your memory returning. We can't all put our lives on hold, waiting for you, Charlotte! Now get your things while I collect the cabriolet."

My things included my hat, reticule, cape, and gloves. I was already dressed in a business smart blouse and skirt with a jacket that had unfashionably small sleeves. I imagined this was less a matter of fashion—I did seem to like clothes—than one of practicality. Practical seemed to be one of my predominant characteristics.

He pulled the horse up before the main entrance of Backus Engineering, which was further down the road from the house's lane, away from town. The entrance was well packed gravel, and the large bay doors were open today as a delivery wagon unloaded bales of sheet metal that we would cut and shape and hammer into whatever our customers needed.

From designing ground-up steam engine assemblies to improving existing waterworks or devising a way to tie the two together, we did that. We conducted our own research in our lab, testing new designs that would increase efficiency, production, and safety. I felt very proud, seeing the facade.

And because I was busy staring, I did not leap out of the cart as I might otherwise have done, so Maurice was able to hand me out, which no doubt made him feel better, though I was rather annoyed. He walked me to the door as two young men took hold of the boxes he directed and we all four went through the front door. "This is a very bustling place when at full production," Maurice said. "I'll see you for dinner, my dear." He doffed his hat with a short bow and left me to the office. I realized he expected me to unpack those boxes and file them correctly.

Seeing no one else about—everyone assured me that following

Sunday's announcement, I would have a full complement of employees—I began to do just that.

A knock on the door interrupted my concentration. It was a welcome distraction. "Pardon me, ma'am, I heard we were re-opening. Can I help you?"

"And who might you be?"

"Stockton, ma'am. Daniel Stockton. I, um, this is my office," he added apologetically. His hat in hand, his suit was not dissimilar to the one Macklemore had worn yesterday, though Mr. Stockton had chosen dark blue and grey, and his waistcoat was of a more restrained tan pin stripe.

I was inordinately happy to hear he claimed this nightmare of paper as his demesne. "I apologize, Mr. Stockton. You've heard that I've lost my memory? I am glad to see you."

His eyes took in my face, my scars, looked away as he came into the room. I would have to get used to that. I vacated his seat behind the desk.

"You really don't remember? Anything?" He hung up his hat and examined the files I'd removed from the boxes. "Glad to see these returned."

"Nothing of import," I said, shoving my fingers into my hair and loosing the style in the process. "I've been trying to re-acquaint myself with the operations, but there is just so much..."

He pulled out more files from the boxes, sorting them into piles by merely glancing at the labels. "Perhaps if you tell me what you'd like to know I can help you find the pertinent information easier."

I looked around the office. "John Macklemore was by yesterday."

Stockton made face. "Of course he'd hear of the re-opening before me. What did he want this time?"

"This time? Safety issues, he wanted to watch or oversee the construction of the new boiler."

"When will it be ready?"

"I think they're doing the pressure test today," I said, thinking of that small room. Trying not to think of that small room.

He nodded. "It'll be the insurance company who'll want to make the final testing and determine how safe it is, not Macklemore."

"What exactly is our relationship with the union? I went over a couple of employee files and we seem to be paying a fair wage."

"A little too fair. That's the biggest problem."

"I don't understand."

He sighed heavily and strode to one of the cabinets in the room, pulling out a thick file. "It's all in here, but the short version is, you and your father have always considered the bulk of your employees to be skilled labor, and pay them accordingly. The industry in general, however, sees it differently."

I was having trouble following the gist of what he was saying, simply because it didn't make sense. To see if I was understanding him correctly, "You're saying the union is upset with us for paying *too much-*?"

"Not the union, no, not per se. But as you know, unions are sometimes subject to... outside pressures. In this case, companies don't want to cut into their profits, so they're pressuring the union to pressure us to pay our employees no more than the average negotiated pay. John Macklemore is caught on the very horns of dilemma. He can't very well call himself a union rep and demand we cut wages."

I shook my head. "I almost feel sorry for him."

He grinned. "Don't worry, that feeling wears off after an hour or so in his presence."

I smiled back. "How do the men feel about this?"

"Pretty much as you'd expect." He shrugged. "Probably the reason the insurance company took so long to pay out was because of Macklemore's interference. We have our inspections every year, like clockwork. Of course, you being missing might have also had something to do with it."

He didn't ask, but I heard the question in his voice. "Without my memory, I had no idea who I was. It was three weeks before I was found and I still don't remember, but people seem to recognize me and call me Charlotte Backus." I smiled wryly. But thinking of those weeks, I was reminded - while my friends had not been willing to pay whatever sum Dr. Sheldon had asked for, I was in a position to pay for my care, such as it had been. "Whom would I ask about reimbursing the asylum for my care?"

"I can take care of that for you, ma'am. In what amount?"

"Enough to cover three weeks room and board. Make it payable to the asylum in Dorset, whatever their official name is. Oh, and I should like to deliver it personally." It was at least one ethical thing I could do. "What exactly do you do here, Mr. Stockton?"

"You hired me to be office manager, ma'am - I oversee all the paperwork, keep everything filed, and I also seek out the best prices and lowest bids for equipment and supplies."

"I thought Mr. Westham was doing that?"

He hesitated, shifting the files on the desk and adjusting the blotter. "Hmm, I don't think so. He had signing authority until six months ago, when you hired me, but his signature wasn't on a lot of the paper work. A Mr. Howard handled most things. He retired seven months ago." He smiled reassuringly. "I can get you my employee file if you'd like?"

"No need, Mr. Stockton. Mr. Westham only took a more active role, then, when I went missing?"

"He wanted to. We had a talk. He came around to the idea that I might know better than he how to keep the company profitable, though he insisted on taking these." He gestured toward the boxes.

"I did take a brief look at what he'd been doing. Everything seemed in order."

"Yes, for the most part."

"But?"

"Some of his purchases were less than satisfactory. They didn't hurt the company, but we could have realized a higher profit... whether it was ignorance or laziness or cronyism... er, sorry, Miss Backus."

I could visualize all three being a factor. I wondered if he had been trying to help, or trying to take over. He seemed to have some plans for the business, after we were married. The idea made me inexplicably uncomfortable. "What is my position, exactly?"

Stockton's cheeks turned a pale rose color as he said, "As owner, you, ah, take an interest in every part of the business."

"I interfere, then. In everything."

"Not at all, Miss Backus. You just take a very active role sometimes, to the shock, dismay and probable enjoyment of your employees. You seem to have become aware of, of your effect in the shop, and recently you've been limiting yourself to the research lab and, of course, the weekly production meetings. You also meet with customers, and, um..."

"Yes?"

"You, uh, like to oversee installations and uh, sometimes, trouble-shoot. On site."

I rolled my eyes at his description of my behavior, finding it all too easy to believe. "That must go over well." I liked learning about this aspect of me, though. At least it seemed honest and enthusiastic.

His cheeks had remained in high color throughout this conversation, though why he should be embarrassed on my behalf, I didn't know. Now he said, "A mixed reaction, from what I hear. Most customers want to be impressed by the personal service, while simultaneously being uncomfortable that you're... you're...."

"Yes, Mr. Stockton, my being a woman has not escaped my notice," I said dryly.

"No, ma'am."

I spent the morning reviewing the employees of Backus. I couldn't put faces to the names, even to the few whom I must have known almost half my life. Then a whistle blew, startling me out of my studies. "What's that...?"

"First break. We divide the men into two meal breaks, so anything that simply can't be left won't be, without depriving anyone of sustenance." Mr. Stockton said absently.

I looked at the time. Maurice was expecting me back at the house. "I think I'd best be along myself. I shan't return this afternoon, Mr. Stockton, so I thank you for your help and I will see you Monday?"

"Sunday, surely?"

I smiled. "Yes, of course. My memory loss must make me sound quite dizzy, sometimes."

He studied my face. "Somehow I don't think that will be what everyone's talking about."

That would have to be something else to get used to.

***

When I returned to the shop, I decided to check on the progress of the lab. I remembered the panic I'd felt when Mr. Lyons had accompanied me that first time, and wondered if it was born of the fear I must have felt when I realized the boiler was about to explode. I'd had enough warning to raise my hands to cover my face, perhaps a scream of escaping steam. I shook my head. Now, the floor was replaced and some of the metal structural elements were in place. Piles of brick had been moved inside for the interior walls. We had decided to put the lab's boiler against the outer walls and brick the interior walls that would separate it from the lab itself so a future explosion—God forbid!—would be more contained.

I stood in the door way for a long time, trying to remember.

Finally the foreman approached me. "Miss Backus, yes? Is there something I can help you with, some change to the plans you wanted to make before we proceed?"

I smiled. "No, I was just curious to see how the work was progressing, I didn't mean to get in the way."

He stared at my face a moment before smiling, and his smile was genuine, so I wondered just what he saw in my face, beyond my scars. "Oh, our customers get in the way all the time, far worse than just standing in a doorway. I would ask you to clear the area, though, we're-" He pointed upward and I realized the ceiling had been torn out as well and new ventilation shafts were being installed.

"Oh, of course. If you have any problems..."

11 First Presbyterian Church of Dorset

WE ARRIVED AT the church early, our steam car drawing fewer looks than I might have imagined. It clearly wasn't the first time it was parked amidst the various horse drawn conveyances tied down the length of the church yard, but still a novelty to be admired or scorned, depending on one's point of view. I was feeling quite flushed and thrilled at having driven here. Elizabeth and Mr. Lyons had taken turns teaching me how, again, as I apparently used to do so before. It was quite exhilarating and I almost missed Maurice taking the pastor aside.

Before I could go find out what he was saying, Elizabeth had taken Mr. Lyons on one arm and me on the other. "There are quite a few people here you know, including the good Rev. Brewer."

"If I am so well known, why did no one recognize me, when I wandered into town all bloody and burnt?"

Mr. Lyons shrugged a bit and Elizabeth said, "I understand you were unrecognizable precisely because you were all covered in blood and soot."

Or I was so unremarkable as to be forgettable? That seemed as unkind to the people of Dorset as it was to me. "Well, they certainly won't forget me now," I murmured, thinking about my scars.

Both my companions stifled noises I chose to interpret as humor.

We were early enough that I didn't have to face down a gauntlet of stares as Elizabeth led the way to our pew. We were at the front, so it seemed that in spite of not being Vanderbilt wealthy, I was still a big fish in this particular pond. I didn't recognize anyone, but I did not fail to see one or two disapproving looks directed our way as Maurice joined us. Elizabeth was a teacher, albeit a highly sought after one, and Gideon Lyons my employee. Maurice Westham was a junior member of his law firm. Any one of us could have been the reason for the raised noses.

The church grew noisy as more people arrived, and, precisely at ten, the doors closed. Reverend Brewer was a distinguished looking man of middle years with a commanding voice. The announcements included the re-opening of Backus Engineering, as well as plans for a spring picnic - Easter had come early this year, it seemed, and I'd been in the asylum. I didn't hear anything that sparked any memories in the announcement and as the service progressed, I found myself stifling a yawn.

The pastor's voice was almost hypnotic and his choice of subject held no interest for me. I was not a deeply religious person, I guessed, but then if I was willing to make love with a man of only two weeks acquaintance whilst engaged to another man whom I had deceived in regards to my interests and occupations, both of whom were in attendance with me, I supposed that was a given.

Everyone stood up abruptly and I hastily rose to my feet with them, staring at the open book Elizabeth thrust in front of me. A hymn book, but as the music started I recognized it. "I know this one," I murmured.

"Try to look a little more interested, Charlotte," she said quietly as voices rose in song. "We are in the front row."

"I suspect that's not the first time you've said that to me."

"Just sing."

I learned two more things of interest about myself—I liked singing, and I wasn't a very good at it. I was mindful of my posture for the rest of the service, keeping my gloved hands folded neatly on my lap, and my head slightly bowed so the veil on my hat obscured my face, and breathed a sigh of relief when it was over.

Outside the church, the day was mild and sunny and I enjoyed seeing the blue of the sky and the faint green haze around the trees that would soon obscure the branches for the summer. "I think this is my favorite time of year," I said, to no one in particular.

"Miss Backus, so lovely to see you in our midst once more!"

I turned to see the pastor smiling genially at me. "It's good to be back, reverend."

"I understand you're suffering from amnesia?"

I smiled. "I don't know that I'm suffering any more than if I remembered."

"Such a pert sense of humor, Miss Backus. I should like to call on you, however, that we might speak more in depth. Just to ease my mind that you are well in yours."

I gave him a short bow from my waist. "Thank you, that would be most kind." He might know things about me or my father that no one else did, and if not, it was an excuse for tea and sticky buns, though I doubted he would play sugar face with me and Elizabeth. I smiled at the thought, even as a woman I recognized from the pew across the aisle pulled me gently aside.

I smiled quizzically at her and she said, "You really don't know who I am?"

"I apologize...?"

"Mrs. Montcalm. Harriet Montcalm. You and my husband do a great deal of business together," she explained briskly.

"It's a pleasure to meet you again, then," I said smiling weakly.

She stared at my face. "My, those scars are really quite... Pardon me for staring, Miss Backus. My husband owns the lumber mill, you and Mr. Lyons designed the, um, for the new saw." She waved her hand dismissively, fluttering a lace trimmed handkerchief in the process. "We are holding a ball, in appreciation for those who've contributed to our success. We would have mailed you an invitation, but what with your disappearance, we weren't sure... we didn't want to seem... well, if worse came to worst, you understand. In fact, had I suspected you would be in attendance today I would have brought it with me, but as I didn't, I should like to personally invite you, and Mr. Lyons, of course, to the ball we're hosting at the Halimond Hotel in Bangor this Friday."

She broke off as if embarrassed. "I know it's an uncivilly late invitation, but we would so love to see you both there. There will be escorts available for you both, of course. I do hope you'll accept?"

"I would be grateful to attend, Mrs. Montcalm, but wouldn't Mr. Lyons have replied by now?"

"He declined, but it was untimely in light of your accident. Won't you entreat him to change his mind?"

"I will do my best."

Her hands clapped together, nearly soundless for her crocheted gloves and lace handkerchief. "Marvelous. I'll send the invitation along properly, of course, but I will count you as having replied!"

She hooked her elbow into mine and we walked back to where

the others were chatting amiably. "Miss Backus," Daniel Stockton said, tipping the hat he now wore. His Sunday best made him quite handsome in his own right and I imagined any man not hideously disfigured must be handsome in the right clothes. I gave him a smile and nod of acknowledgement.

Because I could perform the experiment within the confines of my thoughts, I asked myself—would I kiss Daniel Stockton, a reasonably attractive man with a demonstrated intelligence after knowing him all of two weeks? To my relief, I found it quite difficult to imagine.

"Young men are so bold, these days," remarked Mrs. Montcalm, reminding me I wasn't alone.

"He's my office manager."

A tall silver-haired man with a generous cravat and high top hat suddenly grasped my hands. "Miss Backus! So wonderful to see you again!" He let go my hands and gave a smile to the woman beside me. "Did you pass on our invitation, Mrs. Montcalm?"

"I certainly did."

"It will be my honor to attend, Mr. Montcalm," I said graciously, working out his identity by context.

"Those scars, I must say, make you look quite ferocious." He said, winking at me as if sharing a joke.

"Mr. Montcalm!"

"Sorry, my dear. Miss Backus and I have spent a good deal of time engaged in the dull concerns of business, it leads me to forget she's also a lady." He bowed to me. "And my apologies also to you, Miss Backus."

"No need, Mr. Montcalm," I replied with a smile. "I appreciate your honesty. Many, I'm sure, will consider me disfigured."

"You and Mr. Lyons certainly present some interesting challenges, as guests," he said genially, then flinched as his wife jabbed his ribs with her elbow.

I should have dearly liked to ask after the details of these challenges, though I could guess one or two, but Mrs. Montcalm led her husband away, scolding him quietly for his social faux pas—not that I was entirely sure what he'd done wrong—and Elizabeth was gesturing for me to join her. I think she might have been the only one there to understand how bewildering this was, being greeted and warmly welcomed back by complete strangers.

Elizabeth led me to a man with two children, saying, "You don't remember Mr. Strudwick, but he owns the Mercantile in Dorset and also has interests in the playhouse. He's a widower," she added significantly, though I didn't grasp the significance.

"Recent?"

"No, no, some five years ago. He heard about your condition, and hesitated to renew his acquaintance."

I studied him as well as I could without seeming to stare. He, like most of the men present, was dressed soberly but well and looked quite handsome, albeit slightly anxious. His eyes darted to my scars and down, then he realized where his gaze had fallen and he looked up again, perhaps as far as my mouth. "Miss Backus. It's so good to see you well. You may not recall my children, Sarah and Peter." His attention turned toward the children, the boy looked perhaps twelve and the girl a little younger. Both stared up at me with wide eyes.

I smiled at them. "Hello."

"Are you a pirate?" The boy was staring in rapt curiosity.

"Peter! My apologies, Miss. He's been reading Treasure Island, and..." Mr. Strudwick's face was pink with embarrassment.

I waved it away with a laugh and Mr. Strudwick herded his two children away.

"Mr. Strudwick makes it a point to attend you personally when you come into town, otherwise, he lets the shop ladies run the Mercantile. I thought he might hold you in some deeper regard," Elizabeth said, staring after the man's back.

"You're trying to, to match-make?"

"I thought if you really want to be married to a man of substance, I'd remind you there are better options than Maurice Westham."

"Talking about me, ladies?"

We both jumped, and Elizabeth hastily excused herself. "Maurice. Elizabeth was just wondering where you were."

"How kind of her to notice. Have you given any thought to my suggestion? I was wondering if I should speak to the good Reverend about reserving his church?"

I looked down at my feet, clasping my hands tightly in front of me. "I've barely accustomed myself to addressing you as Maurice, must you press me on this?"

He frowned at me. "My dear, I'll give you another week to accustom yourself to the idea. But I really must press you, yes. This is important to me. To us! Now, I'll be returning to the city this afternoon, immediately after dinner, and I'm not sure I can make it back out here before next Sunday, so you'll have plenty of time to think about it, our history, and what the right thing to do is."

"Thank you," I said meekly, not finding much consolation in this less than generous concession.

I was as silent at the dinner table as I was my first day back at the house, equally at a loss for words, though for much different reasons. Mr. Lyons didn't say anything about the Montcalms' invitation, nor did I, so the meal proceeded in a more stilted fashion than usual, until Westham said jovially, "Charlotte has finally agreed to set a date, for which I am truly grateful. I assume you'll assist her with all that silly stuff women do, Miss Bayfield?"

Mr. Lyons abruptly pushed away from the table muttering, "Excuse me."

Elizabeth was looking at me like I'd suddenly grown a third eye, and after a suitable interval I excused myself as well.

"Charlotte?"

"I, need some air, Mr. Westham. Excuse me!"

I fled outside and up the gnomon stairs, grateful that we'd repaired them. At the top, out of breath, I sank onto the bench and surprised myself by bursting into tears. As much as I hated not knowing what I'd forgotten, Maurice Westham was correct on one very important issue: I could not wait on my memories returning before moving forward with my life. He said it wasn't fair for me to ask everyone else to hold their lives for me, but it wasn't fair to ask it of myself, either. I would have to make decisions about my life based more on what I felt, than what I knew. I did not like having to rely so much on feelings, it was a frightening notion.

So immersed in quiet sobs of self-pity, I didn't hear anyone on the steps, and a sharp voice asking, "Is someone here?" startled me.

I cleared my throat, trying to stop the quaking of my stomach brought on by my breakdown.

"Well, if it isn't the happy bride," Gideon Lyons said, his voice hard and bitter. "Don't bother to invite me to the celebration, I must visit a sick friend that day."

His sarcasm cut me and I hic-coughed before stifling my sorrow. "Go away," I muttered.

"Christ, Charlotte, why are you doing this? Which of you am I supposed to believe? You asked me once why you are marrying that boor. Do you want to know what you told me? That he was the man of your dreams and that marrying him would be the happiest day of your life. You said that with a knife in your voice."

I dared to look up at him. His mouth was hard, his lips pressed tight together. Then he said, "So I lied. I, I had hoped with your amnesia, we could stop hurting each other, if only for a little while."

I sniffed. "Well. I obviously lied when I told you that, for whatever reason. I don't remember."

"And which of you am I supposed to believe? The pre-accident

Charlotte, or you?"

"I'm the only Charlotte left." I said sadly.

He swore, then pulled me into a tight embrace. "I wish I could hate you, the way you hate me."

There was a different ache in my throat now, and I clung to him. "I don't know what passed between us, but I'm as certain as I can be that I do not hate you, Gideon Lyons. I-I think I love you."

After a long moment he said heavily, "I wish I could believe you. But it was quite surprising to learn at the table that you've finally decided to wed." His embrace fell away and I released my grip on him reluctantly.

"It was equally surprising to me," I said stiffly. "I have most definitely not chosen a date. He is pressing me to decide and the more he insists, the more reluctant I am. If he truly cared about me why would he not—" I stopped abruptly. "I don't want to marry him. But for some reason, and I assume some good reason, I decided to do so. Now I cannot remember why or if there is a good reason I should not follow through on this engagement."

"I can think of one."

I didn't say anything, uncertain of his meaning, and uncertain how I felt. I *remembered* meeting him only a very short time ago, but I *felt* something deep and longstanding for him, that did not make sense from what little I'd been told.

"You said it on the gnomon, Charlotte." His voice dropped so low I almost couldn't hear him. "You should be marrying me."

12 FILES

IT FELT QUITE strange to drive up the sweeping curve in front of the asylum. Spring had advanced enough in the seventeen days I'd been gone that the grass was now green, the trees were painted in the yellow and mint shades of early leaves. It looked friendly, inviting. Of course, the front rooms didn't have bars on the windows, which helped.

I didn't remember much more now than I had upon my arrival here, but I knew who I was and I had some small—very small—degree of confidence in that. I walked up the stairs and through the doors. "I'd like to see Dr. Sheldon, please."

"Do you have an appointment?"

"My name is Charlotte Backus, I'd like to speak with him, please."

"I'm afraid if you don't have an appointment..." The nurse frowned at me as if to suggest such verged on criminal.

Small wonder my friends had become impatient. I nodded and turned as if to leave, and when she turned her back, I slipped past her. I wasn't used to approaching Dr. Sheldon's office from this direction, but it was easy enough to find. I knocked on the door, and when he called a distracted, "come in" I did just that.

"Ah!" He jumped to his feet, taking in my attire. "Miss, uh, Miss?"

"Backus," I said, "Charlotte Backus."

"You remember!" He clasped his hands, looking pleased.

"No," I said, "But that's not why I'm here."

"No?" He gestured to the chair I sat in half a dozen times before. "No?"

"No." I pulled the cheque from my reticule and passed it to him. "I wanted to give you this. And I wanted to ask you a question."

He took the cheque and if he was unhappy with either the amount or the fact that it wasn't in his name, he didn't show it. He stamped it and wrote me a receipt. "This is most appreciated, Miss, uh, Backus. What question can I answer for you?" He looked up at me. "Your scars are healing quite, um, well."

"Did you know who I was?"

He passed me the receipt. "No. I can't say I know... wait. Backus? As in Backus Engineering? One of those Backus's?"

"You didn't hear about the explosion, or know I was missing or put together my injuries with the accident?"

"No. That is, I heard about the accident, and heard you were missing, but hadn't known you were there. You were found just outside of town, some five miles away from the site of the explosion. You were wearing the remains of a house dress, not any sort of work clothes or, or anything that might have indicated you were a woman of, um, status." He stared at me. "Are you in fact certain you are Charlotte Backus? Might those people not be using you as a, a fake Charlotte Backus, for some gain of their own?"

I shook my head, thinking of Gideon Lyons specifically. He could not recognize me by sight, but he seemed quite certain of who I was. More or less. And of course, the people at church. "I am definitely Charlotte Backus. I've met too many people who knew me before, no conspiracy could be that big."

"No, I suppose not. I did hear the factory has reopened, that's good news."

I studied him, as I had before, but trying to see him through the lens of what I knew now. "Why would you think they might be using me, my friends? Why did you ask me if the accident might not have been an accident if you didn't even know what kind of accident it was? It's only... I thought you were trying to frighten me into submitting to your even more frightening treatment methods."

"Ha, well. That's honest." He laced his fingers, resting his hands on the blotter. "I was trying to protect you, Miss, uh, Backus. Without your memory, you are in a very vulnerable state, and one of the people asking after you was, shall we say, a former guest of the asylum."

***

I drove home in a mix of fear and anger. I hadn't looked at the file Dr. Sheldon had given me, afraid of what name I'd find on it. I pulled open the garage door and recklessly backed the car in, bumping over something that made a loud screech and the sound of escaping steam. "Damn."

I left the folder on the seat and knelt to look under the carriage. Steam hissed and hot water dripped on the worn wood floor. I reached cautiously underneath to get an idea of what I'd done, and yanked my hand back from the hot metal, scraping the back of my wrist on the bottom of the car. I was not dressed for such work and I wasn't sure I wanted to take the time to figure out the intricacy of a steam carriage anyway. Although it would certainly be preferably to opening that file.

Inside, I put the file with the one containing my father's will, found the first aid kit in my room, which didn't surprise me at all, given my inclinations to play with sharp metal and hot sparking things. I dressed the scrape on my wrist, which wasn't that bad, and checked my fingers. They were red, but not blistering. Thank goodness it was my left hand; I could hide it while eating. As if inspired by the thought, the dinner bell rang. I pulled my sleeve down, letting the lace cuff hide the scrape and took myself to the dining room.

Gideon came in, looking slightly rumpled from his morning at the shop and Elizabeth joined us after closing the door behind her student. "I'll be returning to work next week, Charlotte," she said. "I've resources in the classroom in town that I need to go further. The school has, I'm rather glad to say, suffered in my absence. It's good to be needed."

She sat down and poured some water for herself, offering the pitcher to me. "Water, Mr. Lyons?"

"Thank you," he said. He cleared his throat. "Were your tasks in town successful, Miss Charlotte?"

"That remains to be seen, Mr. Lyons. I'm afraid I," I hesitated, feeling my cheeks warm as I finished my confession. "I broke the car."

"Charlotte, how?" Elizabeth exclaimed.

Gideon's mouth twitched. "Broke it?"

"I backed over something."

"Something?" He raised an eyebrow, giving him a somewhat diabolical appearance.

"Something that crunched," I said, gritting my teeth. "And water and steam leaked out. I would guess in addition to the car, I broke something else. Crunched it, you might say. I'll fix it."

"No need," he said, smiling. "I'm afraid that steam car is a

114

unique piece. The engine has served as an experiment and doesn't bear much resemblance to anything you're likely to be familiar with, after several years of my tinkering. The thing you crunched might be the more pressing concern."

"I couldn't see what it was. I won't be going to the shop today. Is there anything I should know about?"

While he talked, I ate and made faces at Elizabeth as she and I engaged in atrocious table manners that, had Gideon been able to see, might have shocked him to see two adult women engaged in. Fortunately, he couldn't, and there was no one to tell us to stop. Afterwards, with Gideon returned to the shop, and Elizabeth ensconced in the parlor with her afternoon student, I retired to my room to do some reading.

Still reluctant to even look at the new file, I pulled out the other one and opened it. It contained a number of legal documents, including my father's will. It was probably best to read this without my memories, so I would not feel the pain of his loss so intensely. It was very brief document. If I had any other blood relations, they were not remembered by Father. There was one thing about it that quite thoroughly astonished me—the house and grounds were solely mine, but the business he'd left jointly to Gideon Lyons and I. All this time I'd been thinking of him as my employee! Why did he not correct me when I'd said the lab was mine? He was my business partner. I realized that my father had held him in the highest regard and that said much.

My father had also remembered Elizabeth with a modest sum, to be administered as a trust fund until such time as she should wed, when it would be paid out in full as a cheque drawn in her name. An addendum stated that should I die unwed, my half of the business was to go to Gideon Lyons or his heirs, while the reverse was also true.

I could not mention that to Elizabeth or she would have Gideon Lyons painted as a villain attempting to murder me for his own gain. My eyes fell uneasily on the unopened file peeping beneath the document before me. Surely... surely the name on it would not be Gideon Lyons. My father had to have been a better judge of character than that!

The other papers in the file seemed to be instructions to the law firm regarding how they were to proceed in the event of my father's demise and I set them aside.

Drawing a breath and holding it, I pulled out the file from Dr. Sheldon and read the name through squinted eyes. I exhaled sharply. Who the hell was Hiram Clarke? I was overwhelmingly relieved, for I had been terrified Dr. Sheldon meant one of the three who'd rescued me, but clearly he meant someone else, some other person who had been inquiring after me at the asylum.

Puzzled over who this person might be, I opened the file. He was barely a man, his age listed as eighteen, and his condition was listed as megalomania. I took the file with me downstairs to the study, in case there were other terms I needed to look up. The file contained many notations I could make nothing of, perhaps Mr. Clarke's daily vitals or medicines, but after many consultations with various books in the study I managed to piece together young Hiram's problem. He was, it seemed, quick of mind, and believed he was destined for great things. These great things were variously identified as monetary success, wide-spread fame, and particularly to receive the accolades due his greatness, even to the Nobel prize! Yet he felt he should not work to achieve these things, but rather they should simply be given him. His sense of entitlement led to criminal behavior, which I gathered had been limited to theft before his commitment to the asylum.

Further, the file asserted that the staff had worked to instill a work ethic into Mr. Clarke, that is, they taught him that it was perfectly fine to want these things, but one had to work for them. And when he demonstrated to their satisfaction that he had learned this, they had released him.

116

This only puzzled me more. How long ago had this transpired? I checked the dates and frowned. The records began some eleven years ago, just after my fourteenth birthday and Hiram Clarke had been released while I was in Paris. Three years and eight months he'd been in the asylum. Had Dr. Sheldon inadvertently given me the wrong file?

When I heard the parlor door open, I crossed the faded rug of the hall. "Elizabeth? Do you—do I—know someone named Hiram Clarke?"

"No." She paused, frowning. "No, I don't recall ever hearing the name." I handed her the file, which included my summation of its contents, as best I'd been able to determine. She flipped through the pages and skimmed my summary. "What is this?"

"Dr. Sheldon said he was someone I knew, who might wish to hurt me."

"Dark and sullen," she read, then looked at me. "Sounds a little like Mr. Lyons. But the need for admiration sounds more like Westham. Maybe Dr. Sheldon made a mistake?"

Perhaps.

That evening at supper, I asked Gideon most casually why he hadn't advised me that he and I were joint owners of the company. His mouth quirked in a smile and he replied, "What difference would it have made?"

I sucked on my lower lip. I don't think I'd treated him as less than my equal, so from that perspective it didn't make a difference, but even still. "In light of all I've forgotten, it would have been nice to know."

He reached across the corner of the table and found my arm with a light, reassuring touch. "I apologize, then."

It wasn't until we were clearing the plates I remembered to ask him, "Mr. Lyons? Does the name Hiram Clarke mean anything to you?" I explained, with Elizabeth's speculative interjections, why I was asking.

He frowned. "Name doesn't sound familiar. Maybe he worked for your father? Silas Johnson, the night fireman, he's been with your father as long as I can remember, shall I ask him if he knows the name?"

"Thank you."

13 The Steam Car

IT WAS ONLY by chance that I was home when the Reverend
Brewer called. His visit reminded me again that I was supposed to
be a lady of leisure, my sole task to run the house and, and do
needlework, I suppose. As it happened, I was actually in the
gardens, which I imagine was close enough for the good pastor's
comfort. "Reverend Brewer! How nice of you to call."

I pulled off my heavy gardening gloves and tucked them into
the coarse apron I wore to protect my clothes, and gestured up the
gnomon stairs. "There's a bench up there, a lovely view."

"An unusual garden structure," he commented.

I explained it was a sundial and showed him how the shadow
of the staircase fell on the curved walls below, marking the hours.
He seemed quite bemused, perhaps even more convinced of its

oddity, in spite of it having some small practical purpose. "I wanted to see how you're coping."

I settled on the bench, choosing my words with care. "Without my memories, I have no base for comparison, you understand. I feel confused by many things, simply because I do not remember, but it does not trouble me into sleepless nights." I waved towards the house. "I feel secure with my companions, and in my house."

"The congregation is keeping you in their prayers."

"Thank you, but I was hoping you might be able to give me some more, hmm, concrete help. I was wondering if you might tell me what you know of me and my family."

He paused as if to collect his thoughts. "You have always defied the role that God and society has made for women."

I was taken aback by his bluntness, but returned it in equal measure. "Don't expect that to change."

"Not even when you marry?"

His question brought home the fact that Maurice did indeed expect me to fall into those roles. What little work I'd done at the company since the loss of my memory was deeply satisfying and I was looking forward to doing more. I couldn't imagine giving it up. "I may have changed my mind about marrying," I said quietly.

***

The ringing of the telephone was such an unusual occurrence that at first I did not know what I was hearing. I dashed to the study and grabbed the handset from where it hung on the wall by the door. "Yes?"

"One moment while I connect your call, Miss Backus," the operator said cheerfully. Our local exchange consisted of perhaps half a dozen telephones so keeping track of them by personal names was an easy task for our operators.

She sounded too cheerful for it to be bad news—funny that I

associated the telephone with bad news—so I guessed it was unlikely to be the shop. I was a ten minute walk away through the woods, only an emergency would require a telephone call.

"Charlotte? Is that you?"

I blinked in astonishment. "Maurice?"

"My dear, I find I simply cannot wait until Sunday to see you. Would you like to come into the city for dinner with me? You can meet some of my colleagues."

"I, I'd love to," I lied, "But I'm afraid I can't." That, at least, I didn't have to lie about. "I took the car to town yesterday to visit Dr. Sheldon-"

"Sheldon? What did you want to see that vulture for?" He sounded angry or suspicious or maybe both.

"I just wanted to pay for my care. Not the ridiculous amount he asked for, of course, but reasonable recompense. But when I came home, I, um, ran over something and it kind of broke the carriage. G-" I caught myself. "Mr. Lyons has it up on blocks and I believe he intends to repair it tonight, but..."

"Are you unharmed?"

"Oh yes."

There was a silence over the line so long I wondered if our connection had been lost. "Maurice?"

"Sorry my dear, I was just... I'm disappointed I won't be able to see you after all. I suppose this telephone call will just have to do until I can see you on Sunday."

I probably should have told him it was nice to be able to talk to each other while so far apart, but I couldn't bring myself to lie any more. "I'll see you then," I said abruptly and replaced the hand set.

I had to stop this. Using my lost memories as justification for not acting, even if that acting was based soley on something as unreliable as emotions - it wasn't fair to Gideon or Maurice. Or me. I risked losing something I couldn't even remember and I had to consider that at this point, I might never remember.

***

"Come with me, Miss Charlotte," Gideon invited, at dinner. "I want to get that carriage fixed, and I have a story to tell you about Mr. Hiram Clarke."

I could not resist the invitation. Gideon and I were spending little time in company, and my engagement was a vast, invisible barrier between us. The dim light did not bother him in the slightest. "It's always dark, my dear," he said gently, but I needed to light the lantern.

Wearing a coverall to protect his clothing, he pushed under the car until all I could see were his legs. "I spoke to old Mr. Johnson and it seems Hiram Clarke used to work for your father."

"Indeed. In what capacity?"

"Mine." His chuckle was muffled. "Well, not exactly. It seems he was a bright young man your father hired to be his assistant during a conference in New York, more of an errand runner than an assistant. Upon arriving home here in Dorset, he, your father discovered that young Hiram had stolen quite a number of documents from the other attendees, including, Johnson said, Nikola Tesla himself."

"Gracious. Then how did my father become endeared to the great man enough to secure anything of him?"

"Johnson wasn't entirely sure of the details, only that your father left the young man at the asylum for safekeeping. You are not unaware that the asylum and the prison farther upriver once had fairly strong ties? And he, Dr. Backus, returned to New York straightway to return the stolen items. It's a plausible guess that his sincere regret and swift action in returning the goods renewed the respect he was held in, and perhaps Tesla was impressed by your father's humility and honor. Those things mean much to

122

Tesla, they say. We can't really know, of course, but that is the story of Hiram Clarke."

"Where did he go after he left the asylum?"

"Pass me that jar of grease, would you?" A hand emerged from beneath the car.

I found the grease and knelt to place it in his hand, which promptly disappeared.

"Johnson said he heard the young man went to the city, which makes sense. It's a far better place to make a new start than a small town like Dorset. Can you fire up the engine for me?"

I leaned inside to press the igniter and started pushing the bellows stick back and forth. "Don't stay under there too long."

"No, I just want to make sure there's no other leaks. It's a clean break."

A rattle in the engine had him scooting out. "That didn't sound good."

"I,I backed over something. But the engine should be fine." I left the bellows and helped him heft the cover of the engine back. "What the hell is that," I said without thinking.

He tsked at me, grinning, and I was glad he couldn't see my blush.

"Hang on, it's hot in there." He moved to the side of the car and switched off the burner.

The engine resembled nothing I'd ever imagined, though I thought I could detect something like one in the depth of the shadows. "Damn, Gideon." I clapped my hand to my mouth.

He chuckled and slipped his arm around my waist. "Is it wrong I like hearing you use vulgar words?" he said in my ear.

"Probably," I said, my breath catching.

"Hmm," he said, his lips brushing my ear and then he released me, shoving both hands into the mess that was the engine. "Oh my." He frowned. "Someone let a squirrel loose in here?"

"So it's not supposed to look like that?" I said, trying to

pretend his proximity hadn't bothered me at all.

"Can you hold this for a second?"

I peered into the shadowy darkness. "I can't really see..."

"Just slide your hand down my arm, this one," he said jigging his left elbow a little.

Holding my breath I touched his forearm and slowly slid my hand down his arm until it rested on top of his hand.

"Ah," he said, "You, uh make that... just hold this." He placed my hand around a bit of metal tubing that tried to pull back from my grip. It was still warm from the aborted start-up. Then he grabbed a tool unerringly from the wall behind us and put both hands back inside. It was rather strange to have such an intimate experience of how he worked, and within minutes, he was easing the tube out of my hand and attaching something to it. "That was easy enough."

"Still looks like a squirrel got in there," I remarked.

"Aesthetics aren't my strong point." He smiled wryly. "You may not have noticed, but it uses remarkably little fuel, plus there's a rudimentary condenser so it doesn't lose as much water."

"What did I jar loose when I ran over—what *did* I run over?"

Gideon put back the tool he'd used and felt along the table top until he found a rag and wiped his hands. "An old copper boiler. It was part of an experiment Dr. Backus and I were working on in the barn that didn't quite work out. I brought it here to vandalize for the carriage. But no, you didn't jar loose anything, it was deliberately disconnected, though I can't imagine why or by whom."

Deliberately disconnected. "But it wasn't anything dangerous?"

"No. Do you need a rag? I think there's a clean one here somewhere." He started feeling along the work table with casual grace. "As you heard, it went clunk. If we hadn't turned off the burner, it would have built up to a hiss, hiss, clunk, clunk and the engine would have died." He reached the drawers under the counter at the end and pulled out the third from the top with hardly a pause, tossing a clean rag in more or less my direction. "Completely harmless. On a regular engine, though..."

I knelt to retrieve it, wiping my hand as I stood. "Oh?"

"That tube being disconnected would have resulted in a build up of fuel fumes," he said, finding the grease jar with his toe. "Hiss, hiss, boom." He froze with the grease jar in his hand. "You don't think that was what whoever did this intended?"

I had a very uneasy feeling that was exactly what had been intended. "When would it have gone, er, boom?"

He shrugged. "If I was testing my repair, maybe then, if not then when—when you took it out tomorrow." He pulled the work coverall off, stepped out and tossed it on the shelf. "Charlotte?" He reached for me, and I helped him find me, letting his arm encircle my waist. "I hate to give credence to Miss Bayfield's over active imagination, but I'm beginning to feel very uneasy."

"If someone is trying to kill me, he's not very competent."

"You think this Hiram Clarke could be responsible, is that why you had me ask after him?"

I sighed, leaning into him. "I don't know. I feel so, so helpless, not being able to remember."

He loosed his hold on me. "We should return to the house," he said gently.

"So soon?"

"I am taking advantage of your vulnerability, too."

He offered the crook of his elbow as I extinguished the lantern. "You are trying to trick or deceive me?"

"I make love to you when you forget why you'd never allow such a thing." He paused outside to draw the doors closed and pull the bolt down.

"Maybe you should tell me, then."

"If you intend to marry Westham, does it really matter?"

I didn't know what to say to that, or how honest I should be to a man who seemed certain I would not like him, could I remember him. But once we'd crossed the yard and climbed the front steps I stopped, causing him to halt as well. "I'm afraid," I admitted.

"Someone seems to mean you harm, Charlotte. It's normal to be afraid. The county sheriff has a telephone, we'll call in the morning."

That wasn't what I'd meant. "I see little point to that. We have no proof of anything, no suspects, and no suggestions of how to keep me safe. All we would do is provide him with his morning amusement."

"We should do something," he said frustration coloring his voice. He led me to the porch swing and we sat down.

"I will just have to be careful. If-if these accidents are not accidents, then they are being arranged by someone who knows me well. That leaves an awfully short list of names, and none of you have any good reason... "

"I'm on the list, then."

"Not really. You, Elizabeth, and Maurice are the only ones who know me well enough, well, perhaps not Maurice. He certainly was appalled to discover I'd been anywhere near the new boiler."

Gideon sighed and put his arm across the back of the swing. "Perhaps he was appalled that you were with me."

I didn't have anything to say to that. "I really can't believe it of any of you. I could believe the board was something I or you might have somehow managed to forget in spite of how careful we were, and that the unbaked clay blocks were just a mistake and we happened to be in the wrong place at the wrong time. But it's hard to deny that the carriage engine has been deliberately tampered with."

There was a length of silence and in spite of the disquieting discovery this evening, I took comfort in the anonymity of the gathering dark and the pressure of Gideon's arm across my shoulders. "It's possible the connection was loosened by the vibrations of driving, and your backing over the small copper boiler shook it free."

He sounded like he didn't quite believe it himself. I sighed and let myself lean against him. His arm dropped around me without pretense and we sat in companionable silence until the moon rose, dappling the river before us.

14 FREDERICK

MAURICE DROPPED BY without warning the following night, as Elizabeth and Gideon were holding a heated discussion regarding who might be trying to harm me. I was ignoring both of them, trying to read a silly love story that I liked in spite of the improbable plot. Elizabeth was still trying to accuse Gideon, or at least argue about it. "Listen, Miss Bayfield," he said heatedly, "If I was forced to choose between the business and Charlotte, I'd choose Charlotte!"

"Well isn't that touching," Maurice said into the resounding silence, the dripping sarcasm announcing his arrival.

I dropped my face into my book as if I could just disappear inside it while Elizabeth said, "We were just trying to figure out who would want to hurt Charlotte."

Maurice glared at Gideon before sitting beside me. I put my book aside. "They were discussing it. I was reading."

"I thought we'd had this discussion and concluded that no one has any reason to harm you?"

"Mr. Lyons does," Elizabeth said. "He'll get Backus Engineering if anything happens to Charlotte before she marries."

I stifled a groan. I should never have told her.

Since Maurice had handled my father's affairs on his death, this could not have been a surprise to him, yet he reacted as if learning it for the first time, his brow wrinkling in thought. "I see," he said gravely, "but—" He turned to me abruptly, and studied me thoroughly. "Has there been another accident?"

"Someone sabotaged the carriage," Gideon said irritably. "Though sabotage is an extreme word for the minor inconvenience it caused."

Maurice now turned his stare on Gideon, who was happily oblivious. "So no one was hurt?"

"Obviously."

I stood up, and gestured Maurice to remain seated. "Let me get you some tea. What brings you all this way, I thought you said you couldn't make it back to Dorset until Sunday?"

"I was... concerned."

I paused, surprised, at the parlor door. "Why?"

He shook his head, chagrined. "Just a feeling I had." He smiled at me. "I was anxious to see you, I imagine. Tea would be lovely."

"I'll bring the tray."

When I returned with the tray, it was to a silent room. "Mr. Lyons couldn't possibly be the one trying to harm me, " I said conversationally, as if they had merely been waiting on my return.

"Indeed?" Maurice said, his voice hard. "He was with you, for all of your accidents? Made sure you were in the right place?"

"He's far too competent. Take the matter of the car, for

130

instance. If he had truly meant that to injure me, then why would he disconnect the wrong tube? He knows the workings of that vehicle better than anyone."

"A trick? To make you believe just that?"

Gideon snorted, but said nothing. Elizabeth, on the other hand, said, "Oh bosh. It was just an intellectual exercise, Mr. Westham. If Mr. Lyons wanted Charlotte's half of the company, he wouldn't have to kill her."

All heads turned in her direction.

"Charlotte, one of the reasons we got involved in the local suffragette movement—" Maurice now snorted derision, but Elizabeth continued, "Maine's property laws, remember? Oh no, of course, you don't. Only unwed women over the age of twenty-one can inherit property. Once you marry, everything belongs to your husband. Which is completely unfair!"

I nodded thoughtfully while Maurice started three different sentences that never made it past the first word. Arguments against suffrage, I suspected, that he wisely chose not to finish, before grudgingly admitting, "She's correct."

That was why Maurice had talked about his plans for the house after we married as if my opinion didn't matter. After we married, it wouldn't. Which made it even more incomprehensible why I had agreed to marry him in the first place. It wasn't for love, it wasn't for money; it was actually against my best interests to marry him. And yet, I had agreed and made Elizabeth promise to help me pretend to be a lady.

That was what I feared, what I'd meant to articulate to Gideon the night before. The less sense it made to marry Westham, it seemed more likely there must be some extremely compelling reason I had forgotten.

"Besides," I added, "Mr. John Macklemore would be a more likely suspect in the case of the faulty boiler blocks. It would support his contention that Backus Engineering is an unsafe workplace."

Gideon laughed. "The man is a pest, Miss Backus, but surely you give him too much credit?"

"I don't know," Elizabeth said thoughtfully, clearly enjoying this game. "He might be under pressure from," her voice dropped to a conspiratorial whisper, "outside forces." She grinned and continued in her normal tone, "But he wouldn't have had anything to do with the sundial or the steam carriage. Oh! I know—what if the first and third accidents aren't related to the boiler? It's just a coincidence!"

I really wanted to believe they were all coincidence, but couldn't quite bring myself to do it. There were too many unanswered questions. I suddenly saw one more. What if I'd agreed to marry Westham for the same reason someone plotted my demise? Had I agreed to marry to save myself from, from... something? If so, he wasn't much of a protector.

"What about Frederick?" Maurice asked into the silence following Elizabeth's melodramatic outburst.

Elizabeth looked dumfounded. "How do you know about Frederick?"

Gideon and I asked, almost simultaneously, "Who's Frederick?"

I was imagining some beau of Elizabeth's whom I had forgotten so I was doubly surprised when she said, "He's-he's... He was Charlotte's first beau, and I know for a fact he had nothing to do with this."

She had spent a good bit of time regaling me with stories of our long association, and had mentioned Gideon in several negative contexts without details, but had never mentioned anyone, boy or man, named Frederick.

"Maybe he's jealous," Maurice said, "and feels if he can't have her, no one can."

Elizabeth laughed. "Oh, poor dumb Frederick. No, trust me he isn't capable of jealousy. Charlotte, I will tell you all about Frederick later. I know," she hesitated, "I know I haven't mentioned him previously." Her cheeks flushed.

And the matter was dropped, though my curiosity remained.

I changed the subject to the ball tomorrow night. I hadn't mentioned it before, in case Maurice assumed he was invited, too. I made rather more of it being a business affair than necessary. In truth, I was quite looking forward it. I'd had all together too much time to dwell fearfully on what I could not remember; the chance to put it out of mind for a few hours and dance in a pretty dress with handsome men—and I imagined all men were handsome in formal wear—sounded wonderful.

"You're not going," he said as though that were a foregone conclusion.

"I most certainly am."

"But you-you won't know anyone there!"

I bit back a sarcastic reply, wishing I could find the courage to just tell him it was over, and there would be no wedding, and he had no right to tell me what I could or could not do. "It will improve my spirits, to dress up and get out of the house for a bit," I said quietly.

He looked at me a long time, not remarking on the obvious slight of not being invited. Business or no, after a year long engagement, there surely wasn't anyone who didn't know we were affianced. "I suppose you'll be safe enough there. I suppose I can drive all the way out here to at least see you safe to the hotel."

"Mr. Lyons, as my business partner, has also been invited, so I thought he would escort me," I said cautiously.

"It would be an honor," Gideon said, his tone mocking.

A shadow crossed his face. "Lyons. I see. Isn't that... cozy."

My chin lifted in defiance. "It's convenient, Mr. Westham."

"Very," he agreed, his voice cold. He gave me a very long look, as if to memorize my face. "I believe I've become accustomed to your disfigurement," he said, sounding surprised. Then his tone became matter-of-fact. "If I can't talk you out of it, then at least you'll be surrounded by too many people to be in danger. I will see you Sunday, my dear. Miss Bayfield, I bid you good night. Lyons."

He kissed my knuckles and left, with little more fanfare than when he'd arrived. I felt guilty again, mistaking his concern for my safety for jealousy over Gideon.

"Disfigurement," Elizabeth scoffed.

"Tact is not his strong point," Gideon agreed dryly.

I watched from the window as his smart little two-wheeler left the lane in a pretty clip and sighed in relief as he vanished altogether from sight. He'd hardly stayed long enough to make the trip from Bangor worthwhile. "We forgot to ask him about Hiram Clarke," I said, turning from the window.

"Not much point," Gideon said, "that was long before Westham got involved with the Backus family."

I resumed my seat and picked up my book. It had fallen shut and I had not marked the passage. "That's true."

"We also know of no reason why Hiram Clarke might want to harm you," Elizabeth pointed out. "I know it sounds silly, but it does seem too coincidental to be coincidence, even if no one has a reason to hurt you."

That was also true. The coincidences made me uneasy, and I cursed Dr. Sheldon silently. If he knew something specific, he should have told me, rather than hinting ominously and giving me a file he must have known I could not comprehend. I flipped through the pages of the novel not sure I wanted to try to find my place.

Gideon rose gracefully to his feet. "Ladies, it has been a wonderfully entertaining evening." He approached Elizabeth, extending a hand to her that she took after giving me a look of misgiving. He bussed the back of her hand. "Miss Bayfield." He turned to me, and, bemused by this unusual behavior, I took his hand. Instead of kissing it, he leaned forward to brush his lips across my cheek. "Miss Charlotte."

My face was crimson and when he was out of the room and beyond hearing, Elizabeth turned to me, her eyes wide. "Did he just *kiss you*?"

"On the, my cheek," I said. "Just my cheek." I patted both my cheeks, trying to hide the blush.

"Charlotte, please be careful. I have no belief Gideon Lyons means you physical harm, but be wary with your heart. He, he has been careless of your emotions in the past."

"I'll bear that in mind."

***

Friday morning dawned to find me so full of excitement for the ball that night that I stayed at the shop only long enough to ensure I wasn't needed. I signed a few papers for Mr. Stockton, ran into John Macklemore who was poking around the fresh construction of the new lab. The new boiler was in its own room, surrounded by the myriad of pipes and gauges required, half of which were yet to be connected. The exterior shop walls were white brick, and this new boiler was in an outside corner to minimize damage, should anything happen. To further contain the damage, the new interior walls surrounding it were also constructed of brick. I would have preferred the new concrete, but it was simply too expensive for the amount we required.

At present, we were waiting on the insurance company again. Although the boiler had passed our in-house safety standards, we needed certification from the insurance company in order for them to pay out in the case of another accident, heaven forbid. "Not looking to cause an accident, are we, Mr. Macklemore?"

He turned, clearly startled from his ruminations. "Miss Backus, please. Surely your partner, Mr. Lyons, has reminded you of the difficult position I'm in?"

135

"He has. And I apologize if my jest sounded more like an accusation. I just don't see how, as a union man, you can countenance keeping workers from working. They have families, you know."

He looked around the room. "I know." He returned his attention to me and smiled. "I'm mostly just killing time. If I'm here, then I can honestly say I've been here, looking into safety matters."

"I believe I feel some sympathy for you, Mr. Macklemore. Not enough to do as you ask, but..." I shrugged and smiled.

"Do you realize what an unusual operation you have here?"

I raised an eyebrow. "Because we pay well?"

He shook his head and stuffed his hands into his pockets. "Dr. Backus once told me that he came from a working class background and that was why he was always giving his workers in excess of the union's requirements. He was the only man of his stature I've ever met who embraced the union."

"From what I've learned of my father, that sounds entirely consistent." I studied him. "I hope you understand, Mr. Macklemore, that I support the union, too. Which is why I don't understand how you can do this."

"If I don't, they'll just get someone else." He paused. "Have you tried confronting the owners of the other companies? Asking them to leave the union out of their feud with you?"

My hands found my hips and I met his eyes. "I don't remember, but it wouldn't surprise me to find out I did try. However, it might surprise *you* to learn that a woman in business is seldom taken seriously. Do you really think they'd listen to me?"

His mouth twisted into a wry smile. "A fair point. Well, Miss Backus, as neither you nor I can do much to rectify the situation, shall we at least call a truce?"

I sighed and nodded. "Please check in with a supervisor when you come in, that's all I ask."

He inclined his head and offered me his arm.

***

After dinner, Gideon excused himself to return to the lab and I reminded him about the ball. His smile as he said he was looking forward to it was dare I say mischievous. Could Gideon Lyons be mischievous? I sought out Elizabeth, who had no students this afternoon.

"What will you wear to the ball? Oh, you will let me help you, won't you?"

"Of course, I couldn't do it without you," I said, touching my hair ruefully. "But we've plenty of time and I want to know who this Frederick is. You've not mentioned him once, in telling me stories about our history."

Her cheeks reddened and she said, "We should go for a walk."

"There's no one in the house to hear us."

"It isn't for fear of being overheard. Only come with me, please."

I turned my eyes heavenward but refrained from asking *why me* aloud. Instead I followed her through the kitchen, pausing for a cheerful exchange of greetings with Hannah, and out into the gardens with our shawls.

She led me through the maze surrounding the gnomon and out the other side and pushed aside overgrown boxwood to reveal an deep alcove in the corner of where the gnomon and marker dial structure intersected. Inside was a statue of a naked man, in the pseudo-Grecian style popular during the Renaissance. One of those quirky pieces of knowledge I had that I did not remember acquiring.

"This is certainly private," I remarked, staring at the statue. "What an odd place for a garden ornament. Did Father hide it here because he wanted to protect me from..." The statue was carved in loving detail, including the rather prominent private parts, and I tried not to stare. It was a statue, for goodness sake. I'd been three years in Paris with an art student for a room-mate, it seemed likely that I was familiar enough with the male form to forgo gaping at a statue.

Elizabeth smiled. "No, putting him here was your idea. I had him shipped from my parents' garden in New Hampshire, for your twentieth birthday."

"Ah." Intrigued as I was by the idea that this was an appropriate birthday gift—or not, since I'd hidden it away—I was more curious about this first beau of mine. "So, Frederick, what can you tell me about him?"

"Uh... he's... tall. You might say he's a cold, hard man of few words. Charlotte, this *is* Frederick."

"What?" I turned to stare at the statue. "I'm not certain I understand. The statue is Frederick?"

Her cheeks again took some color. "Frederick used to live in my mother's very proper English garden, just off the morning room. Mama loves to pretend she's a great English lady, which has its uses in our society. However...." She stared at the statue called Frederick. "We liked to pretend mother's garden was the Labyrinth of the Minotaur, among other games, and Frederick was a natural part of our games. We would even dress him up sometimes, to be this or that character, when we could filch the clothes. Then, when you were but thirteen, your interest in Frederick became more, um, primitive."

Now I was blushing. "How did he acquire his name?"

"You thought it was, and I quote, wildly romantic." She was grinning again. "I would like to say that I sat by and was quietly embarrassed by your behavior, but sadly I am forced to confess it delighted me in the way mischief always does. We were both curious about the intimate aspects of adulthood, so we practiced kissing, both on Frederick and each other, to see what it was like.

Frederick's, um, masculinity was well placed for us to discover other things, as well."

"Other things?"

"Give him a hug and a kiss," she suggested with a wink.

I studied the statue carefully and guessed that the protrusion of his masculinity must have fit nicely between girlish legs, right at the pleasure point. "This is one of those embarrassing childhood stories we hope to forget as adults, correct?"

She chuckled. "Oh you became quite the hoyden, Charlotte. Frederick was but the first of many statues to know the touch of your delicate hands and soft lips." She petted the curve of his bottom affectionately. "I always thought you channeled your physical desires very effectively. And you did outgrow it. At least, I don't think you've visited Frederick for, um, comfort since we returned from Paris. My bringing him here was kind of recognition of our little joke, a reminder of things only you and I know."

"And Maurice, it seems!"

"He clearly imagines Frederick to be a real person. We were wont to speak of him as your first beau, and to be fair, no other statue captured your affections enough to earn a name."

Still blushing furiously, I walked around Frederick. He was, I had to admit, a nicely carved figure. "It must have been quite difficult to not laugh when Maurice suggested Frederick was the jealous type."

Elizabeth laughed. "Indeed." She looped her arm in mine. "Come, lets get you ready for a night of dancing, in the arms of flesh and blood men."

15 THE BALL

ALTHOUGH ELIZABETH WAS not attending the ball, she was as excited as if she were. She insisted on doing my hair and choosing my wardrobe, right down to the stockings. I couldn't imagine any of that would matter. Who would see what I wore beneath my gown?

She fired up the coal stove to heat curling tongs and dressed my hair into an impossibly intricate style I would never be able to duplicate. Instead of trying to hide the scars, she used my hair to emphasize the shape of my face, which the scars did in their own way. She pulled the scarlet gown from my wardrobe and helped me into it, even as I questioned how appropriate it was. "This is a ball, Charlotte, a ball gown is appropriate."

I turned in front of the glass, hardly recognizing myself.

Again. The Charlotte in the mirror was, well, still not beautiful, but striking in a way I hadn't imagined I could be. The dress had a dramatic decolletage, which only made me self-conscious when I saw it in the glass. I considered protesting, but I would hardly be the only one in such a gown, after all. Then she sparingly applied cosmetics to darken my lashes, define my eyebrows, and blush my cheeks just lightly, not bothering to try to hide my scars. The mirror told me I was not a disgrace to the beautiful dress. I touched my eyebrow, or rather the scar that bisected it. "Should we not draw over it with charcoal?"

"No, I think not." She studied my face, as so many others had in these past few days. "I think they lend you a rather rakish quality. I should very much like to paint you, Charlotte."

"Not something pastoral?"

Her smile grew mischievous. "Well, at least if Mr. Lyons were to walk into the parlor whilst I was doing so, he would never know, would he? But I was thinking of a portrait, in this dress. You look, I can't even find the word. Let me make some quick sketches, won't you?"

"By all means." I studied her creation in the mirror. I didn't know what the word might be, either, but it certainly wasn't plain or homely or ugly.

She returned carrying a large sketch pad and easel. "Mr. Lyons is fetching the car," I reminded.

"Don't panic, Cinderella shan't be late for the ball. I just need to capture this... you look... I should fall at your feet myself," she said absently, which wasn't particularly convincing, but made me smile anyway.

"Oh, wait!" She found a spray of matching red feathers and placed them carefully on the side of my head, so that they fell down behind my right ear. "Perfect."

"What do you think of Mr. Lyons?" I asked, trying to sound unconcerned with her response.

"I would think better of him," she said, concentrating on her drawing, "if he hadn't been so viciously cruel to you when we were girls. You could certainly do worse." She looked up abruptly. "I suppose you weren't asking that."

"Cruel in what way?"

"No sad stories tonight, just sit still."

I turned a shoulder to the glass, wondering if Gideon would like it, could he see. It was past time to stop waiting for my memories to return and start living, starting with following my heart in personal matters. By not breaking my engagement, I was being the cruel one, the deceitful one. I sighed. I would do it soon.

A thought struck me. "Elizabeth? Do I know how to dance?"

"You do. You're quite graceful. We took countless lessons in Paris. Your father hoped you would become a polished young woman."

"Polished. He never expected me to be an arm ornament, did he?" I laughed.

She clucked her tongue. "I'm certain he was aware you'd never want to be that, but I suspect he wanted you to make a good marriage. Do try to sit still—please?"

My mood shifted again. "Do you suppose he'd consider Maurice Westham a good match?"

The corners of her pretty mouth turned down. "Forgive my brutal honesty, but no. He would have wanted you to have someone who knew you and cared enough about you to let you be yourself. I think he would have been happy if you chose a less handsome man, with more common interests."

"...like Gideon Lyons," I suggested playfully.

She nearly choked, and glared at me.

I bent a knee, exaggerating the opposite hip and snapped my fan open, like a coquette. "How about this for a pose?"

"Brilliant!" She flipped a page and began frantically sketching. "You look mysterious, sultry, dangerous," she said, her eyes moving from me to her sketch in rapid movement.

"Miss Backus?" Gideon's voice echoed up the stairs.

"One minute more, don't move," she held up a warning finger as she went to the door and called out, "She'll be right down." She looked at me. "One minute. I'd have thought the car would have taken longer to build up steam."

"There must be some way around that. I think such vehicles would become more popular if they could start faster."

"They'll never be popular no matter how fast they start, so long as they remain so very expensive, but try to limit your conversation tonight to more topical subjects."

"Such as the suffragette movement?" I suggested slyly, looking for my gloves.

She rolled her eyes at me. "Hold still. Have you given any more thought to breaking your engagement to Westham?"

"Truthfully, Elizabeth, I should have done so already, if I only knew why I accepted him in the first place." I pulled on my gloves and checked my reticule.

"You may have to play dress-up again with me, Charlotte. I want to finish this painting."

She passed me a wrap of scarlet wool decorated with jet beads and helped me secure it without mussing the curls hanging down my back. "Have fun for both of us, and try to stay out of trouble."

I hurried down the stairs, eager for the distraction, the women in their beautiful gowns, the men so refined in their black and white. Everyone at a ball was beautiful. Tonight even I, plain and scarred Charlotte Backus, was beautiful.

Gideon was all wrapped in his coat as he ushered me to the car. It was a trifle unconventional for him to escort me, as he wasn't my suitor, or at least, not officially. I was always confused just exactly where I stood with him, and that was in no small part my own fault for leading Maurice on with hopes of a wedding.

I liked driving the steam car, it was a thrill to control in a way that a horse drawn vehicle wasn't. And the road to Bangor was smooth and empty so I did not hesitate to give it full acceleration, to Gideon's chagrin. He clutched at the sides without comment, though, and I deduced that this was not the first time I'd done it. "I might try to find a way to vent some of the steam back this way," he said, teeth chattering as the chill evening air rushed over him.

"There's a lap blanket," I reminded him.

He found the blanket, and slid across the seat until our legs were touching, draping it over us both. "I'm rather surprised you were willing to even get in this thing, after what happened."

"Mr. Westham thinks you're trying to kill me. Inherit the company."

"Clearly you disagree."

"Clearly." I didn't want to expand much more on that. With Elizabeth's words in mind about common interests, and to distract myself from his proximity, I asked, "What is your opinion, Mr. Lyons, on the suffragette movement?"

He chuckled.

"You find it amusing?"

"Only in how different my views are now, from the ones my parents taught me. My family is very traditional, and yours was not, so it was quite a revelation in many ways, coming to live under the Backus roof. I support the aims of the suffragette movement—how could I not when you are living proof of what a woman can accomplish when she is allowed to make her own choices contrary to what society dictates. Why do you ask?"

"You and I, we talk about many things, but rarely politics. I was curious."

"I believe an in-depth discussion would reveal we hold similar points of view. We are both businessmen—er, people—and both strongly influenced by your father. I don't—" I veered to avoid an unexpected pot hole and he grabbed on to the edge of the seat, then continued as if nothing untoward had happened. "—normally consider politics an interesting discussion."

We arrived in the city in half the time it would have taken by horse, and I slowed as Gideon began reciting the directions that had accompanied the invitation from memory. Even in the city, our steam car was noteworthy, though hardly one of a kind as it was in Dorset, and at the Halimond Hotel, a specially trained valet had been hired to take care of the various horseless cars.

Gideon escorted me to the door where we were shown to separate cloak rooms. I wouldn't get to see him in formal wear until later, it seemed, but inside the cloak room were many lovely gowns. The women were an even mix of older married women, as one would expect to find at a ball given for such an occasion, and younger, more colorful single women—daughters, I would guess. I imagined I must know some of them, but although conversations halted and began again, after much staring at me, no one came forward to greet me.

I found some space in front of a mirror to check my hair and the folds of my skirt. The dramatic lines of my scars still seemed striking to me, even if my present companions deemed them disfiguring. With no reason to linger, I followed a mother and her two daughters out to the main ball room, where Mrs. Montcalm quickly found me. "Miss Backus, you look quite, um, lovely tonight. Such a beautiful gown.

"Thank you, you look very lovely yourself."

"Ah well I lack the benefits of youth. I know it is inevitable that you will find yourself surrounded by men tonight. They do love to talk business at a social event! But I would ask you to minimize those encounters. For one, your youth and charm is not at all hidden tonight, so many a woman who has grudgingly accepted that her husband does business with a woman will not be pleased to see him smiling at you."

My mouth twitched in a smile I struggled to hide, amused by the idea that anyone would be jealous of me. Mrs. Montcalm

146

continued: "Also, I know that because of your unique position, you are used to certain rules of propriety not applying to you, but this is a purely social event, and for your own sake, I ask that you be as demure and discreet as possible."

Her words were a rebuke, but her tone was kindly, so I took no offense, only nodded my acquiescence. She introduced me—re-introduced me, that is—to several women, married to men of my business acquaintance who promised to treat me like an adopted daughter, at least for the evening. I just wanted to dance; I would observe propriety as much as possible.

It was unsurprising that my dance card acquired names. The ettiquette of a ball demanded that every girl, no matter her appearance, should dance and enjoy herself, even if the hosts had to single out their gentlemen guests and guide them to us. Gideon's name had been scrawled in three places, including the first. One dance more than was strictly proper.

I searched the crowd, looking for him. He stood out, being the only gentleman in cinder glass spectacles. The Montcalms had paid for a man to serve as his guide this night, which was thoughtful of them. Gideon looked splendid in formal dress, not a wrinkle in sight tonight, though his hair was only slightly tamed. He wielded his cane almost defensively, and his spectacles gave him a villainous appearance. He was a delight to— "Miss Backus, you look most lovely tonight."

Blushing, I turned my attention to the gentleman addressing me, my host. "You're very kind, Mr. Montcalm."

As Mrs. Montcalm predicted, I was at various points surrounded by men, though most of them were my father's age, and all of them were married. While I enjoyed discussing business briefly, it was no hardship to abide by my hostess's wishes and catch the eye of one of the women assigned to be my chaperone and allow her to rescue me.

The band left off playing as Mr. Montcalm made a speech

thanking everyone who had contributed to the success of his business, and wished us all to enjoy ourselves as the dancing began. Gideon's guide led him to me as surely as if he himself knew who I was. The Montcalm's had certainly given a great deal of consideration to his unique circumstance. "Miss Backus," the guide murmured to Gideon, who bowed in my general direction.

"I believe this dance is mine?"

I smiled, aware of the disapproval of the women beside me. "My pleasure, Mr. Lyons."

"I'll hold your cane, Mr. Lyons," his guide said courteously.

Gideon let me lead us to the dance floor, and he murmured, "I must trust you to warn me when we might collide."

"I have eyes, Gideon, but not in the back of my head. We'll have to trust the other dancers to watch out for us." I was forming a high opinion of the Montcalms, to have taken Gideon's disability into consideration, even to dancing, as I assumed they must have.

He sighed and put his hand at the small of my back as the music swelled. "Normally, I don't really feel much disadvantaged by my disability, but at events such as this..."

"Why did you change your mind about attending, then?"

"To dance with you, Charlotte." He smiled. "What are you wearing?"

He danced hesitantly at first, but I noticed the other dancers were indeed aware of him on the floor and were taking great care to leave us plenty of space. "A red gown I found in my wardrobe. The other dancers are giving us room."

"Ah, the infamous red gown. Your father had that made for you. The ensuing argument was quite, hmm, loud. I always wondered what you might look like in it." His smile grew wicked. "Of course, I only have one way of looking, now." His fingers flexed against my back and I was grateful he could not see my blush. "I imagine your dance card is full."

"Fuller than I would have expected," I admitted.

148

As he grew confidant of not running into another couple, it become evident that he was a very good dancer, and surprisingly so was I. "You must look very beautiful indeed in that dress," he murmured.

"Must be the decolletage," I replied absently, enjoying immensely the way it felt to nearly fly across the dance floor in his arms.

"You tease, dear Charlotte. Now I simply must finagle a way to see that for myself."

The thought of his fingers tracing across the neckline of my gown was enough to catch my breath. He wouldn't dare! Would he? I felt a very unladylike thrill, remembering his kisses, and the close embraces we'd shared in private. I expect I should have given my whole self to him already had he not insisted that I break my engagement before we indulge in anything more than sweet kisses and fond petting. I suddenly hoped very much that he intended to do something untoward and blushed, embarrassed and excited by my own imaginings.

All too soon the dance was over and I led Gideon to where his guide was patiently waiting. I wondered if this was his first such job. Gideon reclaimed his cane, and then Mr. Montcalm was by his side as well. "Come, Mr. Lyons, there are some gentlemen I think you should like to talk with."

I didn't have much time to wonder why Gideon would be talking instead of dancing, as my next partner claimed his dance and we whirled away. But not all the spots on my card were filled and I managed to contrive a conversation in the same group of people as Gideon. The topic under discussion was horseless carriages, which we both had opinions on, though I tried to offer mine in a more feminine manner. "Ah," said one gentleman, "This is Miss Charlotte Backus, the other half of Backus Engineering. Miss Backus, allow me to find you a suitable escort."

I bit back a protest and nodded polite acquiescence.

"Escort?" Gideon asked softly. "But of course, I forgot you cannot cross the floor by yourself."

I recognized the dare in his voice, but felt no urge to act on it. Instead, I replied, "I'm bending enough rules of propriety already, Mr. Lyons."

His chuckle, so knowing, made me blush. "As you say, Miss Backus."

Before a suitable female escort could be found, my next dance partner was bowing before me. "There you are, Miss Backus! Might I have the honor...?"

I curtsied and let him lead me off. It was a most wonderful evening, and when the ball broke up for a midnight supper, I was cheerfully exhausted and starving. Gideon, my last dance partner, left me for his guide, while a matron with her own daughter took me in hand to lead us to the buffet table, where she left me with a disapproving grunt. I wasn't entirely sure what she disapproved of.

I spotted Gideon standing behind the table near a large window and unobtrusively sidled my way over. "You ditched your minder, too, hmm?"

"Miss Charlotte," he said with a chuckle upon recognizing my voice. "I sent him to fetch me a plate. I find the necessity of a, a minder as you call him, quite distasteful. But I suppose otherwise I would be in corner, out of harm's way."

"Now you know what it's like to be a woman," I teased.

"Sad comment on our society. Don't expect arguments from me, I've been too long a part of the Backus household to not have picked up some progressive views." He paused. "Is it stuffy in here? I should like some air."

I looked around the room. No one seemed to be watching us. "There's a terrace of some sort behind us."

"Perfect. It would be easier to guide me if you put your arm around my waist," he suggested slyly.

"That sounds like something that might work on a gullible

young woman."

He laughed softly. "These moments with you have made me not regret accepting the invitation."

With another look around the room, and seeing everyone engaged in conversation and food, I led him discreetly outside, through a set of glass doors that were partially opened to keep the room temperate. I guided him over the flagstones until we were out of sight of the window. "Better?"

He drew a deep breath. "Mmm. Can anyone see us?"

I looked around, but there was no one else outside. "No."

"Good," he said, "Now let me look at that dress."

I should have stopped him, but I didn't. Instead, I stepped closer to him, thrilled beyond speech as his fingers walked from my waist, up over my bodice and then slid delicately along the demarcation of flesh and gown, over the curve of my breasts. Shock and delight—what a heady combination. "Gideon," I whispered.

He swallowed some strong emotion or desire of his own and his head leaned forward for a kiss, a kiss I gladly gave. My arms went round his neck as I'd been wanting to do all evening, and he kissed my ear and down the side of my neck and the base of my throat. I clutched his shoulder as he kissed mine. Then he straightened to kiss my face, my scars, and my mouth. At that moment I did not care if the doors should be thrown open and the entire populace of the ballroom see us. "I love you, Charlotte," he said, his voice husky as he declared himself for the first time.

Before I could reply, the doors flew open and half a dozen pretty young women in bright gowns exploded into the shadows, like a Chinese rocket. We stepped away from each other, and stood side by side as if sharing an innocent conversation. "We should go in," I murmured.

"Come to my room tonight," he whispered before saying louder, "If you would be so kind, Miss Backus," and extending his arm stiffly.

I led him past the giggling girls with as much dignity as I could, and I was grateful when his hired guide appeared at the glass. "There you are, sir. I've prepared a plate for you." He purposely avoided looking at me as he took my spot at Gideon's elbow.

"Thank you. Miss Backus, I appreciate your kindness, as well. I hate to ask you to leave so early."

"I understand completely, Mr. Lyons. I am not used to these late nights, myself. Until we've said our good byes?"

He and his guide went one direction and I waited too long, hearing one of the girls say scathingly to her friends, "Who else but a blind man would kiss a face like that?"

Then Mrs. Montcalm descended with a smile, "My dear Miss Backus, there you are. I missed your glorious gown for a moment!" She lowered her voice, ushering me towards the table. "I know Mr. Lyons is your colleague, but it was very foolish of you to leave the room alone with him!"

I opened my mouth to make an excuse, to lie, and couldn't. "My apologies. I didn't think anyone would notice or care."

She took a breath and laced her gloved fingers together, fan dangling from her wrist. "You're so young, not much older than those gossipy girls, yet so independent. I should have—"

I place my hand on her forearm. "You done much more than required, and I thank you. I will be making my good-nights early, I am not used to late nights, and Mr. Lyons has indicated he finds the company a little tiring, given his disability. Uh, Miss Bayfield waiting up for us."

"You really should have an older chaperone, but I suppose she does well enough. There is certainly no hint of scandal and Dorset is too small to hide anything. Now you just need to get married and your life will be well arranged."

Mr. Montcalm suddenly interrupted. "Pardon my intrusion.

152

Miss Backus, might I ask a favor of you? Mr. Hillman has fallen under the weather, as it were, and I don't want him on the road tonight. Would you mind very much taking him back to Dorset with you?"

"Mr. Montcalm, I've just been encouraging Miss Backus to observe the rules of propriety and you want to send her out, alone, with two men?"

"Propriety be damned if it saves Mr. Hillman from a possible accident, my dear. I trust Mr. Lyons will defend Miss Backus's honor if Mr. Hillman should be so far, er, ill as to mistake her for less than a lady."

Mr. Hillman, if I recalled correctly, was with the railroad, negotiating freight services or something like that. He made his home in Dorset because, as I understood, he could have a grander home for less money.

With a passenger slurring his way though tales of his own epic greatness, Gideon and I could do little more than snicker at each other.

16 ILLICIT LOVERS

GIDEON MANAGED TO get coherent directions to Mr. Hillman's house and the two of us practically carried him to the door. He managed to open it with nothing more than a dangerous sway, but he was home and safe. A very sort time later, I pulled the car up to the garage and we sat in silence, listening to the engine. "I'll put it away, I know Miss Elizabeth must be eager to talk to you," Gideon said, his voice neutral. "Should I expect to see you, in a little while?"

I nodded, forgetful he couldn't see it. "Yes," I forced myself to say. I had just agreed to an assignation from which there would be no turning back. I didn't care if it was wrong. Practial Charlotte seemed also to be passionate Charlotte. But I loved him, I was certain of it, and he was the one who would have my maidenhead.

155

My first important decision based on my emotions. It felt good, and somehow correct, in spite of how wrong I knew it to be.

So it was to Elizabeth's room I went, that I could leave when I desired, and I had so many things to tell her, it was not difficult to pass the time until I imagined Gideon should have the car put away and be waiting patiently in his room. I described the ballroom and gowns, the food and the dances and how lovely it was to fly across the floor, remarking perhaps a bit too enthusiastic on Gideon's dancing, and I told her of the rude comments I'd overheard with a carelessly dramatic heavenward gaze to indicate how silly I'd found them. "We should host a ball, Elizabeth! Have we ever done that?"

"No," she said smiling at my enthusiasm. "You haven't seemed to feel like celebrating for quite some time."

"Oh. We should." Reminded that Maurice had suggested it as a way to announce our upcoming nuptials, I changed the subject. "It's late, Elizabeth. I had such a wonderful time tonight, but I'm exhausted. We can talk more tomorrow?"

"Charlotte, I could not help but notice how often Mr. Lyons' name crept into your narrative. I think we should have a long talk about him before, well, before you grow too fond of him."

"Much too late for a long talk. Perhaps in the morning?"

She gave me a troubled look. "Very well. And we will talk more about our own ball, too," she said forcing a smile and kissing my cheek. "Good night, Charlotte."

***

I nearly flew down the backstairs, my dressing gown fluttering behind me, my heart pounding in anticipation. At Gideon's door, I hesitated. This was a momentous act, one that could never be undone. I wanted to be reckless—I *was* being reckless!—but I forced myself to reconsider at this last minute. There could be very serious consequences, particularly if Gideon wasn't being honest in his affection. But it was he who until tonight had resisted more than few precious kisses, whilst I was engaged. Of the two of us, he seemed the more ethical.

And the truth was, I felt that I was being given a second chance at an opportunity missed before. Something I should grasp in both hands whilst I could. The consequences I would accept.

Satisfied that I had duly considered the consequences of my recklessness, I tapped lightly on the door.

"I wasn't sure you'd come," he said, his voice low and rough. He was wearing his lovely banyan, but I couldn't tell any more in the deep shadows.

"I wasn't sure, either."

He swept me into a tight embrace, the warmth and strength of his body against mine took my breath away. "This is madness."

"Yes."

"You can still leave."

I let my hand slide inside the smooth brocade of his banyan, touching his skin with held breath. Gideon Lyons was not a brawny man, but he worked hard and his physique bore that out. For some reason I thought of Frederick. "I want to look at you," he whispered, tugging at my nightgown. I helped him pull it over my head, feeling reckless and excited and a little afraid.

He stood behind me, my bare shoulders against his equally bare chest, and he tilted my head back towards his shoulder that he might kiss me. With one hand resting gently on my shoulder, his other traced the scars on my face and my eyes closed as if to enhance the exquisite sensations of the flesh. His fingers grazed my jaw, then slipped down my neck to trace my collar bone. The fingers of both his hands now began to trace the contours of my arms, hesitating over the new skin on my forearms. "I nearly lost you," he said softly in my ear, his a breath a tickle that warmed me.

He took my right hand and lifted it to his face, pressing it against his cheek, still smooth from an evening shave. I pushed my fingers further back, into his unruly hair as his finger tips alighted on either of my hips, drawing a surprised gasp from me. Slowly he traced up, hips to waist to chest, drawing another quick breath. I found myself alternately sucking in a breath and holding it, then panting when I let it go, his touch was so light, and teased the very surface of my skin.

Sliding now towards the center of my torso, his fingers danced across my breasts and as he touch my nipples, his breath was hot on my neck, and as ragged as mine, I noticed. He cupped my breasts, which spilled over a little from his hands, and his exhale was a rough version of my name.

I wasn't sure how much longer my knees would hold me, but now instead of just using the tips of his fingers, the entire palms of his hands returned to my hips, before one arm embraced me fully, holding me against him tight enough I could feel the hardness of his masculinity. His free hand slipped across my belly and down, and I tightened my legs reflexively. As he continued to stroke and quest ever so gently with his fingers, I relaxed and let him do as he would. Words fail to describe the sensation, like electricity with pleasure instead of pain and my arms flailed for something to grasp.

I stumbled out of his hold, breathless, afraid, and wobbly, saw in the dim light the planes and angles of his face and body. "Gideon," I said, not meaning to speak aloud. I wasn't afraid anymore of the irrevocable act, but of my own reactions. The intensity of sensation staggered me. Standing here, apart from him, staring at him, I understood that I wanted to be joined with him in every way possible. It was the intensity of the emtions, the feeling of being out of control, that alarmed me.

"I will not force you," he said softly, standing still as a statue. As a statue.

"No," I said, my voice shaking, though I wasn't sure what I was saying no to. I opened my mouth to explain, and changed my mind. Instead, I put my hand on his arm, to let him know where I was and that I wasn't afraid. I reversed our positions, standing behind him, and traced the contour of his back, marveling at the feel of his skin. I impulsively kissed him between his shoulder blades. "May I?" I whispered, my head angled upward, the corner of my mouth still touching him.

"Please," was his hoarse reply.

I copied his earlier motions, with the flat of my hands. I felt his pulse, the warm, yielding nature of flesh, and the hair across his chest that no statue had. I pressed my bosom into his back and was gratified by his hiss of indrawn breath. I brushed his nipples, finding them as firm as my own and almost as sensitive. I held my breath exploring the firmness of his stomach, the indent of his belly button, and my hands paused at his hips, nervous. That part of a man was far more different from a statue and I froze again with virginal fear.

Finally my hand closed round him, and I drew a shocked breath, surprised at the length and hardness, but also by the silken texture. I had not expected that. His hand closed over mine as he groaned. He squeezed both our hands, and then pulled mine away, turning me to face him. Our bodies touched, front to front, flesh to flesh, and now he stroked my back as he kissed my mouth.

He stooped just low enough to lift my from my bottom until his hard masculinity was pressed against my place of self-pleasure, sending a thrill through my body, even as my legs wrapped wantonly around him, almost of their own volition.

He lay me down on the bed, taking my hand and putting it with his between his private parts and mine, so I could feel both. "Is the spell broken if we speak," I asked in a low whisper.

"Your voice only makes this more real," he replied, his voice low and intense. "I'm going to kiss you," he said, "from here—" He kissed the larger of my scars and then my mouth, "—to here." He laced his fingers through mine, pressing into the dampness between my legs.

"Is that... quite... proper?" I asked, thrilled and scandalized all at once.

"My darling Charlotte," he murmured, his mouth against my neck. "Proper was left on the other side of my chamber door. But I will stop if you ask it."

I had thought the touch of his hand had been pleasurable, but now I learned new sensations. Not only from the pressure of his lips but the tickle of his hair as he slowly eased down my body, his weight holding my legs open when my first instinct was to close them. Then, his mouth was on my pleasure point and my body arched, even as I tried to stop him. I'm not sure when my hands stopped pushing at his head and started pulling, perhaps when I realized this sensation was familiar, one I had brought on myself, only so much more exciting for being done to me! "Gideon!" My voice was wonderment, but my thought was lost as he brought me to my pleasure.

When it had passed enough to leave me sensible, he mumbled against my hip, "I love your passion, my dear, but you could strangle a man with the strength of your thighs."

I blushed and stammered an apology and he choked laughter as he brought his face to mine. "Don't apologize for your enjoyment. Would you kiss me now?"

His kisses tasted strange, but I desired them too much to protest and when he moved over me, my fear had me halting him. "May I not kiss you as you kissed me?"

He smiled. "Oh my darling. I should be undone if you did so just now."

"Will it... hurt much?"

160

He kissed me then, and guided himself inside me in one smooth motion, then froze. It took me a few seconds to realize that we were hip bone to hip bone and it... felt... wonderful.

"I'm all right," I whispered, when he remained still.

He coughed or laughed and said in a rough voice, "I'm not sure I am."

Before I could ask, he pulled back and then pushed in again and it felt strangely magnificent, and my hips again seemed to know automatically what to do, and my legs wrapped around him to make the motion fiercer, harder. Such an animal act, yet so exquisitely beautiful and I wept when he clutched me tight to him, tension releasing inside and out.

"Charlotte. Did I-? Hurt you?"

"I love you, Gideon Lyons," I said, sounding fierce to my own ears.

He rolled off me, pulling me so I was half on top of him. "I hope you would not have come to my bed otherwise."

"No," I confirmed in a small voice, though I suspected he was tesing me again.

Then we were both laughing and holding each other tightly. When the high emotions began to settle and something resembling logical thought was again possible, I realized something vaguely shocking. "We've done this before."

His body beside mine tensed, but he asked gently, "What makes you say that?"

"I was clearly not virginal, and you were clearly not surprised." I had not made this decision lightly. I certainly had not forgotten the censure for indulging in physical intimacy without the benefit of marriage, and it was mildly alarming to discover this wasn't the first time I'd made the decision. It was only his lack of surprise that kept me from assuming the worst of myself. There was only one way he could have known this wasn't my first time.

He sighed heavily and sat up. I missed his warmth and pushed myself up as well.

"I suppose I should have told you this before. Before we did anything you'd have cause to regret."

"Trust me, Gideon—I regret nothing." I leaned forward to kiss whatever part of him was closest, it seemed to be his shoulder.

"I-I feel that I have taken advantage of your memory loss. But I must tell our entire history now, and submit to your judgement."

"That's very melodramatic," I said, trying to lighten his mood.

"I was nineteen when your father brought me here. It was an honor he paid me, to live under his roof. You must understand that I was raised to be very traditional and it in no way excuses what I did, but perhaps it might explain some of it."

I pulled the soft wool blanket up and draped it over both our shoulders, positioning myself beside him on the bed. So far his words made little sense, but I trusted that would change.

"I thought you were a silly girl, in a blossoming body. I thought it over-indulgent of your father to allow you come to the lab, especially as you were no longer a child and the men working there might get the wrong ideas."

"That's sweet of you," I murmured, unsurprised by his characterization. At fifteen, I probably *was* a silly girl, though I trusted the men working for my father at the time weren't so insulated as to have never seen one before.

"No," he disagreed. "I thought you were a pest, and I hated the way you seemed to follow me around." He paused, as if deciding what words to use. "One night, the anniversary of my arrival, your father introduced me to a case of liquor in the storeroom, sharing it out with a few others of the men. Our work was progressing, or so we thought, and we were both happy he had brought me here. But he went home and I continued to drink. I don't remember exactly how I got back here that night. I remember you, though. Clad only in a thin nightgown, you came rushing down the stairs to quiet me, that your father not know what a fool I'd made of myself.

You hoisted me to my feet and half dragged me down the stairs to my room. And I, I dragged you down on the bed and stole your virtue."

I had to repeat his words to myself to make sense of them. He was telling me that he had taken me by force? His story inspired no shadowy memories to grasp at, it was as if he were recounting something he'd done to a stranger. I was as certain as anything that I loved him, so if he spoke true—and I believe he did, for who would tell such an awful lie on his own self—forgiveness must have come at some point. I leaned in to offer my sympathy, and he shrugged me off, but gently.

"There's more. While I don't remember the rest of that night, the next morning we met in the hall. You looked so, so strange. Almost happy." He sounded puzzled, but continued, "I felt horribly guilty for what I'd done to you, and by extension your father. I had sullied the daughter of the man who took me under his wing, shared his home with me! Under his own roof, while he slept, I'd betrayed him and done injurious harm to you. I did not want him to know, and I admit there was more than a little selfishness involved. I did not want to lose my position. I was angry at myself for being so stupid! " He paused, his jaw tight as if this were a difficult story to tell. "So I berated you for taking advantage of me, I accused you of trying to ensnare me in marriage, and the way you flinched under my words, it was as if I were physically striking you. I saw your pain at the lies I spoke, and I could not unsay them."

I cringed as I imagined what it must have been like to hear those words from a man I had surely been infatuated with, who only the previous night I must have imagined some love tryst where he recounted theft by force. "I must have forgiven you at some point," I said reasonably. "Because I only remember meeting you some three weeks ago, but the depth of my feeling for you could not have grown in such a short time."

163

"If you did, I never knew it. You went off to Paris, and I was relieved; I didn't have to face my guilt on a daily basis. In the three years you were gone, I found a way to reconcile myself with what I'd done. And when you came back, you were no longer a child in any way. You were cool to me, as was only to be expected, but eventually we discovered that we worked well together in the lab. When I wasn't working with your father, you and I, we worked almost like one being, hardly needing to talk because we both thought the same way. You would hand me a spanner I never needed to ask for, almost before I knew I needed one. When things didn't go right, as they so often do not, we cursed and commiserated together. But when we came home, it was like I was invisible to you. I remember the day I realized that you were the woman I wanted to be with for the rest of my life, and how desolate I felt, knowing I had no right to say anything. I dared not speak. A year later, my feelings had not faded, only grown, and I could suffer no longer. I resolved to ask your father for permission to court you, even if all I expected was to be forced to endure your rejection. I had stepped outside the research lab, trying to find the right words, when the boiler exploded."

"Oh!" My free hand went to my heart, more upset to hear this than any other part of his tale. His feelings for me were all that had spared him my father's fate. "Did you ever say anything?"

He turned from the waist and hugged me. "I grieved for your father almost as much as you did, and felt guilty that I had survived when he hadn't. And of course, I was no longer a whole man, Charlotte. What use was a cripple to you? And when I returned from my rehabilitation, Maurice Westham, a handsome man by every account, was all solicitous and bent over your hand," his voice grew bitter at Maurice's name, "and suddenly you were engaged. What would have been the point?"

I hugged him back, squeezing him as tight as I could until he grunted. "Seems like there might have been a point, else I would not be here now, would I?"

"Perhaps you're only here because you did not remember?"

I drew back a little. "I would like to think I'm not that free with my person. I have a depth of feeling for you that most certainly has not developed only within the short time I actually remember knowing you." I repeated myself since he seemed to have missed my words the first time.

"Then... why are you engaged to Westham?" He sounded both curious and hurt.

"I don't know, but by tomorrow's end, I won't be. Or is that later today? I..." I hesitated, trying not to hold him to a course he might not wish. "I don't know what is to become of us, but I cannot marry Maurice Westham and I cannot pretend to him that I might change my mind." I was feeling guilty again, for the week of deception, for I had known before tonight that I loved Gideon Lyons and could not marry Maurice. I was simply too cowardly to act, based solely on my feelings.

He kissed me, stroking my hair, and said, "This should have been our wedding night."

A lifetime married to Gideon Lyons, now that I had no trouble at all imagining.

17 Breaking Up is Hard to Do

I WAS ALMOST asleep in his arms when Gideon said with soft reluctance, "You need to return to your room, Charlotte. We can't be found together until..."

"Until?" I asked sleepily.

"Until we're married," he said, and his mouth curved in a smile I could feel against my forehead.

If I hadn't promised Elizabeth an early morning talk, I'd have said to hell with propriety. I loved the warmth of his arms and I could sneak up the back stairs to my room before anyone was the wiser. If I hadn't promised Elizabeth. I sighed and found my nightgown and wrapper. I kissed his forehead and his eyelids, his nose and his mouth, feeling sultry and wanton and sleepy and sad to leave him.

It felt like I had just closed my eyes when a rapping on my door woke me. "What?" I said crossly, forcing my eyes open. I was still wearing my wrapper—my bed had felt cold when I finally crawled into it. The door opened and Elizabeth came in with a tray that I had to admit smelled good. As I swung my legs out of bed, the soreness of my thighs caught me off guard and I blushed, feeling my cheeks burn, and I swung my hair over my face to hide what I was sure was a bright red face.

"Are you quite well?"

"Yes, I must have danced too much," I said resisting an urge to giggle. I put my slippers on and hobbled to the writing desk. After this talk, I had to write Maurice a most difficult missive.

"I didn't feel like firing up the stove, so this is just made on the little gas burner," she said uncovering two bowls of fresh oatmeal, topped with canned pears and two steaming cups of tea. "Mr. Lyons is on his own for breakfast."

We'd told Hannah yesterday to not worry about today—with the ball last night, breakfast at six-thirty was no certain deal—in fact the giant sundial outside said it was nearly nine and I could have slept at least two more hours. I yawned and took a cup of tea, drawing in the rich scent appreciatively. "Thank you, Elizabeth. What was it you wanted to talk about."

"Gideon Lyons."

I smiled before I could stop myself.

"And that's exactly why. You should not be smiling like that over him. Last night you were practically gushing, as besotted with him as you were at fifteen."

Ah, as I had suspected. "Gushing? Nonsense, I was just describing how he danced, with such grace, among so very many other aspects of the ball that had very little to do with Mr. Lyons."

She shook her head. "I've been watching you, and I can see what's happening. You shouldn't spend so much time with him."

"I'm engaged, I know." I looked to the ceiling with a slight shake of my head before setting aside the tea for the oatmeal. I was tired yet, but hungry, too.

She gave me that pretty frown and pout combination that said she was troubled. "He hurt you, deeply."

I ate my oatmeal, debating whether or not to tell her that Gideon had confessed his crime to me. Deeply hurt me... nearly ten years ago. I must have held a very large grudge. "I think I can take care of myself."

She sighed and picked up her own bowl. "I, you were so determined that you would never let him hurt you again. I'm trying to protect you."

Which is probably why I never said anything when my anger or hatred had turned to love. I nodded. "Maybe it's different this time. I think he has some affection for me."

She said nothing, just ate her oatmeal thoughtfully. When it was done, she said, "He does seem far more kindly inclined to you. He—it's difficult for me to gauge him sometimes, because of his blindness. He has sought out your company and I have not been as vigilant in my chaperone duties as perhaps I ought." She narrowed her eyes at me. "Has he been courting you?"

"I wouldn't say courting." But now that she had, I supposed his behavior could fit in that category. "Is it really so strange to you that he might be fond of me?"

She gave me a glare over her tea before setting the cup down. "I meant to question his ability to care, not your worthiness to be loved. Given how you looked last night, I'm sure you had plenty of admirers." She thrust one of her sketches at me.

I was speechless. The woman in the sketch was strong, yet alluring. She looked like the queen of thieves, or something equally dangerous yet her stance suggested a woman of carnal pleasures and I blushed. "That isn't me. And while I had plenty of men wanting to dance with me, most were my father's age. And married. Business contacts." I touched my scars, glancing at her sketch. "Certainly no line up of love-sick men, such as that woman might have."

She sighed. "I hope you aren't suggesting Lyons only likes you because he's blind."

I shook my head. He had been trying to find the words to ask my father's permission... "No, I don't think so."

She patted my arm. "Just be careful, Charlotte. I don't want you to get hurt again, not by him."

Lately it seemed I was more likely to be hurt in a freak accident. "I'll be careful."

After she left, I wrote a carefully worded letter:

Dear Sir, You have been most kind and patient with me through these many days of my amnesia, and I feel I must be honest with you - you deserve no less! Though it might hurt you now, I hope you will someday be able to think of this day with gratitude. I cannot marry you, Maurice. It isn't merely that I cannot find it in me to feel what surely I must have once felt, but I also think my heart and interests lie in other directions. You are such a well-favored man, surely you should have a wife who not only shares your views, but also appreciates all the things you can offer her. One who will host your dinner parties with elan and do you proud with her mild manners and exquisite taste, things we both know I lack. You deserve far better a wife than I, kind sir, and I must, with most humble apologies, decline your offer of marriage.

I tried to be as gentle and flattering as I could, he deserved that, at least. I was engaged to this man, regardless of how I felt about him, and I had passed the night wantonly in another man's bed. Thinking about it still made me smile broadly, in spite of my guilt. But I had taken a road from which there could be no return and I owed Maurice my honest feelings and a clean break.

Satisfied I had put it as kindly and definitively as possible, I walked up the lane to post it personally, ensuring with extra postage that it would be delivered this day. I wanted no further delays.

Even so, I was more than a little surprised when he called at the house after supper, clearly upset. "I must speak with Charlotte alone," he said, pushing a concerned Elizabeth out of the parlour and closing the door after her. "What is the meaning of this?" He brandished my note.

I folded my hands across my stomach. "Exactly as it says, Maurice. I, I cannot marry you."

He stepped toward me, his face a study of angry confusion. "You," he said, his voice tightly controlled, "are a plain, disfigured woman with little idea of what a woman is supposed to be."

I blinked in surprise at his harshness.

"You should be grateful," he continued, his voice grating, "that I would stoop so low as to pretend I care for you. You should be begging on your hands and knees for me to take you to the church before I change my mind. You should be honored! Honored!"

"Uh..." His words were so brutal, and so precisely aimed, and so very unexpected. I knew he found my scars difficult to get used to, but this contempt took me completely unawares. I blinked back tears, and told myself he was only saying these things because I had hurt him. My throat tight, I said, "Since I'm not honored, then we are in agreement, we should not marry."

"Clearly," he said his voice tight and cold, "you have forgotten why you are marrying me in the first place."

"Clearly," I said, careful to keep my voice neutral. I had deceived him and now he was hurt, angry, as he had every right to be, and he couldn't possibly mean those things, or so I kept telling myself.

He grabbed my shoulders, startling me. "You will marry me or I will tell the local papers and I will tell the city papers, and I will tell the New York and Boston and Chicago papers what happened in Paris. Your *health problem*," he sneered, "and Miss Bayfield's scandalous secrets. You will be implicated in the worst sort of perversion, shunned by society, unable to procure any kind of work, save selling your disgusting body to sex-starved sailors."

His words, brutal and cold, struck me quite dumb. My health problem? What scandalous secrets? My knees grew weak at this sudden assault of all I did not remember. And Maurice, he lowered me gently to the settee, as if he'd not uttered such a threat.

He knelt before me, the loving suitor, and forced my chin up to meet his eyes. "Carry on your dalliance with Gideon Lyons, by all means. Let him between your legs, if his blindness has left him so desperate, for I will never sully myself with you but the idea of a child I can give my name to pleases me. But you will marry me." He let go my chin and I blinked back tears. "Now, lets go pretend to be a happy couple, shall we?"

"I-I'm not feeling well," I said, hating the tremble in my voice.

"No, I imagine not. It must be quite traumatic to not remember what an emasculating tramp you are. Go to your room, like a good girl, and I'll have Miss Bayfield bring you some laudanum."

I hated being so vulnerable to the things I did not know. But not enough to forget whose house we were in. "Get out of my house. Now."

He stood up and bowed from the waist. "Very well. But soon it will be my house, and you will have no choice but to do as I say."

I sat unmoving until I was certain he'd left, then I left by the front door myself, to avoid Elizabeth and Gideon. I went to the back of the house and climbed the stairs of the gnomon to the top. The sunset may have been beautiful, but I did not see it. What had I done? What did I have he wanted so desperately that he was willing to marry a woman who clearly disgusted him profoundly?

Gideon found me first. I recognized his tread on the stair.

"Charlotte? What was that about? Westham stomped around like he was quite put out."

"I told him the engagement was off."

"Ah. I-I thought you might be more pleased about it." He seemed confused, and how could he not be.

I couldn't look at him, feeling shame over things I could not remember. "He threatened to tell everyone about the scandals Elizabeth and I had created in Paris."

He leaned on the rail beside me. "What scandals?"

"I don't know! I don't remember! I was taken quite unawares. He-he called me..." I could not repeat the phrase. *Emasculating tramp.* My throat was tight and my eyes were burning but I would not cry. "Why does he want to marry me so desperately he's willing to blackmail me into it?"

Gideon was silent, his expression unreadable in the shadowy twilight. "I don't know, Charlotte," he finally said in a low voice. "I-I can't imagine."

I turned to him, clutching his arm. "If you love me, Gideon, please don't abandon me now."

He was very still, then he covered my hand with his. "I won't. If you can forgive me the horrible mistake I made, how could I be upset over any scandalous thing you might have done in Paris?"

"Your mistake—? Gideon, I was sixteen, old enough! It seems as likely that was as much my mistake as yours."

"The mistake was mine," he insisted softly. "And I was twenty and should have known better."

"Perhaps. I feel so helpless, being unable to remember. I remind you, we have not known each other long enough—that is since my memory loss—for me to have developed this depth of feeling for you, so I must have loved you before, no matter what you say."

He sighed and put an arm around my waist. "It troubles me that Westham seems to think whatever you did as a youth in Paris is terrible enough to ruin you today."

Fear fluttered in my stomach. "Do you imagine that I perhaps am the type of woman who would find herself in a compromising position with a man after say less than three weeks acquaintance?"

Again he hesitated before answering, allowing my fear to grow. "You were not when you returned from Paris. You were a polished, confident woman, who was also fearless when it came to hard work and unembarrassed to get dirty and sweaty. That was the woman I fell in love with."

His words did not completely reassure me.

He tightened his embrace. "Charlotte, I think perhaps you should find out the precise nature of his blackmail."

He was right. I allowed myself the comfort of his embrace several minutes before pushing away with a sigh. "I must speak to Elizabeth. She is the only one who could know exactly what happened in Paris."

18 Miss Bayfield's Account of Paris

ELIZABETH WAS IN her room. The curtains were drawn against the falling darkness and the gas light had been lit and turned up brightly. Her easel was set up by the window and a canvas drop cloth covered the floor beneath it. Beside was the smaller easel with the sketches she'd made of me. She was at her dressing table, squeezing paint onto a well-used palette. "Tell me about Paris."

She looked up from her palette; I thought I caught a fleeting expression of dismay. "Paris? But what did Mr. Westham want?"

I pulled out the chair from her dressing table and sat down. "I need to know, Elizabeth."

"Well," she laughed, not sounding amused. "Your father decided that since your heart lay in maths and sciences, you should go to Paris to be educated by the best minds in those fields. I wanted to study art and literature, so Dr. Backus determined we should go together. I would keep you from being too studious, and you would keep me from causing a scandal."

"That didn't work, though, did it?"

Her mouth dropped open at my bluntness. "You remember?" Her voice was low, and her cheeks flushed.

"No. Elizabeth, Maurice Westham was here because I broke our engagement by post this morning."

She blinked at the change of subject. "That's...that's good!" Then she frowned. "Not because of Lyons? Please say it's not because of Gideon Lyons?"

I ignored her comments regarding Gideon. I was having enough doubts now. "He said I would marry him or he would tell all the papers about what really happened in Paris. He implied I was sent to Paris because I..." I stopped, reluctant to say it aloud. There was only one sort of health problem that sent a girl overseas. "Because I was in the family way," I said harshly, "and that you were involved in some scandal."

She gasped, setting the palette aside. "How could he know that?"

"You ask me? I don't remember what happened in Paris! Is it true, was my father's real motive in sending me to hide the fruit of my shameless conduct with," I paused and added with pained reluctance, "with Gideon?"

Her eyes widened. "So you have remembered some things?"

Some things, trivial things. None of the things that really seemed to matter. "Gideon told me."

She gasped again. "He did?"

"He felt I was becoming too affectionate towards him and that when I recovered my memories, I would be appalled. He..." I stopped. Gideon had said, the day he nearly drowned us both, that our relationship was complicated. I rubbed my temples tiredly.

176

She regained a degree of composure and said in a measured tone, "Your father never knew about, about what passed between you and Lyons. I didn't even know the full of it, until... you did not know you were in trouble until after we arrived in Paris, and then you told no-one. I found out only when the doctor in Paris botched the job."

I closed my eyes. "Please, from the beginning."

"It is as I've said; the plans to go to Paris were in place before your night with Gideon Lyons. We left within a week. You, you had told me then only that he had said hurtful words to you, made accusations, I didn't know that you had been intimate with him," she said awkwardly. "When you found out that your actions had far more serious consequences than a broken heart, you certainly didn't tell me," she said, the memory of hurt coloring her voice. "So no, your father never knew."

Elizabeth sighed and picked up her palette and a paint knife. She mixed colors with great concentration, avoiding my eyes as she carried on the story: "We'd only just begun to settle into Paris with some comfort when I returned from classes one day to find you on the settee, doubled over, nearly unconscious, your skirts soaked in blood. I had no idea what was wrong with you, until the doctor took me aside to ask which abortionist you'd gone to."

"I-? I aborted?" The word came out hoarsely.

"You had no choice, Charlotte. While many an American girl of means goes to Europe for her ahem, health, we were too young and unsophisticated to make such arrangements on our own. We had no connections, no knowledge of what to do. Can you imagine attending your classes, most in which you were the only woman, with a growing belly? I was upset you hadn't told me, your best friend, and I was angry that you were forced to go to a man who nearly killed you, but I support to this day your decision as the only reasonable one you could have made."

"And it is certain that the father was...?"

"Oh yes, without question. Gideon Lyons has always been the only man ever to make you lose all sense," she said dryly. She picked up a brush and started painting broad strokes across the canvas in a dark red color. "You confessed the whole of your indiscretion to me whilst recovering. He has caused you so much grief, it worries me to see you with him now. Though," she added almost reluctantly, "if he told you what he did, he must care something for you."

I sat silent, staring out the window. I was trying to imagine the situation. Far from home, suddenly discovering I was in the family away, alone, and I managed to find a physician willing to perform the illegal operation. My heart ached for that girl whom I couldn't quite imagine as me. I could only imagine how deeply I must have resented Gideon Lyons. And yet, I had no need to imagine the love I felt for him, running just as deep. "He never knew?"

"Lyons? No. You said you'd never tell, and made me promise to never breath a word. This day is the first I've spoken of it to anyone." She frowned down at her paints. "The surgeon assured me the matter would have no formal record."

Then how did Maurice Westham find out? He would have had to have gone to Paris, or hired an agent there to search into our history. It would have been a deliberate attempt to discover something scandalous. Deliberate and successful. But... why?

"I think I love him. Gideon, I mean," I said.

"Oh, Charlotte," she said, resignation in her voice. "I wish I could say I'm surprised. If events hadn't happened between you, when you were so young and vulnerable, I would have called it a good match. I've seen you two work together, and I've eavesdropped on you talking, I know you have much in common. But he always pretended nothing happened, and you were never quite able to forgive." She sighed, dropping her brush into a can of thinner or cleaner and setting down the palette again. "Now, the matter of my scandalous behavior," she paused, staring at brush marks on the canvas. "That was the following year of our Parisian adventure. I-it was my turn to fall in madly in love. And naturally, having spent a good year scolding you for your foolish choices in matters of the heart, I could not tell you of mine. My art teacher, so smart, so passionate, so beautiful. Her name was Mariette." She raised her eyes to meet mine, her brow furrowed in worry. "Does that shock you?"

It didn't, not really, though the full extent of Maurice Westham's threat began to resolve. I gave her long consideration, before asking curiously, "Did you ever feel, hmm, romantic, towards me? You did say we practiced kissing each other."

She blinked at my sudden divergent comment, and laughed. "My dear Charlotte, we've been the best of friends since we were very small, you are far too much like a sister to me." She winked at me. "I hope you're not disappointed."

I smiled back. "Relieved to not be counted among your unrequited loves. But I interrupted you."

Her smile faded and her eyes grew wet with tears she refused to let fall. "The scandal was mostly confined to the art community, and the school accepted it as a vicious rumor. I was terrified that word would somehow come back here, but..." She dabbed at her eyes. "It seems such mad affairs are also common for young American students in Paris. We could not, neither Mariette nor I, survive the scandal, should we continue our relationship, so we agreed to, to pretend it had not happened, that we were not inclined that way, that it was silly game. You never took me to task for my foolish choices, Charlotte, only comforted me through my own heartbreak."

Her story had a familiarity to it, like it was something I could almost remember. I struggled to grasp those memories and they slipped away, like wet soap. Letting it go, I asked, "Have you kept in touch over the years?"

Elizabeth nodded. "I suppose she is my Gideon, though she

never caused me the heartbreak he caused you. She will always be the only person I will ever love. We write often, and sometimes she crosses the ocean as curator for some art show or other and we can steal a few days together."

We sat in silence for a while, as I digested her story. "Well," I said, patting her knee. "Aren't we a pair."

Although her eyes were glassy with sorrow, she laughed. "That we are, dear friend."

Now that I knew the story behind Maurice's threat, it seemed less frightening and I could see where his intent lay. Apart from the scandals of our youth, which in light of our youth, might possibly be forgiven, he meant to imply that because she and I lived under the same roof, we were lovers. That would indeed destroy our reputations and our independence. I would have to tell Gideon the truth, and I could not even guess what his reaction might be.

We sat in companionable silence for a long while, until I realized that although I finally knew why I was engaged to a man I did not like, I still had no idea why he was determined to marry *me*, particularly when it was clear that he disliked me intensely.

And it was some time after that before I realized that so long as all our livelihoods were threatened, I was still engaged.

19 Secrets and Plans

ELIZABETH DROVE US into Dorset for church on Sunday, and Gideon sat beside me. "You didn't come to my room last night," he said in my ear.

"No."

"You asked me not to abandon you, might I ask the same?"

I gave him a tired smile. "I had much to think on. I will tell you everything, and submit to your judgement," I said, repeating his words back to him.

He gave my hand a quick reassuring squeeze.

Maurice had the audacity to meet us at the church as if nothing had changed. He bowed and smiled, but his grasp of my hand was nearly crushing. More than a few looks were thrown our way, so perhaps Elizabeth had been right in supposing my behavior at the ball had been too forward with Gideon, but today we were carefully ignoring each other.

I smiled over gritted teeth after the service, and as the pastor approached, Maurice said, "We should speak to him about a wedding, don't you think? Darling?"

I swallowed panic. I could not commit to any such thing without talking to Gideon. "Next week," I said calmly. "I want to arrange a ball, and I need to compile an invitation list. You must provide me with the names and addresses of your friends, so I am sure to invite them."

"So very glad you are finally seeing sense," he said, and his low voice sounded genuinely pleased.

I had an idea in my head, but it all depended on Gideon. If he was still willing to marry me after hearing about, about the things that had happened in Paris, then Maurice's threat held little power. Some might believe I was marrying Gideon as a cover, but I was certainly willing to smother him in kisses publicly. Just to quell any doubts, of course.

If he wasn't... "I should like a new dress," I said.

"Oh really?"

"You are always so perfectly turned out, Maurice. I should like to not embarrass you on our wedding day."

"That's... thoughtful," he said, clearly puzzled.

"If there is no help for it, I see no reason why not to make the best of it," I said, minimizing my irritation.

"You are ever practical, Charlotte. Perhaps I should never have tried to convince you this was a match of the heart."

"It certainly would have saved me considerable soul-searching," I agreed acerbically.

We were strolling towards the street, where my steam car was waiting, with Maurice's sleek two-wheeled cabriolet. As we talked, his grasp of my hand had eased considerably, to my relief. Then he bade me good-bye and kissed my knuckles, saying he'd send by post the addresses I needed, and he would see me next Sunday. Relief and relief.

"We've full pressure," Elizabeth said. "What was that about?"

"He wanted to book the church for our wedding," I said, and saw Gideon's mouth tighten.

"You're not going through with it?"

"I hope not, but for now it is easiest to let him believe he's gotten his own way. If," I hesitated. If I had known Maurice was going to be here, pressing the issue, I'd have gone to Gideon last night and explained everything. Now I was in a bit of a corner, choosing my words carefully. "If another option does not present itself, I have no choice. Backus Engineering will be no more, and no one will ever trust you with their children again, Elizabeth."

She glared at me, but Gideon's expression turned puzzled.

"I may not be able to preserve your secret, Elizabeth, but I will try."

Her eyes narrowed. "If the only way to protect me is to marry him, then it's not a secret worth keeping. Surely I have proven my worth beyond a youthful indiscretion."

I realized then that she had not fully grasped the extent of Maurice's threat. I studied her profile, her pretty mouth tight in determination. She need not know, it would only distress her further.

***

Gideon volunteered to make the midday meal and it was such a treat to sit in the kitchen and watch him put it together. If he had not been blind, he might have found our interest a bit nerve-wracking, but then if he had not been blind, it would not have been nearly so interesting to watch. "John Macklemore took me aside this morning," he remarked, finding the matches to light the small gas burner that Father had installed for convenience. It wasn't one of the sleek new models available to those with ostentatious real estate, but rather his own invention, a modification of the burners

183

we used at the lab.

"Macklemore? I thought he was Catholic?"

"He is, but he knew where to find me."

The Catholic church was only half a block away. If he wanted to talk, the church yard would be one place where no one would make a ruckus. "What did he want this time?"

He opened the ice box and touched the contents lightly, looking to see what Hannah had left us. "He seems concerned about you, apparently your amnesia is a danger to your employees. You'd think he'd have made some outcry over a blind man being project manager, wouldn't you?"

"So he's what? Attempting to use my amnesia as an excuse to persecute me for the crime of being female?"

He sighed. "I just don't see how he can make this a union issue."

I hesitated. "Westham hasn't been entirely truthful with me, regarding the managing of Backus. I hired Daniel Stockton six months ago. Did I discuss this with you at the time?"

"Yes, we interviewed him together. He seems quite competent. You said his references were in order."

"He is competent, yes. He mentioned some purchase orders that Westham had placed that seemed dubious, but not inherently harmful to the company."

Elizabeth seemed to be listening to our conversation with more interest than I'd have thought, given we were talking about work. Gideon started slicing bread, using his fingers as a guide. I flinched, but managed to not remark upon seeing the knife used so dangerously. He knew well by this time what worked and what did not, and the bread fell in slices of even thickness with his technique.

"I feel like I've been sleeping since my father died. Of course, that is largely because I can't remember anything."

"You have not been sleeping, Miss Charlotte. You've been

working behind the scenes and playing secretary whenever Westham makes his rare appearances. You do know his running the business is largely in his mind?"

"So I've gathered. Mr. Stockton said these particular purchase orders looked a bit like cronyism, but otherwise Maurice stayed out of the affairs of Backus Engineering. Not in our best financial interests."

"As long as the goods themselves are quality, I suppose we can forgive him for that as a minor indiscretion. He hasn't been drawing a salary, has he?"

My jaw dropped. "Oh! I think he's been taking a stipend from the estate, rather than the business per se—I didn't see him listed in payroll, but..." I needed to look more closely into my father's estate. I had read my father's will, but not the rest of the folder, distracted by the mysterious Hiram Clarke.

Gideon sliced cheese and the left over roast and put it between bread, which he fried with sliced onions, and served us unselfconsciously. "So nice to have a man in the kitchen," Elizabeth sighed happily.

After lunch I offered to help Gideon take the scraps to the midden. Elizabeth gave us both a narrow-eyed look but said nothing.

When I was confident we were out of earshot of anyone, I took a deep breath. "I need to tell you about Paris. Please know this is what Elizabeth told me, I don't remember. Which is to say, I think she told it true, but I remember nothing of it."

His arm hooked around my waist. "Just tell me," he said gently.

I looked at our surroundings. "Not here." Now might be a good time to introduce him to Frederick. Or Frederick could serve as a distraction or a way to lighten the mood. "I know a place that's private."

He let me lead him through the boxwood to the hidden alcove

where Frederick the statue made his home. I stared at the smooth lines of the statue. "Charlotte?"

I couldn't put this conversation off any longer. I took a breath to steady my nerves and said, "It seems... that night, that you told me about?"

"When I forced myself on you?" His voice strained, his body tense.

"I, um, came away with more than a broken heart."

"Wh-what?"

Whatever he'd been expecting to hear, I guess that wasn't it. "I found out after we, after, when I was in Paris. I didn't tell anyone. I-I didn't know what to do, so I... somehow I found a doctor willing to help. Even Elizabeth didn't know until she found me on the floor of our rooms, soaked in blood. She says..." my voice faded away in my uncertainty. What I'd done was illegal, and could be considered immoral. But how would Gideon judge me?

He let go of me and walked away, hands over his face. I waited, heart in my mouth, until he turned and said, "Oh God, Charlotte! How can you possibly think you love me after what I've put you through?"

I swallowed my relief. "That was a long time ago, Gideon. I was sixteen. I, I'm glad you didn't ask who was responsible," I finished in a small voice.

"I try not to make the same mistakes twice. Your first beau, what was his name? He certainly hadn't— " He broke off, unwilling to finish the sentence.

I smiled as I realized he still believed Frederick to be a real man. I was glad Gideon couldn't see it. "Gideon. I do not remember how, but I would guess I came to love you in much the same way you came to care for me—by mutual admiration and respect."

"But you never said anything."

I took his hands in mine. "And you never said anything to me, did you? All I know is that I only remember meeting you a few weeks ago and yet my feelings for you go deeper than such a short acquaintance can account for." It seemed I was doomed to repeat myself, in order to make him understand. "So while I cannot remember and you don't know, it happened and I know it, here." I put his hands to my heart.

"That, that's not very rational of you, Charlotte."

"Actually, Gideon, I rather think it is. But if you prefer me to be practical, then I have to tell you the exact nature of Westham's threat. You see, while my actions might be forgiven for the mistakes of the young girl I was, Elizabeth had a mad affair with one of her instructors."

His hands did not linger on my chest, but circled around me, and I think after the heightened physical desires we'd been feeling, this affectionate—rather than lustful—gesture touched me deeply. "It was not your mistake, Charlotte, but mine. You can't accuse me of taking away your right to be responsible for your choices when that, none of that, was your choice."

"Society would not see it so." We both knew that was the plain truth.

He sighed. "Could not Miss Bayfield's romance also be forgivable as a youthful mistake?"

"Perhaps." I hesitated to share Elizabeth's secret, but I trusted Gideon, and if she really wanted me to not marry Maurice, then I had to tell him the precise nature of the threat Maurice represented. "Under normal circumstances, but Elizabeth is a, a sapphist," I finished quietly.

"What? She is?" He drew back in surprise, still holding me gently by the arms.

I smiled. "You didn't think it a bit unusual such a beautiful and accomplished young woman has no suitors?"

"I really hadn't thought about it. I don't really remember what she looks like; she only became part of the household after I returned from New York, so all I know is the sharpness of her voice."

"She is a good cook," I reminded, amused at his admission.

"Granted." He smiled a little, but it was forced.

"But the substance of Maurice's threat was to imply an improper relationship between us. That would destroy her living, and ours."

He frowned. "If you don't marry him, we will lose everything. That's what you meant this morning. That's why you're still going through with this." His voice rose slightly with each sentence, his words coming a little faster.

"Unless another option presents itself," I said, not daring to voice the idea that had occurred to me. I hoped Gideon might see it himself. "A way to prove without a doubt that Elizabeth and I are not lovers."

He cupped the back of my head and held me close against him. "I suppose we could reveal our own affair...oh!" He released me and slapped his head. "I'm an idiot! The solution is obvious!"

"It is...?" I didn't want him to feel he had to marry me—I would have preferred him to actually desire it—but I must confess to being nervous that his solution might differ from mine.

He picked me up so abruptly I squeaked, and kissed me. "Why," he said, "Did I not want you to marry him in the first place?"

"Uh..."

"I want to marry you!" He sounded a trifle irritated with me, as if that were the most obvious thing in the world. He set me down. "Foolish woman. Did you not begin this conversation reassuring me yet again that you love me and have for some time? Do you think I just forgot the previous times you said it?"

I was genuinely confused now. "Yes?"

"Of course not! But when something sounds too good to be true, it can be difficult to believe or one can be reluctant to believe it. Has it been thus with you as well or have you truly not heard me express my desire to marry you? Even from that day on the gnomon, when I agreed it was confusing as to why you weren't marrying me!"

I blushed because he was right. Oh, not about that day on the gnomon, that hadn't been clear at all, but other times since, yes. I had been so focused on his insecurities, I had ignored my own. "You want to marry me," I repeated, just to make sure I was finally understanding.

"Yes! And if we marry, then Westham's accusations fall apart."

Relieved and happy, I threw my arms around him. "Brilliant!"

His exuberance faded a little, though he returned my embrace. "If he makes the accusations first, though, won't it seem like we're marrying just to save face?"

I took a deep breath. "I would be willing to behave scandalously with you in public to convince them."

He didn't react at all for what seemed a full minute, then to my very great joy, his mouth twitched and he suddenly started laughing. "Being married to you will surely be a great adventure," he said, grinning widely.

Happy that something in my life was making perfect sense, I said, "He has given me a week to begin planning our wedding and a ball to announce it."

He clapped his hands. "Do so. Plan the wedding, plan the ball. For us. Should we go back to town and talk to the pastor?"

I frowned at him. "Well. I should still like a proposal."

He laughed again, though his cheeks reddened. He knelt gracefully, catching up my hand and looking at me as earnestly as if he could see my face, he said, "Charlotte Backus, I would be honored and humbled if you would do me the kindness of becoming my wife."

"Hmmm, let me think about it."

He pulled me off my feet and kissed me. "You shouldn't tease, when we both know I'm not good enough for you."

"I disagree, Gideon Lyons, and I'll not have you say such things about the man I'm going to marry."

Reverend Brewer seemed surprised to see me again so soon. "I was going to call this week, Miss Backus. Mr. Westham said you might be ready to set a date, I was going to bring the church event schedule to help you decide." His glance shifted from me to Gideon, whose hand was resting familiarly on the small of my back. "Mr. Lyons," he acknowledged.

"'I'm not going to marry Maurice Westham," I said abruptly.

"Oh." He gave me a stern look. "I hope this isn't a hasty decision."

Hasty. I almost laughed. "Not in the slightest," I assured him. "Believe me, I have struggled with this for quite some time. Mr. Westham is, um, not a man I could live with and to marry him would be a, a mockery of the institution of marriage."

"I see. I had rather thought marriage would be good for you, help you to find your proper role, but I appreciate the wisdom of self-knowledge. Having made no arrangement with me that you need to cancel," he spread his hands wide and asked, "What can I do for you?"

"There is some slight hope for me," I assured him. "I do intend to marry."

Gideon filled in smoothly, "Miss Backus called off her engagement with Mr. Westham nearly a week ago, though he seems determined to proceed as if she'd not spoken. In the meantime, I have asked for the privilege of her hand in marriage."

Reverend Brewer gave me a startled look. "Is this true?"

"It is." I held my breath, surprising myself by how much I cared what Reverend Brewer thought.

He looked from me to Gideon and back again, his silence making me nervous and Gideon, too, evidently, for he took my hand in his, and held it tightly.

"This is a love match?"

"Yes," Gideon said as I nodded.

Finally the pastor smiled, a slow, happy smile. "Let me offer my congratulations to you both. And if I may be so bold to say, Miss Backus, this is a match I think your father would heartily approve."

I released my breath with relief and smiled up at Gideon to find him already smiling down at me. He was so familiar with me now that he knew exactly where to angle his head so that I might have the benefit of his smile. I resisted the urge to hug him. I thought it best to not tell the good reverend that marrying Gideon wasn't going to put me in my proper place, but he'd discover that soon enough and for now, we needed his help. "Reverend Brewer. We were wondering if we might ask you...."

The saintly man was reluctant at first to fall in with our plans, but upon learning that Maurice had only secured my hand by odious blackmail he agreed to everything.

***

Arranging the ball and wedding and such gave me plenty of excuses to be sending missives to the city. For some of the arrangements, I could use the telephone, such as for booking the hotel ballroom. It was less grandly modern than the Halimond, and less expensive, but the Collingwood Inn dated from the forties and the ball room still carried royal grandeur in its darkly rich decor. Either of my two gowns would look magnificent in that room, but having so recently worn the scarlet, I would wear the gold and cream one.

Maurice's list of invitees was small. He apparently had no family, either, for the only names were those of the senior partners whom he worked for. Since they were my father's choice to oversee the legalities of his business—and his death—I saw no reason not to invite them, though we would be announcing my upcoming wedding to Gideon, not Maurice Westham.

Before I sent off official letters regarding my power of attorney and Maurice Westham's history, I opened the drawer where I'd put the file of my father's estate and Hiram Clarke's asylum file. Maurice had indeed been drawing a stipend from father's estate as "manager" until six months ago. I had evidently already asked for my power of attorney back. Why I had continued to let him have such a hand in running things I wasn't sure. Perhaps I had only just hired Daniel Stockton and needed time to train him? I would ask Mr. Stockton when next I saw him.

That Maurice had not mentioned such to me filled me with misgiving. He was a hateful man and I could not imagine what Backus Engineering—only half at that, as Gideon had been an equal heir to the business—and this house and lands would mean to him. Did he mean to sell it for his personal gain? Gambling debts? If he'd ever told me before, I did not remember. And truly, did it really matter?

Perhaps it was the loss of the stipend that had inspired him to rush the marriage, though of course, from his point of view, he had been a very patient man, indeed.

Uneasy without knowing why, I decided to use the telephone to call Mssers Walton and Bright and arranged to meet with them at the Collingwood Inn, for a question I had about my father's estate. This was agreed to and I felt some easing of my tension.

Elizabeth helped me with the rest of the invitation list, providing the names of those whom should be invited, and gently suggesting a few of the names I'd come up with on my own be removed. "Not everyone has or can afford formal dress," she said gently. "I praise your egalitarianism, but those people would actually find your invitation a mockery or insulting."

I nodded and adjusted the list accordingly.

When I pressed Gideon for whom he wanted to invite besides

his parents he paused for a little too long before saying, "You seriously mean to go through with this, I wasn't just dreaming?"

I set my pen down. "Is there some social incompatibility between your family and mine?"

"No. But Charlotte, I'm blind. People will question this match, for many reasons."

"Nonsense," I said picking up the pen. "My father left the company to us jointly; most people undoubtedly expected us to marry, and Westham was the odd, questionable thing. Whatever else gossips want to say about it, we'll just have to prove them wrong by being happy and brilliant."

"Supposing your father did hope we would marry, would he still want that, knowing I was blind?"

"Yes," I said, staring at him suspiciously. Was he trying to back out? "I don't even remember my father and I know that wouldn't matter to him."

His mouth thinned, then twitched into a smile. "I believe you're right. I better get you my sister's address."

"Do you think we should hold the wedding closer to Boston? For the sake of your family?"

"I believe it's traditional for the bride to choose the church."

"Will it be big enough?"

His smile broadened and he pulled me to my feet. "Invitations to the church will just have to be very exclusive," he murmured. "Extremely sought after. Duels will erupt on the streets of cities from Bangor to Boston over who deserves to be invited."

He emphasized his words with gentle kisses, and I returned them in a state of happiness completely inappropriate to the situation.

"Charlotte, I have those— Oh!" Elizabeth broke off, as she realized what she'd walked in on.

Gideon did not rush his last kiss, and when he drew back, his mouth was quirked in a smile. "She's still here?"

"She is our chaperone. She's to ensure we don't so something scandalous."

"And I'm clearly not doing a very good job!"

Gideon released me with a chuckled and bowed in Elizabeth's direction. "So sorry, Miss Bayfield."

Elizabeth composed her features with an obvious effort and said, "I don't wish to be the scold, and the change in your relationship is, well, it makes me nervous. Charlotte is vulnerable-" I snorted very unladylike at that, "and, and... this sort of behavior must be stopped before it goes too far!"

I blushed, even as I wondered at her words. Was she pretending not to know Gideon had claimed my maidenhead? Nor did I really see what we did in the privacy of our own home could matter. Publicly, I was still engaged to Mr. Westham, though we three knew better, so I suppose if we forgot ourselves while out, it could be damaging to our reputations. Perhaps restraining our behavior would be to our benefit a while longer.

"She has a point," I said to Gideon.

Her face flushed, and she looked at the ground. "Yes. Well. I don't care to be the scold, it's not my nature. But I remind you that even here, propriety..."

My expression must have communicated something to her, as she broke off to give me a hard stare, before turning the look on Gideon. He was blessed, in some ways, to be ignorant of that piercing look. "You haven't...?"

I confess, I could not meet that gaze. My blush deepened, and yet I could not hide a smile. I so enjoyed the intimacies shared in the warmth of Gideon's bed.

"You, you've been intimate? Oh my God, no."

Gideon cleared his throat and said quietly, "I don't believe that's relevant. Or any of your business."

But she was staring at me, now, and I, cheeks burning, but grinning, said nothing. She scowled. "Charlotte, quit smiling like that."

Gideon's face angled in my direction, his cinder-glasses creating the illusion he could see me. "Smiling in what way?"

Elizabeth huffed slightly, then replied, "A very smug, self-satisfied smile."

He tilted his head. "Self... satisfied?"

I collapsed into some extremely inappropriate laughter.

***

At the height of the lumber industry, Bangor had been known across the land as the Queen of the East and the Collingwood Inn had been one of the jewels in her crown. Constructed—naturally—of timber, the exterior was clad in pale green wood siding, only now showing signs of aging, and adorned with a grand porch of white painted elaborately turned spindles and pillars. The large windows were graced by dark green shutters, pinned open to permit the spring breeze.

Inside, the lobby's wood floor was polished to a high gleam and protected from foot traffic by a slightly worn red carpet, edged with gold curlicues and pale pink roses. I was ushered into the ball room to inspect the facilities and conferred with the chef there as to what I should like to serve for a light supper and beverages. Every facility necessary was clean and tidy, and I was most pleased with my choice.

Across from the ball room was a tea room, empty this early in the day, but suitable for meeting with whichever of the senior partners chose to make our appointment. I was surprised to see two gentlemen, in the older style of hat and wearing gloves as if it were a formal occasion, step into the room. My own gloves lay to the side of a teacup, and I surreptitiously touched my hat, self-conscious in the face of their formality. "Miss Backus, a pleasure to see you again," said the more portly one, and I belatedly offered my hand for him to bow over.

"You seem to have had some adventure since last we met," remarked the one with the silver sideburns.

I touched my scars. "Yes, and I'm afraid I lost my memory as well, so might I ask after your names?"

Portly said, "Edward Walton at your service, miss."

Sideburns bowed and said, "Robert Bright. I am sorry to hear of your mis-adventure."

I shook my head. "I have some good friends who are helping manage well enough. Tea?" It was surprising that both had come at my request.

"Thank you. We were surprised to receive your invitations, both here and to this, this ball of yours."

"As you might imagine, being unable to remember has left me with numerous questions. I beg your indulgence as I ask things which might seem obvious or even silly."

"Of course my dear," said Mr. Bright of the snowy sideburns. "I wonder that it took you so long to contact us."

I leaned forward, frowning. "Mr. Westham said he was taking care of things on my behalf." My words caused the men to exchange a look. "What can you tell me about him?"

Mr. Bright gestured to Mr. Walton, who said, "I will not prevaricate, though I know you are engaged to marry him. Out of respect for your father, I must be honest. Mr. Westham is not a very diligent worker. We hired him as a patent lawyer. Dr. Backus was not our only inventor client, you see," he smiled at me, and the smile faded as he continued: "We would have let him go, but he convinced us that the problem was the type of work he was doing. When your father died, he asked to be allowed to handle the estate."

Mr. Bright picked up the story along with his teacup. "Dr. Backus seemed very conscious that if anything happened to him, you would be alone in this world. He had left his estate in excellent particulars, so we saw no harm in letting Westham try. That is, there was little harm he could do, should he prove to be inadequate."

"That is not the impression he gave." But if Maurice was not the socially upward rising man of law he boasted of, then that explained better his desire to marry me and acquire by said marriage all my property, including half of Backus Engineering.

Mr. Walton frowned. "Mr. Westham has always felt entitled to more than his work deserves—a better title, more pay, and so forth. We were pleased when you applied to us to have him removed from control of your affairs, though I suppose he will have that back after you wed."

"The ball is to formally announce my wedding," I said, "and if I may entrust your confidence, it shan't be to Mr. Maurice Westham."

There was a pause, and the two men exchanged another look. "At the risk of repeating gossip, would you mean Mr. Gideon Lyons?"

Startled, I assumed the gossip he was referring to resulted from our short sojourn outside at the Montcalm's ball. I had no innocence to protest so I lifted my chin, cheeks burning, and said, "Yes, I would mean Mr. Gideon Lyons."

They grinned at each other and Mr. Bright said, "We should be honored to attend."

Mr. Walton added, "It was your father's fondest wish that you two should see a way to unite. Keeping his company whole, as it were."

It was gratifying to know my father would have given his blessing to our match.

***

It had been my thinking that Gideon and I would announce

our upcoming wedding at the ball and I would thoroughly enjoy Maurice's thwarted outrage. I began to see that, as satisfying a scenario as that was, it wasn't the most prudent from a business perspective. True, many would be happy to see Gideon Lyons become the full owner, and some might be relieved to think they would not have to deal with me quite so directly. But it would look quite the spiteful act on Mr. Westham, who, so far as anyone else knew, was an honest man honestly engaged to me.

Anyone who spent more than a few minutes with him seemed not to care overmuch for him, but most of these people, clients and employees of Backus Engineering, had not had the misfortune and knew him only by name or the reputation he spread of himself. Yet no immediate idea of how to handle it, without giving Maurice the time to spread his lies, presented itself. Fortunately, I no longer had to come up with all the answers alone.

20 Falling In and Out

THE NOTE ON the study desk bore my name in a curious scrawl. The hand was that of an adult, but staggered as if the writer had been under the influence. I opened the note. "Meet me in the loft, I have something for you." It was signed with a large G. I smiled. That explained the haphazard scrawl. It was hardly a billet-doux, but I pressed it to my heart anyway.

"I got your note," I said as I reached the top of the ladder to the loft.

"Ah, I apologize for the hand." His voice was wry.

I chuckled, "Unnecessary. It was legible. My father's handwriting was very neat, almost mechanically precise—and utterly illegible."

He grinned. "I remember. And so, it seems, do you."

My smile faded. "So it seems. Little things like that come back to me all the time. It's the important things I cannot seem to bring to mind."

"I don't know if I think that's good or bad."

My smile returned and spread into a grin. "You still think I'll change my mind simply for remembering?"

He gestured me forward, toward the work table. "Now that you know the entire history between us, and still seem to regard me fondly, I am less worried. But I confess, the fear does haunt me."

I turned and threw my arms around his neck. "I won't."

He returned my embrace, his lips pressing lightly on my scarred eyebrow. "Then I shan't try to convince you again of my unworthiness." He kissed my mouth softly. "I have something for you."

"Mmm." I drew his head down for another kiss and slipped my other arm inside his jacket, resting my hand on the small of his back. He pulled my hips against him and I felt his lustful response to my forwardness.

"Do you mean I should take you like farm hand takes the milkmaid, on the straw?" he murmured.

"Only if you've been a thoughtful farm hand and provided a heavy blanket," I teased.

He hugged me tight and said in my ear, "I'll keep that in mind, the next time I invite you to the barn, vixen. But I actually have something tangible I want to give you."

I shifted my hips, wishing I was just a bit longer of leg to more effectively tease us both. "Feels tangible to me."

"Careful," he warned, "Or I will throw your skirts over your head and take you against the table."

I gasped, torn between being scandalized and intrigued. "Promise?"

He groaned. "You make being a gentleman very difficult."

"Only for you, Gideon. I love you."

"Here. Before you distract me so I'm as memory lost as you."

He was offering a, a... I took it to see what it was. It looked like a feather puffed winter bird, only all in metal. "Gideon! This is exquisite!" Each feather was a separate bit of hammered metal, copper or bronze.

"I started making it for you, when I realized I loved you. I set it aside after you accepted Westham's proposal. It winds up, you see?"

His hands around mine, he showed me the key and how to wind the toy, and the wings of the bird slowly opened out and spread as if would take flight. Then just as slowly, they folded back, the metal feathers folding across one another almost identical to the real thing. I was speechless.

"It's not very intricate, it doesn't sing or do anything more than that. I am by no means a master, nor shall I ever be. But I thought you might like it."

"It looks very intricate to me, I, it's just beautiful and so delicate!" I held it both hands, as if it were a real bird and walked to the edge of the loft where a beam of sunlight lit up dust motes like gold. The little metal bird sparkled like it was precious metals. And then the board beneath my feet gave way.

The fall seemed to last forever, my cry of surprise caught in the sun beam above me as I turned in the air, trying to fly myself, perhaps. My lovely gift fell from my hand and Gideon was shouting my name and suddenly everything I had forgotten was remembered. It was like being struck in the head, and then I crashed into the floor.

As I lay breathless and gasping in amidst the straw and splinters, I could not decide what hurt more—my ankle, which was surely broken, or the wash of memories. I moved my head cautiously and nearly fainted to realize how close I'd come to being impaled on the tines of the pitchfork, buried in the shallow layer of hay. Beams of sunlight pierced knot holes in the barn and speared my eyes, until the whole barn seemed to glow. The glow faded into grayness then pulsed back strong and I tried to turn my head away. If I closed my eyes, I wasn't sure I would open them again, and under the weight of my memories I wasn't sure I wanted to.

Whatever I might want, I could do nothing at the moment. I tried to sit up but the desire to do so resulted in a sort of flopping as a fish out of water might do. I lay still, trying to ride out the pain shooting up my leg and feeling so very, very tired.

"Charlotte! Charlotte!" Gideon's voice came from so far away, I wasn't sure it was real. I closed my eyes, swallowed by the pain. Gideon was alive, though, that was good, because I... thought he was dead... behind the door...

I let my newly restored memories wash over me, matching them up with what I'd been told or concluded with hopes of filling in or explaining. I thought I felt someone holding my hand, but my eyes were now far too heavy to open. My memory seemed to spool backwards, unwinding, and I remembered the horrible realization that the boiler was about to blow, and Gideon was in there and I didn't want to live with both him and my father gone—I guess that's why I forgot, instead.

I was there to talk to Gideon, I wanted to ask him—to ask him if he might have any feeling for me, enough to enter into a marriage of convenience. Then, as now, I had thought of him as a means to escape Maurice, but then... I'd no idea he cared for me, and I would have died before telling him I loved him.

Tears on my cheek. Mine? I could not tell. At least, if I was dying, he knew I loved him. But oh, we had had so little time!

Maurice... yes, he had come into my life after my father's death. He'd waited not one day past the year of mourning society decreed appropriate to press his suit on me. I accepted finally, because he wore me down with his constant asking. I was lost without my father. He was all the family I had. Even my three

202

years in Paris, away from him, we'd written faithfully, long letters full of the strange mix of technical and household matters that was characteristic of our in person conversations. Maurice could not seem to understand how I could grieve so long. "It's natural for a parent to pass on, Miss Backus, though your father left this world too early, he was destined to do so, sooner or later." What did that even mean? My father had been all the parent I had, and the only thing that made his death at all bearable was that Gideon had not been killed as well. The two most important men in my life...!

Gideon was still in New York learning how to navigate a society designed for the sighted when my mourning ended, and the longer he was away and the more insistent Maurice was to court me... and when Gideon finally came home, he was bitter, so bitter, at his loss, and more distant to me than ever he had been.

I never warmed to Maurice's suit because I was in love with another man. Yet he persisted when many other men would have given up and finally proposed, though I'd given him no indication I wanted to marry him. I politely and respectfully declined. And then his true self had finally shown, some two years after knowing him as merely a persistent, handsome, but ultimately dull man. In that time, he had sent letters of his own to France and discovered all the troubles Elizabeth and I had brought upon ourselves, and he offered up his ultimatum for the first time: Marry him or he would destroy us all.

I could not tell Elizabeth why. I could not bear for her to feel guilt or blame for my entering into a loveless marriage. I was not so awful a person, after all.

I suddenly felt weightless, floating, but oh so much pain. Was this the separation of body and soul? Had my father suffered this? Such pain... I fled deeper into the dark recesses of my memory, now opened to me.

The day Father brought Gideon home... he was so handsome. So disapproving of me. I smiled—I think I smiled. I was instantly infatuated, my first real infatuation, which for a girl of fifteen was sad. I had never met a boy my own age or even Gideon's age, for that matter, who didn't strike me as a complete fool.

Four years older than me, he was not only handsome but clever. His hair had always defied him, dark and curling. His face hovered over me, brows creased, as if cross with me. Nineteen year old Gideon had little use for a fifteen year old girl. I was a nuisance, a pest my father over-indulged. It did seem strange that I should remember him with his cinder-glasses, though. Or was Gideon really there? Maybe I said his name.

The loss of my virtue—oh, I remembered that quite differently from the story Gideon had recounted. True he had over-indulged in liquor and true also I rushed to silence him, to spare him Father's disdain, in nothing more than my night gown. It was as much to spare my father disappointment as it was to save Gideon. He had fallen in the hallway, tripped over the umbrella stand. I helped him to his feet, forgetful of how I was dressed until his hand accidentally fell upon my breast. I was suddenly brought to mind of my voluptuous occupations with the Bayfield's garden statue. Far from being shocked, I was suddenly overtly aware that this man, this man was real, not made of stone.

Gideon's lustful gropings and crude talk had the opposite effect of deterring me, only stirring that dark shameful desire in me. I tried to force it all away, something to rub out with a fistful of nightgown after I had him safe from his own foolishness and Father's disapproval. I closed the door to his room behind us with relief, surprised again when he pressed a kiss on me, foul with drink. I pushed him away, startled by the organic feel of it. "Not gonna leave me wi' my clothes on, lovely? Perky, pretty lovely..." He squeezed my breast again, and I pushed his hand away...oh but how I enjoyed reliving this memory. I helped him out of his jacket, and pushed him onto his bed. "Feisty," he grinned, head swaying. "No bed, my lovely, not without you..." He laughed blearily and pulled me onto the bed.

He was bigger than me, yes. But he was drunk, and I worked in my father's lab. I was no wilting flower whose only exercise was banging on piano keys. I could have easily escaped him. I chose not to. It hurt, the loss of my maidenhead, and he passed out on top of me, but I'd felt enough from his drunken kisses and caresses to suspect that a sober man could make this intimate act all that my body had promised me, in the heating of my blood and the ache between my legs.

I was fully complicit in my undoing, and I never blamed Gideon for that, contrary to what he'd said.

No, what had hurt me beyond trusting was his accusation the next morning. The way he looked at me as if horrified that he'd been intimate with a thing as ugly as me. I hadn't thought the previous night that I'd been the one taking advantage of him, but I certainly believed it when he said it, and I was humiliated. I had never wanted the ground to open up and swallow me as much I did that morning on the stairs.

He said he hated himself for what he'd done—painfully funny that I hated myself for what I'd done, for being vulnerable, for having hope, for daring to love, as I saw it.

Seeing him every day just reminded me constantly what a fool I was. It never occurred to me that I might bear more than humiliation as a consequence of that night, not until Elizabeth and I were in Paris. I didn't want to examine that memory too closely— the fear, the shame, the over-whelming sense of solitude...but I remembered something that no one else had known, except perhaps Maurice, if he talked to the right doctor: that abortionist had not only nearly killed me, he'd ruined any chance I had for future children. The surgeon Elizabeth had taken me to afterwards had informed me before she came into the room: "I'm afraid you will never bear children, Miss Backus." I touched my stomach.

Which was frankly a relief. I loved my work at the shop and in the lab, how could I do that with a child? And new relief—I would not have to pay for my most recent indiscretions with Gideon Lyons. "Gideon," I muttered and felt a sense of doubt overtake me. Would he consider it a good thing...?

Elizabeth helped me through my pain, with far less recriminations that she recalled, and I helped her through hers. We might have been counted young women when we left Maine, but we only truly left our childhood in Paris, in pools of blood and tears. It wasn't all horrible, though. Elizabeth's art studies had instilled a great appreciation for the male form in me. It was another sort of scandalous, the half-naked men in our rooms, though of course Elizabeth had no interest in them apart from drawing and I dared not do more than look. I satisfied my curiosity as to how those beautiful bodies felt by abusing statuary, as Elizabeth put it. Ah, how do you tell anyone you were caught at the Louvre with your hand on a statue's private parts? Even remembering I blushed, I think.

I had resolved to hold my heart absolute, because caring had landed me in a vast amount of pain and trouble.

"Charlotte, do wake up."

That sounded like Elizabeth. Dear sweet Elizabeth. The beauty to my brains though she was clever enough herself. She guided me through the social intricacies my father had been unable to teach me, and she helped me have fun, when it seemed I was destined to be only plain, practical—misfortunately passionate—Charlotte. She understood that under the practical was someone desperately afraid of her own emotions, and she gave me an outlet. And I showed her that she could be more than the sum of her appearance, that she had as much intelligence and drive as I did, only in different fields. Our friendship saved both of us, I think. It grieved me that I had found a way to my love, while she would be forever denied hers. That is, if I lived.

"You must live, Charlotte." The was my father's voice. I will never know why he let me follow unnatural pursuits, as Gideon had once put it. Gideon had learned much from my father, a progressive understanding uncommon to men of their status and education. "Why did you remember now?"

Father? Why would he ask me that? "I fell," I said, or tried to.

The blackness cleared into a faded memory of the study and I was perhaps ten years of age. "Why did you fall? Think it through, Charlotte—or shall I make you return to your piano lesson?"

Oh, how I hated that piano. Elizabeth played it, and beautifully. When she gave me Frederick, I gave her the piano. I only managed to learn enough to be counted socially graceful after Father explained the mathematics of it. But I still felt that had been a trick. "Board...broke..."

Why was my throat so dry?

"And why did the board break? Another coincidence?"

"No, Father, but... no one...wants me dead."

"Think, child! I have to go now, but I expect you to figure this out, or to have mastered your piano lesson."

"Don't go!"

But the room faded and so did my father. Tears on my cheek. Mine? If not mine, whose? Perhaps if I figured it out, he would return.

Gideon loved me. He did not want me dead.

Not Elizabeth.

Maurice? No, why blackmail into marriage if he wanted me dead?

And then I was walking on the path in the woods to the lab, my heart heavy. Maurice had run out of patience as I'd used excuse after excuse to delay our wedding. "Pick a date, book a venue for a ball to announce to the world our happy union, and soon, before another horrible accident like your father's gives you yet another excuse to delay."

His words didn't register with me at the time, I was distressed enough at the idea of being bound to such a man for life. Marriage to Gideon was my only hope of saving us all, and if he could see that, a marriage of convenience, though I loved him so, but I couldn't tell him that....

What had he said? Like an echo, "...horrible accident like your father's..." *Maurice? What did you mean by that?* Was my father's death not an accident?

But Maurice did not live in my head, just memories and ghosts. If Maurice had caused my father's accident, then was he the cause of all mine, as well? And still, it made no sense that he would want me dead.

Suddenly I was falling again, in slow motion, the little metal bird slipping from hand and we both fell into a giant mouth ringed by teeth made of piano keys....

21 RECOVERY AND LOSS

I WAS SWIMMING in a dark lake that dragged at me, and I hoped I was struggling to the top of it, not the bottom. As my face broke the surface and I gasped for air, I realized I was sitting bolt upright in a cot at a hospital. I hoped it was a hospital. I sucked in another great gasp of air, as if I had literally been drowning, shivering like I hadn't shivered since...

I fell back, clutching my ribs, unable to think clearly. My head was still a fog, wisps of half remembered voices and dusty memories. Memories! The room seemed to spin about and I closed my eyes. That stopped the room from spinning, but left me with the strangest sensation that the bed was spinning. I grabbed both sides of the mattress and opened my eyes in a panic, gasping for breath though a mouth dryer than stale toast.

As the room stilled and my heart slowed so that it didn't feel like it was trying to escape, I took in my surroundings. There were three other beds in the room, only one of them occupied, and Elizabeth was asleep in a chair by my side, her chin sunk into her chest, making her look older than her twenty-five years. "Elizabeth!" My voice came out little more than a croak.

She jolted awake almost as abruptly as I had and stared at me. "Charlotte! You're awake!"

I stared at her, not quite sure where I was, or what had happened, and my mouth was so very, very dry. "Water..?"

She jumped to her feet and poured from a metal pitcher coated with condensation that awaited on a table. I watched droplets of moisture trickle across the surface of the pitcher and wondered if there was a mathematical formula that described drops of water sliding across a convex surface. My reverie was interrupted when Elizabeth pushed the cold glass into my hand. "The doctor said you might be disoriented from the chloroform."

I took the glass in both hands and sipped gratefully, sloshing the water around my mouth. "I fell?" As I looked at Elizabeth, I seemed to see two of her, the one I remembered forever, and the one I got to know over the past two weeks. With a click that I thought audible, the two slid together like perfectly machined parts and I gave her a smile that only seemed to work on one side of my face. "Bessie."

She glared at me. "I haven't missed hearing that." the scowl vanished and her eyes widened. "Charlotte? You, you remember?"

"I, I think so." My head was still a-fog. Gideon, he'd given me a bird.... Gideon whom I would never give the satisfaction of... Gideon whom I had given everything and gotten plenty of satisfaction in return... my cheeks burned and I closed my eyes. Complicated, he'd said. I almost laughed, but my mouth was too dry and my ribs hurt even considering it. I would be able to at last put his worry to rest about my feelings for him, though. I opened my eyes, took another sip of water to wet my mouth that I might ask after him, and Maurice Westham came into the room, the very model of a concerned fiance.

Something skittered across the fog in my mind, something about Maurice being an awful man, but then I knew that. Twice, I'd had to listen to him denigrate my appearance, my behavior, and my morals, while being forced to marry him. At least this time, Elizabeth knew what was going on. And Gideon! Knowing I would not have to marry this odious man made it easier for me to compose my features. So as not to cause a scene, of course.

Elizbeth glared at him and excused herself with a tone so cold it should have turned him to ice.

"I'm surprised you're awake, my dear. The doctor thought you might be out longer." His hat was in his hand, his hair smooth and perfect, not even the elbows of his jacket bore trace of a wrinkle, and his voice was neutral.

"How long was I out?" I asked, matching his tone. My hands went automatically to my hair, which was loose and in need of a good brushing.

"Twelve, perhaps fourteen hours."

"Oh."

He sat on the chair Elizabeth had vacated and his brows drew together in a frown. "Why were you anywhere near the barn, Charlotte?"

"I-" I stopped. My recent memories were still trapped in a fog. Gideon had left me a note, had he not? And a magical bird... what had happened to that exquisite little bird? "G- Mr. Lyons was doing something or other up there and asked to speak to me."

"About what?"

"I don't recall," I said, not quite a lie. I didn't recall the words. "Something about the shop, no doubt," I said dismissively, not entirely sure why. After what he'd said so crudely about Gideon, I couldn't see he'd be jealous; he wasn't after my heart. Just my assets. Something flickered in the dim corners of my mind, like a leaf swept by an autumn wind, too swift to be captured. I shook my head to clear it.

"For what it's worth," he said, in that same neutral tone, "It matters to me that you are alive."

I laughed, a short humorless sound that hurt my ribs. "Yes, well. Rather difficult to marry a dead woman."

Beneath his perfect mustache, his mouth thinned until his lips almost disappeared. "Yes," he agreed, his voice clipped. "Have you mailed out our invitations?"

I had to think for a minute. I remembered everything, except the details of the last few days. It wasn't the same complete absence as my previous amnesia, as I remembered those days before the fall, and even the fall itself, dimly. I was just having difficulty recalling the specifics. "I do believe so. I-I remember going to town specifically to do so. But I will check again upon my return home. Do you know when I should be released?"

He shook his head. "I am pleased to see you are resigned to this. You are so very practical." He rose to his feet. "I will see you later, my dear. I have some... old business to take care of, before we begin our journey of wedded bliss," he said, his voice lightly mocking. He didn't bother with so much much as a kiss to my hand, simply turned and left, settling his hat on his head before he'd even left the room.

It was only then I realized that if the glass of water had been of less sturdy construction than glass, I might have crushed it, my knuckles were so white around it. I released a long breath and drained the glass.

Beneath the thin blanket, I wore a thick flannel night gown that Elizabeth must have brought me from home. My left leg was encased in plaster from just below my knee to my ankle. It ached but the pain was dull and far away yet, still held at bay by the chloroform. I hated the cloudiness of mind caused by the anesthesia and the opiate based pain relievers and I hoped the break was clean enough that I could avoid more. If there was nothing more wrong with me than bruised ribs and a broken leg, I should be on my way home tonight.

I considered trying to get out of the bed, but decided that waiting for Elizabeth's return might be wiser. A cheerful nurse came into the ward and smiled. "You're awake at last! How do you feel?" She took my pulse with gentle efficiency, then lifted my chin and turned my head side to side, staring at my eyes. "I've had better days," I said dryly, blinking away some disorientation. "Everything seems a little...wrapped in flannel," I said, hoping she understood.

"That will wear off. Does your leg hurt?"

"It aches. Will that get worse?"

"The doctor will tell you more," she promised, then went left me to attend the other patients.

I fretted. I had no idea when Elizabeth would return, and could not get out of bed. I had no book to read. I sighed and lay back on the pillow, bored. Fortunately, Elizabeth chose that moment to look cautiously inside the room before coming in with paper sack. "Sandwiches," she said.

They smelled of sweet and spicy condiments and my stomach roiled in protest. I wondered if I actually turned as green as I felt. "No, no thank you."

"Oh! I should have thought. Do you mind if I...?"

"Please," I said, my stomach easing as soon as it realized I wasn't going to abuse it with food. I tried to be patient while she ate, but finally could restrain myself no more: "Where... um, is Gideon here?"

Her expression darkened, and she set her sandwich down, as if her appetite had suddenly fled, and fear began to creep along my spine with dark fingers. "I, I'm sorry, Charlotte. He's, he left."

"Returned to Dorset, you mean? To look after the shop." I so wanted that to be true.

She looked down. "No, I mean, he left. I don't know where he went. He said something about not being enough of a man, not being able to protect you," her voice took a bitter twist. "Couldn't even tell you to your face, so I guess he was right about not being enough of a man."

I had never told Gideon how I felt prior to my memory loss because I hadn't wanted to offer my heart up for him to scorn. I swore I would not open myself up to be hurt again. But he—he had told me he wanted to marry me. I could not believe he would lie, not about that, not to me. Something must have changed. I blinked back a sudden onset of tears. "He-he said no more than that?"

She slipped off the chair to kneel beside the bed, pulling out a carpet bag from which she extracted an envelope that looked strangely familiar. "He left this for you."

My name was scrawled across the envelope in large, uneven letters. "Thank you." I stared at the envelope, not sure I wanted to open it in front of anyone.

When it became evident that I wasn't going to open it, Elizabeth deliberately picked up her sandwich and finished it. "I talked to the doctor," she said conversationally. "They want to spend this afternoon teaching you how to get around with crutches and give you instructions on how to take care of your, um cast." She paused, looked at me and away.

"What is it, Bessie?"

She stuck out her tongue at me for the childhood nickname and said reluctantly, "Mariette is in Boston tomorrow, for a day or two. I-well, of course, I shall just have to tell her I can't come to see her."

"When was the last time you saw her?"

She didn't answer me. Instead she wrapped up the second sandwich and stuffed it in the single drawer of the beside table.

"You might be hungry later."

I searched my newly restored memory. "It's been over two years, Elizabeth. You should go. I'm not an invalid!"

"Technically, you are."

"No, I'm not. I will never forgive you if you give up this chance just because..." another leaf of memory skittered across my mind and vanished. "Because I fell out of a loft."

She pulled her lower lip in under her teeth for a moment, giving me a searching look to ensure I actually meant what I said. A smile trembled across her mouth and she threw her arms around me as best she could, given I was in a hospital bed. I stifled a grunt of pain as her weight hit my ribs, but returned the hug. "I'll stop by tomorrow before my train leaves," she said happily. "I'll make sure you can get in and out of the car, and," she dropped a quick kiss on my cheek, "Thank you!"

I spoke to the doctor, who told me that my leg had not broken all the way through, and not to put weight on it, or get the plaster wet. He advised me it would itch, and finally brought in two female orderlies to teach me how to walk with crutches. I admit, I was not masterful with them, but at least by the time they left, I could get out of bed, raise and lower myself into a chair, and move around from one room to another. When I was alone again, I was tired and my body ached so that I did not resist the small dose of medicine the nurse brought.

I was too far down the path of drugged sleep when I finally remembered Gideon's letter. It would have to wait.

*** *** ***

Sun filtered through the hospital ward windows as I pulled the curtains back from around my bed. I had been given a basin of warm water, a mirror and a washcloth for my toilette and upon completion of that I pulled the carpet bag out from under the bed with one of the crutches. I dressed myself with only minor difficulty and sat on the bed to rest. I had no hairpins or brush, so I finger combed my hair and coiled it at the base of my neck, securing it with a pencil.

I chewed on the sandwich Elizabeth had left me, my stomach still queasy, but it was better than the mysterious food offered by the nurse. The bowl might have contained a thin oatmeal, but it reminded me too vividly of my three long weeks at the asylum. I looked at Gideon's letter with dread and hope. Surely there was an explanation within, one he felt he could not trust with Elizabeth.

He had said he would not abandon me. I opened the envelope and pulled out the papers within, not in Gideon's uncertain hand, not a hand I recognized at all. I skimmed the elegantly written words, both pages, and again, and finally a third time, reading every word as if there might be some between the lines message I had missed. It was nothing more than a legal document, giving me full power to run Backus Engineering as I saw fit, for as long as necessary. There was no personal message at all. None.

Somehow that hurt more than if it had been a letter saying, "I'm sorry, I can't forgive you for..." or "I'm sorry I don't love you..."

I wasn't even worthy of an explanation.

22 Dying A Little Each Day

THE HOUSE WAS very empty without Elizabeth or Gideon. I used the telephone to confer with Mr. Stockton for the few days the doctor had absolutely forbidden me to do anything more strenuous than make my way to the water closet or kitchen. I might have given Hannah a few days off but she cheerfully insisted I could not cook for myself, and even brought up my breakfast as if I were a spoiled heiress.

I wished I had forgotten everything again. And for a few days, the laudanum bottle looked very much like forgetfulness. But every man who worked at Backus Engineering depended on me for a living. If I did not want to be present for myself, I needed to be present for them.

In the small room that might have been a nursery, I put my

mother's pink wedding dress away. Neither of my parents would be proud to see me marry against my will to a man I did not like, and I had no choice but to marry Maurice Westham now, for the same reason I could not hide in an opium bottle.

He sent a card asking to call, but I told him I could not see him until Elizabeth returned from Boston. The need for a chaperone was ridiculous, given his disgust for me, but one he accepted without question, nonetheless.

Elizabeth's good spirits were subdued upon learning of Maurice's impending visit, and she grudgingly joined us in the parlor.

"Mr. Lyons does not seem to be about, lately...?" Maurice remarked, helping himself to my liquor.

"Mr. Lyons," I said stiffly, "has left town."

"Indeed. And where has he gone off to? See the sights of Europe?" Maurice said, his voice richly mocking.

"He did not see fit to inform me."

He laughed. "I see. Well, you should have expected that. Even Miss Bayfield said he was only playing sweet to get your share of the company. Once he discovered you were not going to break our engagement, he had no need to keep up the pretense of actually liking you." He leaned forward until I could smell the whiskey on his breath. "I'm sure he didn't leave town without care of his share of the business?"

"It's in my care," I said quietly.

He laughed again, even heartier. "Perfect! Just perfectly delightful! Tell me, did he make you buy his half, or did he give it to you as a guilt price?"

"Neither!" I snapped. As little as I owed Gideon for breaking his word, I could not bear to hear him slandered so. Even if Maurice might be correct. "I have a legal document authorizing me to act on his behalf."

Instantly, Maurice's good mood vanished, like the sun behind a swift moving cloud. "And you have no idea where he went?"

Oh, I had two ideas where he might be—Boston, where his family was, or New York, where he lived for a year and half, learning through the New York Institute for the Blind. However, I saw no reason to share that with Maurice. "He left me nothing but the legal document giving me authority to act in his name."

He was in a dark mood when he left and since I had not caused it, I did not much care why. I did not care much about anything, anymore.

Without the pretense of courting me, Maurice Westham made no further visits and as soon as I was able, I spent every minute possible at work, mostly in the lab. I had tried working on the floor, but too often I would turn to ask something of Gideon only to remember he was gone. The constant reminder of his inconstancy was too much. Once married, I would no longer be allowed here, and I wanted to, well, store up the memories, I supposed. I was five and twenty, with many many years stretching ahead of me, empty of anything that mattered.

When I thought I could bear it, I went to the barn. I was hazy on the details of that day, and the drugged dreams before I woke up, but I remembered the clockwork bird, and I wanted it. After I was bound to Maurice, it would be all that I had that was mine. I would take Frederick with me, too, when Maurice moved us to the city. Or, given his thoughts on my appearance, maybe he planned for me to live here alone while he lived in the city. I dared to cherish the hope that he would leave me here and in his absence, I could sneak over to the shop and play with the boys in the dirt.

That thought cheered me, a cheer that lasted only until I entered the barn. There was the saw horse we'd used to cut new stairs for the gnomon and—enough of that. I limped across the floor, no crutches or cast now, but a cane and a leg that still ached if I walked too long on it. It was foolish, but I wanted my little metal bird. Gideon had left me without explanation, left me after

219

saying he would not. I wanted the little bird to remind me that for a very brief time I had known happiness.

The poor little bird had not survived the fall well. One wing had broken completely off, the other was missing almost the entire lower half. This tiny little thing of exquisite beauty had been mine for such a short time and was now broken beyond my ability to repair.

I spread out my handkerchief on the straw and started searching for the pieces, relying more on touch than sight to find the tiny parts amidst the straw, until I realized I was sobbing and beating the floor.

When Elizabeth came to find me, I was sitting, injured leg sprawled forward, the remains as I had been able to find in my lap. "I can't fix it," I said, dry eyed and meaning more than the tiny metal pieces in my handkerchief.

She knelt, touching the pieces gently. Then she took the corners of the handkerchief and tied them together. "Gideon Lyons can."

I held my silence, certain she meant only the bird.

"You should at least ask him," she added, helping me to my feet.

I tucked the handkerchief in my skirt pocket. "How can I do that, he...he..."

"Honestly, Char—when have you ever just given up, when you wanted something bad enough?" Elizabeth scolded and I felt my eyes begin to burn again.

"You, you are saying I should go after him? After Gideon Lyons?"

Her mouth tightened. "It would not be my first choice, no. However, he, in his blindness, has lost the ability to keep his emotions from his face as perhaps he might had. I know he cares for you and I think it was cowardly of him to leave you as he did. But I hate to see you pining like this."

I swallowed my pride, my pain, my tears. "He abandoned me, he left me with no choice but to marry Maurice Westham. If that is the measure of his love for me, then it's not enough to go chasing after him."

But later, looking at the remains of the bird and knowing it had taken at least two years of working on it several hours a night, could I really believe his affection was so shallow?

I left the remains on my writing desk, still tied in my handkerchief, and cried myself to sleep.

***

"New York," Elizabeth said firmly at breakfast.

I swallowed my oatmeal and scooped another spoonful. "What of it?"

"That's where he went. I went to the train station and asked."

"Ah." I kept eating.

She frowned. "You knew?"

I shrugged. "It was either there or Boston. Look, Elizabeth, if he wanted to be with me, he'd be here, yes?"

"Maybe he had a good reason."

I gave an unladylike snort. "I'm sure he did. But he didn't consider me even worthy of an explanation, so again." I gestured shortly with my spoon and resumed eating.

"Look Miss Stubborn. Why did you not tell me why you were marrying Maurice Westham? Did I not deserve to know?"

I frowned as I thought I had already explained that to her. "I was trying to protect you. I didn't want you to ever feel like it was your fault."

"It wasn't because you considered me unworthy of an explanation?" She stared at me pointedly.

Against my will, I began to chuckle. "Very well, Bessie. What would he be trying to protect me from?" I spread my arms wide.

"What is worse than marrying Maurice Westham? He cannot save me from that if he is not here." I took a piece of toasted bread and spread blueberry jam on it. "I'd have settled for a marriage in name only, one we could annul later. That's why I was going to the lab that night. I..." my voice faltered from its matter-of-fact tone and I took a second to steady my emotions. "I was going to ask him if, if he would consider such a thing."

She looked surprised. "Indeed." She studied her oatmeal and added another spoonful of preserved peaches to it. "You should still find him. Force him to tell you face to face."

I smiled without humor. "It will have to wait. We have a ball to make ready for, remember?"

She sighed. "Ah, yes. To announce the unhappy event." She stabbed the contents of her bowl with her spoon. "Westham ordered those silly masks?"

I nodded. Maurice had for some reason decided the ball should be a masquerade, far too late to advise any of our guests. He'd ordered a box of gold and silver Mardi Gras masks from New Orleans to be given out upon arrival. He wanted a midnight unmasking for the grand announcement of our nuptials. I suppose it fed his vanity.

The ball was the announcement of my doom. It would be a disaster.

***

I took a cursory walk through the shop, noticing that everyone still kept the tools in their precise spots, as if Gideon were going to come back soon. Several of the men with perfectly good eyes were able to grab exactly what they needed while keeping their attention fully on the parts in front of them, so it seemed an efficiency that would stay, even if—. Well, best not think about that now. He was probably waiting until I was married and out of the way before returning.

A knock at the door caused a thrill of hope to run through me but I quelled it and calmly said, "Come in."

It was Mr. Stockton, of course. Who else would it be. "Ma'am.The insurance company has given us our certificate. We can go into full production." He scowled.

"You don't seem happy about that?"

"Macklemore is here."

I shook my head. "If he wants to talk to me, have him escorted here."

He paused a moment as if he might say more, then nodded. He left the door open. The lab was a little different from the shop floor. In the center was a large table where we could either lay out blueprints, or build mock-ups of certain parts, if necessary. It looked more like a mad chemist's lair, but we used the chemicals and burners in here to test or enhance fuels, etch metals, test stresses, and the like. Everything gleamed, being less than a month old.

John Macklemore knocked on the open door as a courtesy. Today he wore a variation of his brown suit and a more subdued waistcoat than normal. I didn't invite him to sit, and stifled annoyance when he did so anyway, knowing he would be standing yet, were I a man. "What ails you today, Mr. Macklemore?"

He looked at me, perhaps examining my scars yet again, then glanced deliberately at the cane I kept nearby—after a few hours on my feet, my leg would begin to ache. I wondered how much dancing I would be able to do. Then again, if I had to sit out, would it matter?

"You're a very accident-prone woman, Miss Backus."

I wasn't able to prevent my sigh, but it was smaller than I would have done unrestrained. "Then you will no doubt be pleased to hear that Mr. Westham has chosen a date to take me away from all this."

Instead of pleased, he looked taken aback. "Then... to whom will I take my concerns?"

"Until Mr. Lyons returns, I suppose you'll have to deal with Mr. Stockton. I have no idea how much my new husband," I could not keep the bitterness out of my voice, "will wish to involve himself." Seeing his expression I added, "He is not a business man, Mr. Macklemore. He will likely sell my half of the company to Mr. Lyons, and for a tidy sum, I've no doubt."

"I see. Well, you are of course, fortunate to be marrying... uh..."

I forced a smile. "Indeed. Until that glorious day, you'll just have to deal with me. The insurance company has granted our certificate on the new boiler." I nodded at the new door, heavy as a bank vault door. It was probably stronger than the walls it was set in, which had been quite amusing. I sighed, forgetting Macklemore for a moment.

"Yes, well," he said, clearing his throat. "As long as you know my concerns." And he left at a brisk walk, no doubt looking forward to having a man to deal with. I sighed again and rested my head in arms on the table.

In one of my silly women's novels, Gideon would come in and find me there and say something that would make it all right, but this was not a dime novel and Gideon did not come.

***

I could not do as Elizabeth urged. I could not bear to throw myself at Gideon's feet only to be brutally rejected once more. But I couldn't entirely dismiss her hypothesis that maybe, just maybe, he was trying to protect me from something, though I couldn't fathom what.

Every time I looked at the pile of pieces that had once comprised his gift to me—and that gift alone must have meant

224

something, the many hours he'd spent on it—was a fresh heartbreak. I would send it to him and ask him to fix it, and hope against hope that he understood. Or if he didn't then at least he'd repair the delicate toy and send it back.

I wrote a dozen notes and discarded them all, laying my head on my arms in recognition of the futility. If I laid my heart bare, then whoever read the note to him would also know. Would he understood what the bird meant to me? I'd had only moments to appreciate it. Finally I drew a clean sheet of paper towards me and wrote simply, "It is broken beyond my ability to repair. Only you can fix it." No pleading, no begging, not even asking please. Just a statement. I stared at the words and nodded, my eyes stinging.

Then I called Dr. Borden's office at the New York Institute for the Blind and asked if it was permissible to forward Gideon's mail there—in that way I both confirmed that Gideon was in New York and that he would get my package.

I wrapped the remains of the bird and the dozens of fragments I'd been able to recover carefully in my handkerchief, tied with silk thread from a long unfinished embroidery work, then packed it in straw into a small wooden box that I'd asked Hannah's husband to make up for me. I folded the note so it would fit on the outside of the box and pressed it there with a staple. I sent it the next morning, confident Dr. Borden would see Gideon got the package, would read to him my note.

After that, there was nothing to do but wait.

I will admit I truly had no idea how Gideon would respond. And as the days passed, drawing the date of the ball ever closer, it seemed he would not respond at all.

23 WE WOULD LIKE TO ANNOUNCE

ELIZABETH AND I had packed an inordinate—to me—amount of clothing and toiletries to the Collingwood Inn. We would be staying the night there, as would many of our guests. The following day I had a fitting for the new gown Maurice had promised, which would only be bearable because of Elizabeth. She had chosen the fabrics when I couldn't muster an interest, so I had no idea what to expect.

We had adjoining rooms and both were heaped with boxes—hats, cosmetics, fans, gloves, shawls, each piece designed to match another. Bags of unmentionables, bottles of scent, boxes of hair appliances. Our gowns, however, were hung and waiting. Elizabeth chatted amiably, sorting through boxes for the just right this or that, while I stared into the dressing table mirror. It reflected the rich damask curtains hiding us from the evening flow of traffic outside.

I went through the motions of getting ready, only finding it in me to be interested in Elizabeth's gown. Mine for some reason dipped as low across my bosom as the scarlet dress, while her gown of blue-green silk left her shoulders bare, but showed not a hint of the valley between her breasts. It was a beautiful dress, and because of Maurice's last minute insistence that this be a masked revel, she was dramatic with the cosmetics, hers and mine. She used peacock colors to complement her gown and stuck with black and gold for me, highlighting my scars with a dusting of gold powder that made me smile.

She piled her hair on top of her head, "to make me look taller," she said, using hair rats to give her exaggerated volume, and I helped her fasten in the peacock plumes she scavenged from one of the hats.

My hair was pulled back over my ears and pinned into a pile of curls over my forehead, while the rest fell down my back in curls only slightly more tidy than nature had given me. I refused to wear any kind of padding in my hair. I liked pretty clothes, but a fashion plate I would never be. Instead, the youthful style contrasted with my scars in such a way I looked... well, interesting, at the very least.

Elizabeth's attitude towards my scars, as symbols of survival, something to if not be proud of, then at least not be ashamed of, had allowed me to accept them as part of myself. So I was still startled when people, meeting me for the first time, would look away. Most of the men at the shop, those who saw me daily, thought no more of them than I did. I grasped Elizabeth's hand and smiled, startling her. "I probably don't thank you enough for all you've done for me."

"What I've done for you? Charlotte, you're doing more for me than I can ever..."

"Don't say it—don't ever speak of it. I kept Maurice's blackmail from you specifically so you wouldn't ever, ever have to feel that or think it. I'm sorry that my memory loss forced me to—"

"Confide in your best friend?" she finished sarcastically.

I sighed.

"Sorry," she said, not sounding sorry at all. "I would rather know than not."

The ball should have been so beautiful. I loved the ballroom of this hotel, and I had to admit that Maurice's gold and silver masks added a mysterious element, working with the rich decor to lend a Venetian glamour to the proceedings and not a little theatricality. It would have been grand theater indeed, were this night happening as planned.

The band was talented and I as hostess was able to dance as much or as little as I wished, and I wished for it not so much, my heart aching at the thought of a lifetime married to Maurice Westham. Though his contempt was contained so long as I was biddable rather than rebellious, I could not imagine making that compromise daily, for the rest of my life.

I carried a cane of black stained wood with a carved ivory head that Elizabeth had acquired for me as a gift. Like my scars it was not intended to blend in but to stand out. Plain Charlotte Backus wasn't going to blend in the background anymore, if Elizabeth Bayfield had anything to say about it. I could not imagine a truer and more dear friend. Maurice dismissed my appearance with a flare of his nostrils and urged me to keep my mask in place—it occurred to me that hiding my face might have been his sole motivation for the masks. How bleak.

When Edward Walton and Robert Bright arrived, Maurice was all beaming smiles, and immediately gave up any pretense of hosting this party with me, thankfully. I enlisted Elizabeth's help to greet our arriving guests. With my memories restored and Maurice's special guests already here, I expected to know at least half of the rest. Along with the Montcalms were numerous other clients and their wives, some of whom I'd only met once or not at all. Some had come with those of their eligible daughters, those already introduced to society, and others with their equally eligible sons. Balls for whatever occasion were also for match-making. Elizabeth's mother was in attendance, with her current husband— Mr. Mathers? Meaghers? Something with an M. Or was that the previous husband? The former Mrs. Bayfield seemed to have a new husband every two years; I think even Elizabeth had trouble keeping track.

Through the doors came a party of five that I did not recognize at all, but before introductions could be made, the manager of the hotel gestured frantically at me. "Elizabeth, do you mind?"

"Go see what he wants," she said smiling happily.

Concerned, I followed the manager to the kitchen. "Madam— Miss, there's been a problem in the kitchen. You originally asked for a much simpler meal, which we are well able to provide, but the last minute additions—we couldn't get a delivery in time!"

"What last minute additions? I was perfectly content with the menu, we settled it last week." I was perplexed; this being my first time hostessing a ball, I had been extremely careful to ensure all was done well in advance.

"Your, your fiance telephoned yesterday with your changes!"

Maurice! I restrained my reaction to something relatively lady-like, but my anger must have shown. "Miss Backus—we tried!"

"I do not doubt," I said gently. "Forgive Mr. Westham, he knows nothing of how these things are done. Assure your staff that all is quite well, and the originally agreed upon menu—that can still be done?" He nodded, and I finished, "That will be perfectly satisfactory."

He looked relieved that the problem was so easily resolved, but then, he didn't have to find Maurice and take him aside to inform him that whatever he'd ordered last minute wasn't going to appear. He stepped away from his employers, glowering thunderously at me. "I wanted salmon," he said through gritted teeth.

"You ought to have told me, Maurice. These things cannot be done at the last minute, that is why we plan them."

"You mind your tone, Charlotte. I don't wish to cause a commotion, so I shall let it go this time, but we shan't be using this hotel for any future entertainments!" He stared at my face. "Not that you need to worry about that," he said. "Put up your mask, dear Charlotte." He brushed past me, jarring my shoulder deliberately and I closed my eyes.

Perhaps after the wedding Maurice would indeed sell my half—his half—of Backus Engineering to Gideon. Then, what happened to me would affect no one. I could hide from my horrid husband in a laudanum bottle if I wished, or even end my own life, should my marriage prove beyond bearing. Ah, I was being melodramatic. Once Backus Engineering was safe, I could leave Maurice. Go to Canada or cross the ocean to England or France. I resolved to hide some money while I still could, to finance my eventual escape.

I stood in the doorway to the ballroom, contemplating these desperate measures, until Elizabeth clutched my arm, drawing me out of my dark thoughts. Her mask in one gloved hand, her brow creased in worry, she said, "Mr. Lyons' family is here, Charlotte! They want to know where he is!"

I winced, drawing a hand across my temple. My headache was as yet figurative, but I expected it to be literal soon enough. I had for some reason supposed Gideon would have advised his family not to come, so it never occurred to me to do so. Now—now, I simply didn't feel up to trying to explain what was going on.

"Mrs. Lyons in particular seems anxious to speak with you."

"Thank you for the warning, Elizabeth," I said, leaving her with a distracted smile and the beginning of an elaborate dance that only partially took place on the dance floor.

As hostess, I couldn't hide, so I did my best to be seen, mask in and out of hand. But I stayed in one place no longer than the few minutes it took to smile and exchange a greeting, always avoiding the tall dark-haired woman with steel grey streaks in her hair. I had no answers I could give her without tears, and I would not give in, not in public.

As midnight approached I could not help my agitation. Although it had never been a secret that we were engaged to marry, making a formal and public announcement would create social expectations that until now did not really exist. It would be almost as binding as the wedding itself. Seeking reprieve, if only for a few moments, I fled the last dance to the anonymity of the shadows outside. The glass doors were open to the early June night, circulating the heat generated by so many dancing bodies within. Outside was a stonework balcony style construction, though it was on the ground and only a few steps above the impenetrable shadows of the gardens. Come July and August, the curtains would be pinned back to allow the maximum airflow, but for now it was cool enough to keep them closed.

I went to the darkest corner, propped my cane into it and rested my arms on the smooth stone rail, feeling the cool stone through the thin fabric of my gloves. The gold mask, a nice match for my gown, looked up at me with empty eyes as I grimaced, my face aching from the big fake smile I felt I'd worn all evening, in spite of Elizabeth's constant remonstration. The night air smelled like freedom and I briefly considered leaving this very minute, with nothing but the gown on my back, so much the dread I felt at the coming announcement, but that might have as negative an effect on those I wanted to protect as my refusal to marry Maurice. I realized that I had hoped, throughout this evening, that somehow... and a torrent of tears I'd been holding at bay for weeks broke through my desire to hold them back.

I knew the noise of the ballroom would cover my despair, but I did not realize my despair would allow someone to approach through the garden without being heard. "Miss Backus? Is that you?"

Horrified to be discovered in such condition, I dabbed futilely at my face with a handkerchief and counted on the night to hide the ravages of tears as I turned to face the man who'd spoken. He was dressed in workman's clothes, a newsboy hat shaded his eyes from the little light that reached this part of the hotel gardens. I sniffed and cleared my throat. "Yes? Is there a problem? Are you with the hotel?"

"No, ma'am. I have a delivery for you." He held up a small box wrapped in silver ribbon.

A delivery? Here? At this time of night? He stepped forward, set it on the stone rail, tugged the brim of his hat and disappeared into the shadows. I stared at the box. Since my fall from the barn loft, I had not experienced any untoward accidents, and with the pain of Gideon's desertion, I had rather forgotten them entirely, but now I eyed that box with the utmost caution. What if another accident awaited beneath that pretty ribbon? It would delay the wedding, I thought with bitter humor.

I opened the box. Nothing happened. Inside was something small, like a ball, wrapped in fabric. I lifted it out cautiously, set it on the rail. Still, nothing happened. I was being paranoid. I pulled the corners of the fabric away and gasped. It was the little clockwork bird! The fabric, my own handkerchief. I spun about, wondering what it meant and if the man who delivered it knew... and I gasped again.

A man stood there. He was tall, and elegant in his formal clothes, and he held a silver mask to his face. There was not enough light to tell more than that. "Who are you, sir, and why have you sought me out against all propriety?"

"You didn't think I'd miss this, did you?"

The sound stuck in my throat was half joy, half rage, and when I threw myself at him, I wasn't sure if I mean to strike him or embrace him, but he caught me, and found my face with his hands, and kissed me. Joy won that moment, and I kissed him and held him that he might not vanish into the shadows.

For many moments I was content to exchange long, slow kisses with him, reveling in his presence, from the solid body beneath my hands, to the familiar scent of his soap and the sweet taste of his mouth. But as his hands began to "look" at me, I pulled back. "I thought you'd abandoned me." It came out as an accusation, which I suppose was better than a whine.

"I told you I wouldn't," he said softly. "I'm sorry I couldn't tell you—"

"I felt, I thought you didn't think me worth the bother of an explanation."

"No!" He squeezed me tight against him until I could scare breathe. "Charlotte, no, never. I-I couldn't tell you the truth, and I couldn't lie. That didn't leave me many options."

His explanation, such as it was, warmed a part of me I'd tried to freeze. I reached up to cup his face in my hands, and touched the arms of his cinder glasses. "May I?" I asked, my voice very soft.

He nodded, and I gently unhooked the spectacles from his ears. I folded them and tucked them inside his waistcoat, making sure he knew where they were. Then I pulled my right arm back and slapped him. Hard enough to snap his head around. And before he could do more than rub his cheek in surprised pain, I stomped down on his toes and he grunted. "You lousy son of a bitch," I hissed.

He grabbed me about the waist and spoke right into my ear: "I've missed your vulgar mouth." And then he kissed my vulgar mouth, hard, before letting me go. And he smiled! "I guess I deserved that. May I say I'm grateful you didn't, uh, use your knees."

My eyes dropped to the front of his trousers and I knew what he meant and I knew he hadn't meant for me to start thinking about what was between his legs in the perverted way I was. "I have rather fond memories of that particular part of you," I said, and to my delight, he blushed bright enough for me to see it in the dim light available to us.

I resisted the urge to be too forward or familiar, in part because I did not want him to think I could forgive that easily. I touched his cheek, wondering how much of the redness was embarrassment and how much was from my slap. "Why did you leave me?"

"To keep you safe. How much time do we have?"

I cocked my head to listen to the sounds of the ballroom. "Perhaps a minute?"

"Damn. Not enough time to do either."

"Either what?" I asked suspiciously.

"Explain," he said, finding my waist and pulling me against him, "or ravish you." He kissed me again and I almost forgot I was angry with him.

"If your explanation is not very, very good, there will be no ravishing," I said, but it was difficult to sound as stern as I intended whilst being held in his arms.

"As you say," he agreed with a wry smile.

I'd meant what I said, but I kissed him anyway, and we passed some precious moments exchanging breaths. "I love you, Gideon" came out of my mouth before I could check myself.

"For now," he said, "and I'm glad. "After your memories return—we'll see."

Ah, he didn't know. I wondered if I should tell him. "I should be more angry with you, but I'm also angry with myself for, for not trusting you." I thought maybe I had told him my memory had returned, for only a Charlotte who could remember how deeply his words had cut would be so mistrustful, but he seemed to miss the subtle point and I let it go as the curtain parted violently behind us and we dropped our arms from each other.

"Charlotte?"

Elizabeth. I turned, handing Gideon the mask he'd put down on the stone rail. "I was just taking some air." I scooped the bird and my handkerchief together in my left hand; it would not be broken again. I hoped.

"What's he doing here?" She asked quietly as I drew closer to her.

"How do you know who...?"

"Char, please. Who else would you be kissing in the dark?"

"Then you know why he's here."

"I can't wait to hear the story," she murmured as Gideon came in behind me, the silver mask over his face.

"Me, too," I agreed.

Maurice called everyone's attention by tapping a goblet with a serving fork, then bowed to me, "My dear, go ahead." I imagined he anticipated hearing the words from my own mouth.

I smiled and hoped I would find the right words to pull this off without disgrace for anyone. "Ladies and Gentlemen, I want to thank you all so much for coming out tonight. You are family, friends, business associates without whom Backus Engineering would not exist. Tonight I would like to make a very special announcement. You may be aware that I have for a long time been engaged to marry the very handsome Maurice Westham."

Maurice dropped his mask and bowed, smiling, toward the crowd.

"I finally realized however, that the reason I kept delaying our nuptials was because, in spite of my best efforts, I was deeply in love with someone else."

Maurice's head nearly spun off his shoulders as he turned to glare ferociously at me.

"I confessed my feelings to Mr. Westham and advised our local pastor that to go through with such a wedding would be a disservice to Mr. Westham and an insult to God and the institution of marriage." I was feeling rather pleased with my phrasing; it saved face for everyone.

But he had other ideas. "Charlotte, you know what I said, should you defy me." His voice was low and cold, but did not go unheard by the at least some of our guests.

"I told you I can't marry you," I said quietly, keeping a smile on my face.

"And I told you that you will marry me whether you like it or not!"

The room gasped and swelled in surprise.

His voice dropped slightly, but he spoke to be heard. "Or do you want me to tell these good people, these friends and business associates, about your dear and intimate lover?"

A silence fell, the kind that anticipated the revelation of something scandalous. And Gideon stepped forward, lowered his mask and said, "I'll tell them myself."

My cheeks reddened at the implication. I knew Maurice was referring to his threat to tell everyone that Elizabeth and I were romantically involved, but Gideon had preempted him. Our gathered friends and acquaintances made all the gestures of shock, quickly smothered with smirks and smiles as if this were not at all a surprise. I was somewhat bewildered—had not we been the very definition of discreet? Except for disappearing for no more than twenty minutes at the Montcalm ball, and that kiss that might or might not have been seen at the shop.

"You better make an honest woman of her, Lyons," shouted someone from the crowd, using the anonymity of his mask to call boldly.

"Two weeks Saturday," he replied. "I'd invite you but it's

rather exclusive."

There was laughter, the men seemed to find it all quite amusing, the women far less so. Maurice's face was red with fury. "This isn't done, Charlotte," he said quietly, his tone ominous, before he smiled at the crowd and bowed mockingly in Gideon's direction. He disappeared into the crowd and I did not see him again that night.

But staring down at me was the woman I'd been avoiding all evening—Eleanor Lyons. When our eyes met, her chin lifted disdainfully and I felt my cheeks redden. She grasped Gideon by the arm and I lost sight of them as other people moved in to offer their congratulations.

Mrs. Montcalm said crossly, "You have given the ball of the year, all of New England shall be talking about it for months! Such a bar you've set!"

I gave her a crooked smile. "I really...I don't seem to have quite grasped the knack of being a proper society lady."

"No," she agreed, "But you certainly have," she paused, as if searching for the right phrase. "A flair for the dramatic. This really doesn't excuse your behavior with Mr. Lyons, you know, though it is, I suppose, understandable."

I didn't know what to say to that, and I was saved from trying to formulate a response by the approach of Mrs. Lyons, her husband, I presumed, and Gideon. Perhaps saved wasn't the right word—now that the specter of life with Maurice had been lain to rest, Eleanor Lyons was almost as terrifying. "That was quite a spectacle," she said briskly by way of introduction.

"I explained, Mother," Gideon began, only to be cut off.

"Yes, yes. Miss Backus. I rather expected more, from the smattering of gossip I've heard tonight, and my son's descriptions of you."

"How do you do, Mrs. Lyons. It's a pleasure to meet you."

"Is it? Well, I'm not sure I can say the same."

"Mother!"

"Please forgive my wife, Miss Backus. You are quite, hmm, unconventional." He smiled, and I saw the resemblance to Gideon. "Andrew Lyons."

I offered my hand, and he bowed over it formally. Then I was introduced to Gideon's sister, Cleodie, his cousin, Randall Black and his wife Caroline. Conversation proceeded somewhat more in the normal manner and I began to feel more at ease. Then as they moved away to allow others to offer their well-wishes, I heard Eleanor Lyons remark, "At least she has decent hips. A grandson should be nice."

I blanched.

24 Explanations and Preparations

I PACED MY room, a rather awkward gait after the long evening but I could not pace effectively with a cane. I plead fatigue to Elizabeth, and I was exhausted, but I had to hear Gideon's explanation. So I remained fully dressed, less only my gloves to minimize any temptation I might feel to, to indulge my wayward passions. I told myself I would not marry a man who didn't love me, but that wasn't true—I had been prepared to ask him for a marriage of convenience, to save us all, and I would do so if that's what he truly wanted. Not that I believed that, after his kisses on the terrace, but I was trying to prepare for the worst.

I opened the door so swiftly at the light tap that Gideon was left to finish the knock in midair. He, too, had left behind only his gloves and I was relieved. Also unreasonably happy at this indication of our similar thinking. He was a dashingly handsome man in formal wear, particularly with his hair so unruly. "Please come in," I said formally, curbing my admiration.

He inclined his head and stepped over the threshold, hesitating within as I closed the door behind him. Regardless of what actually passed between us now, if it were discovered we were alone in a hotel room this time of night—we were not yet married. I was a fool to have let him in. Too late, now. "Your explanation had best be impressive."

"May I at least sit down? It's been a long evening."

Kind of him to understate it so nicely. I touched his hand to lead him to a chair and that was it—a simple, innocent touch and all my good intentions were swept away. I stared at him, saw his jaw flex as he swallowed. I guessed him to be having as much difficulty as I, remembering our purpose was to talk. For some reason, that allowed me to strengthen my resolve, even as passion and desire struggled to dominate me.

His other hand unerringly found my face and my eyes closed automatically as he lightly traced its contours with his fingers. His kiss was not unexpected and not unwelcome, and my newly strengthened resolve crumbled like a castle of sand besieged by the tide. Intoxicated by our shared kisses, we broke apart only far enough to fumble with each other's clothing, leaving our finery layer by layer in a pile by the bed until there was no barrier between us.

Those novels young women are not supposed to read would have this removal of clothing almost a magical thing, but Gideon and I, we fumbled. In our fumbling we roused each in the other a fire, a fever, so that when we fell to the bed, flesh to flesh—and it must have been I who showed him where it was—my legs opened to him in natural readiness. I wanted nothing more than for him to be inside me, with force and vigour, and we came together in wicked wantonness.

When we both lay panting from our exertions, he ran his fingers lightly over every part of my body, allowing me little time to rest before bringing me to new heights of pleasure. I reciprocated, when the trembling of my body eased enough, for I found that touching him, pleasing him was yet another kind of pleasure.

We exhausted the pleasures of Venus, but before sleep could claim us as was its right after such activities, Gideon kissed me softly, this time with a depth of affection not entirely conveyed by the kisses of passion we'd already shared. Affection such that I could not fail to believe him when he told me he loved me.

"Why did you leave me?" My voice was soft, the pain of his leaving not entirely abated by his return and affirmation of both his passion and love. I needed to know.

"To protect you, my love. I did not know how else to do it." He stroked my hair away from my face and traced one of my scars. "I could not tell you the truth—you would follow me. And my dear Charlotte, I could not bear to lie to you. That left me nothing to say."

As Elizabeth had hypothesized, but—"You must know what I read into your silence; that you found me unworthy of the kindness of an explanation."

He pressed me close against him, whispering, "I'm so sorry, Charlotte, I didn't know what else to do."

Safe in his arms, like a soothing ointment that eased the hurt but hadn't quite banished it. "But what were you protecting me from?"

He hesitated, as if unsure how to begin. "The accidents that have befallen you—recall how we considered they might not be accidents?"

"Yes, of course. But the puzzle remains—who would want to kill me?"

"I don't believe anyone does. When, when you fell from the loft, I realized that—I was so terrified, Charlotte. I couldn't see, and you wouldn't answer me. Forgive me, that day was terrifying enough but to have realized.... Charlotte, the loft is my personal workshop, a place only I go. The day you fell, that was your second visit to the loft, in the entire time since your father and I constructed it. Do you understand? The board had been cut; I was the one meant to fall. It was so obvious. As I sat in the hospital waiting to learn the extent of your injuries, and if you would live or die, I considered all your other accidents. Every one, Charlotte, happened in places where I was known to be often, and you were not. Possibly even..." his fingers traced my scars again. "Even the boiler explosion. After all, you weren't supposed to be there. But I was. It was only happenstance that I was at the house. I still don't know why you were there. We might never know, if your memories don't come back."

If he had not been holding me, I might have sat bolt upright, so stunned I was by what he said. He was quite correct. Even the sabotage on the car had been done after I ran over the small copper pot in the garage—it had been meant to hurt Gideon as he repaired the damage I'd done. Everyone knew the steam car was Gideon's special care, and in large part his creation.

He must have felt my body tense, for he stroked me soothingly. It was a measure of my concern that I felt no spark of passion from his touch, yet I did find small comfort in it. Except the same piece of the puzzle was still missing: "But there is no one who would want you dead, either!"

"There is clearly at least one person," he said dryly. "I had to leave. I-Charlotte, I couldn't tell if you were alive or dead until I crawled across the floor to find you. I felt so helpless in my blindness, such as I have not felt since that first year. How could I protect you, without being able to see? If I was the intended victim, distancing myself from you was the only way I could think of to keep you safe."

I bit my lip, wanting to argue with him. But I would have followed him, had I known the reason he left; he was right about that. It was also true that in his absence nothing life threatening had happened to me. "And apart from breaking my heart," I said, not quite forgiving him, "What outcome did you expect? Did this person make another attempt on your life?"

He sighed, pulled the covers more tightly around us. "No."

"So the accidents could have been coincidence?" I fervently hoped so.

"No," he said firmly. "Not at all. It only means the person who wants me dead was unable to follow me. While I've been away, you've been safe, but there has been no attempt on my life, either. I kept waiting—I know he'll find me sooner or later—but I could not leave you to the mercy of Westham's machinations, my dear Charlotte."

"I-I wasn't sure you'd come."

"Surely the arrival of my family must have reassured you? I would have advised them not to attend, had I intended to abandon you."

"I thought perhaps you'd forgotten," I admitted in a very small voice. I was so blinded by my hurt feelings, I couldn't see what had been right in front of me—just as I should have seen the pattern he saw.

"Now, he would certainly benefit from my death," Gideon said thoughtfully.

I frowned. "Maurice? Yes, now that we have made public our intention to marry," I agreed. "But before? What benefit to him when he was assured I would marry him?"

"If I die, you inherit my half of the company," he reminded me.

I closed my eyes and sighed again at my own foolishness. With Gideon dead, I was sole owner of Backus Engineering, and when I married, it would belong to my husband—lock, stock, and barrel. We had dismissed Maurice as a suspect before simply because we thought I was the intended victim, and Maurice so very much wanted me alive. His unmistakeably genuine concern for my health had given him a patina of innocence.

"Think, Charlotte," he said, unconsciously echoing my father, "Isn't it odd that he thought you would need some comforting the afternoon after I repaired the car?"

I did remember thinking it odd. But Gideon's use of my father's favourite injunction had recalled to me the fever dream I had, in the grip of the chloroform. "The boiler!"

His brow wrinkled. "The one that rolled on you?"

"The explosion at the lab. I—Maurice had reached the limit of his patience with me, he was insisting I set a date, book the church and organize a ball—all of this." My gesture was limited by the blankets, but at least he felt it. "I was, I went to the lab to ask if you would consider a marriage in name only, as a way around his blackmail. I had thought of it as a solution earlier, and realized it would save Backus Engineering, if not Elizabeth, but it was the only solution I could see."

"You were-? Charlotte, you remember?"

"Yes, Gideon. My memories came back as I fell. All of them, at once. It was quite overwhelming, and I let the pain of my injuries swallow me."

He was silent a moment, as if realizing that I had remembered, yet was still naked in his arms. "I suppose it's just as well we hadn't wagered on that," he said finally.

I grinned. "You can't be right all the time, my love. Gideon, I was certain you were in the lab. I...when that door shattered towards me, I didn't want to live in a world without you in it. I think, maybe, that is why I couldn't remember. I wasn't injured enough to die, so I shut out the pain of the memory."

"But why wouldn't you remember when you saw I was alive

and well?"

I shrugged as best I could, lying in his arms. "I don't know but maybe because it was a traumatic event that caused me to bury my memories...." I frowned. "I think—Maurice said that I should plan the wedding before I needed to grieve for another accident like the one that killed my father. I think, when that board broke in the loft, that on some level, subconsciously, I knew—I knew it was meant for you. I had a fever dream, my father urging me to think, memory giving Maurice's words more emphasis than I had at the time. I was distraught, and so terrified to ask you what I had to ask, his words hadn't really registered."

His body had tensed as I spoke, and after a pause, he asked in a tight voice, "Do you think he sabotaged the boiler that killed your father?"

A chill settled on my heart. That was the logical implication of Maurice Westham's words, wasn't it? If Gideon had not been trying to find the words to ask Father for permission to court me, it would have killed them both. Could it really be true? Maurice was unpleasant, to be sure, but could he really be willing to murder for what he wanted?

"I-" I began and cleared my throat. "Are you absolutely certain it's Maurice?"

"No," he said, clearly frustrated. "But now that I'm back in Dorset, I worry he—or whomever it is that wishes me dead—will try again. It worries me that you may be put at risk and I cannot even see it coming!"

I snuggled against him, as if everything were all perfectly right. Because, "Tonight, my love, we're safe. Tomorrow, we can puzzle out a plan—together."

"Together."

***

247

The door between my room and Elizabeth's opened with a bang as she seemingly exploded through it at what felt like the very crack of dawn, startling me to rise half out of bed. My motion caused the covers to drop revealing not only my nakedness, which I'd rather forgotten, but also Gideon. I snatched it up and met Elizabeth's horrified expression. She squeaked a sound and spun on her heel so swiftly that the skirts of her tea gown flew out most unfashionably and slammed the door again as she returned to her room.

Gideon turned his head, his face still soft with sleep. I smiled down at him, no longer seeing anything shocking about his eyes, just the face of the man I loved. "Miss Bayfield, I presume?"

"We have adjoining rooms," I explained. "I'm sure she'll give us some time to, um, make ourselves presentable."

"Hmm. I may have to return to my room for something presentable."

I peered at the pile of clothing on the floor. "I believe you are correct. What a shameful treatment of such fine clothing."

"So very careless of me," he murmured, sliding across the sheet to place a tender kiss upon my hip, which caused no small amount of tingling in other parts of my body. I knew Elizabeth would be listening at the door to judge when we were presentable, she would not wish to hear any celebrations of Venus.

A similar thought must have occurred to Gideon, for he made no other motion in the arts of love, but instead asked, "Do you know, my love, where I put my cane?"

It gave me salacious pleasure to watch Gideon remove himself from the bed and use his cane to poke cautiously ahead of him as he found his way to the bath in his natural glory. Whilst he was within, I sorted our clothing, laying his neatly on the bed and shaking out my gown as best I could before hanging it up. The pile of undergarments I hastily stuffed into one of the many boxes littering the room, and those I tried to close and stack between pulling on various bits of clothing. I put on the teagown I'd brought for today's traveling and dragged the chair out from the writing desk in a deliberately noisy way when Gideon had donned some two thirds of his evening dress, leaving off the tie and jacket.

A knock on the adjoining door soon followed and Elizabeth came in as if she'd seen nothing, as if Gideon in my room even dressed was not unusual nor unexpected. "I took the liberty of ordering breakfast for three to your room," she said, looking at nothing in particular.

"Very kind," Gideon murmured, "But perhaps I should be going."

"You might as well stay, Mr. Lyons. I should have realized— and knocked. Besides," she added, finally looking at him, though he could not know that. "I wanted to thank you for what you did for me."

He shook his head with a smile. "I'm pleased that my marrying Charlotte helps you, Miss Bayfield. But I'm marrying her because I love her, not for your sake."

"I would hope so," she said dryly. "I was referring to your swift actions at the ball last night. Because of that, no matter what Mr. Westham may say of me, there is not even a whisper that might support his claims." And I had thought her unaware.

Elizabeth allowed room service to push the cart in the room, but the server himself she stopped. I'm certain hotel staff knew better than to speak of anything they might see, but I appreciated her desire to protect my pretense of a reputation. Gideon told her what we'd discussed the night before regarding Maurice as we applied ourselves with gusto to the food.

"So this Hiram Clarke fellow that Dr. Sheldon warned you about is not a possibility? He might not see you, Mr. Lyons, as someone who usurped his rightful position with Dr. Backus?"

Gideon frowned. "If so, then his revenge is a little late. Charlotte says he was released from the asylum eight years ago.

249

Wouldn't he have chosen to act then? It seems very unlikely."

"I think we need not worry about Hiram Clarke," I added. "All the accidents were devised by someone with access to both the shop and the outbuildings of our home. It seems unlikely that Hiram Clarke would have gone unnoticed."

"Dr. Sheldon said he was asking after you, though, right?"

I shrugged. "But the accidents were meant for Gideon, not me."

She nodded. "Indeed. Very well, I just needed to be sure in my mind before we begin accusing people. If Westham is indeed the culprit, and his motive is to secure Backus Engineering, then are you not still in danger, Mr. Lyons?"

"I'm more concerned for Charlotte, but yes, that would be correct, Miss Elizabeth."

"Only until we're married," I said, covering Gideon's hand with mine.

There was a silence, broken finally by Elizabeth. "Char, if he's willing to kill to get what he wants, it's unlikely he'll be happy once he's thwarted. That could make him very, very angry, in an if I can't have it no one can sort of way."

"I do hope you're being melodramatic."

"As do I," Gideon agreed quietly. In the following hush, he added in a more normal tone of voice. "Ladies, it has been a pleasure and a privilege to break fast with you in this manner, but I must make myself somewhat respectable and see to my family. Charlotte, I know my parents would love you to join us for dinner. Because of the threat to my life, I will try to hurry them on their way back to Boston this evening if I can. I will stay here, until the wedding... she's got the stubborn look on her face doesn't she?" he finished, addressing Elizabeth.

She grinned at me, for I was indeed about to protest. "Mr. Lyons, it occurs to me that you would actually be safer if you stayed close to Charlotte. After all, if Maurice is indeed our would be killer, he has a vested interest in keeping her alive and well."

I mouthed a thank you at her and said aloud, "Exactly so."

"May I remind you both that being close to Charlotte nearly resulted in her death! Several times!" Gideon's voice was hard.

"And that is precisely why I think he will not try again, if you remain close to her. He's come too close to losing her. The further away from her you are, the greater danger you're in."

His brow furrowed fiercely over his spectacles. "I do see some sense in that," he admitted reluctantly. "Fine, I'll send my family on their way and return to Dorset tonight. Meanwhile—dinner in the hotel dining room, at one?"

I squeezed his hand. "Yes, though I think your mother will never like me."

"I can't reassure you otherwise," he said, rising to his feet and kissing my hand before releasing it. "But if it makes you feel any better, she doesn't care all that much for me, either. Losing my eyes was a great disappointment to her."

I suddenly remembered that I would be disappointing her in yet another way, and that I hadn't yet told Gideon. What if he wanted children? Didn't every man want at least a son to bear his name forward? Of course, Gideon wasn't "every man" any more than I was "every woman" but it worried me all the same.

When he was gone, I had no time to think on it as Elizabeth grabbed my hand, saying, "Come—we have a dress fitting!"

"Bessie! That dress was to marry Maurice—I can't wear that!"

"You needn't get married in it, but a dress is certainly the least he owes you, so you'll take it and wear it at some other occasion."

After the long night and intense discussion of the morning, I could only laugh.

***

Gideon's cousin, Randall Black, turned out to be an amateur

auto carriage enthusiast and raced the things so it wasn't long until the three of us were engaged in a lively conversation about steam cars, condensers, acceleration rates, fuel efficiency and so forth, until I belatedly realized that the senior Mr. Lyons, his disapproving wife, and Mrs. Black were all staring at me. Only Gideon's sister Cleodie seemed to enjoy the fact that I found the men's conversation more interesting than whatever the rest of the table was speaking of. I interrupted Gideon and Mr. Black with a hand lightly on Gideon's arm. "I do think we're being dull company."

Having cemented Mrs. Lyons impression of me, I made my excuses and returned to the hotel to finish packing. My little clockwork bird, the most wonderful engagement present I could imagine, had nearly been forgotten in all the fuss, but now I could show Elizabeth how it worked. Like me, she was astonished at the intricacy and how the wings could spread and retract, each metal feather sliding across the other in sleek realism. "And he says he is not skilled. Not perhaps a master to create clockwork pieces for a crowned head of Europe, but skilled, yes."

"Imagine what he could have achieved, had he not lost his eyes," she said absently, staring at the bird as it spread its wings again.

"I think he could achieve whatever he wished, as long as society was willing to grant a few concessions. You've watched him at home, Elizabeth—you can't tell me you believed a blind man could do what he does, until you saw him."

"True and true. I often forget he cannot see. Particularly when I glare at him."

"I've often thought him quite lucky, missing the impact of your glares."

She made a number of faces at me as she set the bird down carefully. The door between our rooms was open and we were packing things more carefully to take home than we had to bring them here, to make unpacking at home a simpler proposition. "I wonder if my reminding you of the past so often kept you two apart. If you had managed to get together sooner..."

I thought about her words before replying. "I don't think so. I was too proud and stubborn to forgive enough to trust either myself or him. It seems forgetting allowed me to express my feelings without all that, the weight of our history."

Our task was interrupted by a knock on the door to my room, startling us both. "Charlotte?"

I opened it, surprised to see Gideon there. "What is it? You look harried."

"My mother, sister and cousin-in-law have decided they need to spend some time with you alone, and hope you will stay another night in Bangor that you might show them around the quaint little shops tomorrow."

Ah lovely, another day to awkwardly try not to be myself. I nodded, and said very softly, "You will stay with me tonight?"

A smile crossed his face. "My pleasure."

With a short discussion, we decided to load up the car that night with our trunks and bags and keep only the bare necessities in the room. Gideon brought a small carpet bag to my room and Elizabeth merely sighed in resignation. For the sake of propriety, he paid for the night for the room rented in his name. It was perhaps over cautious, but it would not do to have too much talk about us until after we were good and properly wed.

Contrary, I'm sure, to Elizabeth's expectations, passion was not present in the hotel room that night. We had had a long day after a long night with very little sleep and now I had to talk to Gideon one more time about what had happened in Paris. "Gideon, we, we've never talked about children."

"I hadn't really thought about it, but I guess—" he broke off, then grabbed my shoulders. "Charlotte! Did I leave you—again?"

"No, no, I'm not."

He let out a breath and released his grip on me. "Thank goodness. Well. I must admit, when I thought of us married, I imagined us working together side by side, and spending our nights together, but children. I suppose they're sort of... inevitable?"

"If we didn't have any, though, would that disappoint you?"

He frowned. "What do you mean? You wish to have a celibate marriage?"

"Oh no! Most certainly not! Gracious!" I was almost distracted from my point, imagining the horror of such a thing. "No, I heard your mother say something about grandchildren and—you recall what I told about Paris?"

"Yes." His voice was clipped but I didn't want him to revisit his self-anger.

"I was recounting to you what Elizabeth told me, but she didn't know the entire story. The, the abortionist, he did something irreparable to my womb. The surgeon had to remove it. I-I will never be able to have children." I just blurted it out and hoped for the best.

He said nothing for a long time, and then he spoke in a carefully measured voice. "When I realized you actually believed I wouldn't come back for you, I was, I admit, wounded. But then I am reminded of the horrible things I have done to you, and I wonder that you can love me at all. Did-did you want children?"

"Gideon, if I can forgive you, you should forgive yourself. My only concern was that if you had your heart set on children, I wouldn't be the best choice of a wife. And no," I added with a frown. "I never imagined myself a mother." I'd never imagined myself a wife, to be honest, but I didn't want to muddy the matter. "And you're right to be hurt that I didn't trust you. But you left just as my memories came back, I think I can be forgiven that?"

"I hadn't particularly imagined myself a father," he said, taking me gently in his arms.

I breathed a sigh of relief. "What, um, should we tell your mother?"

"Nothing. Our personal life will be discussed quite enough among my family," he added with a wry grin I could feel against my forehead. "And I think the days are past when a man's greatest concern is the passing on of his name. We will, how did you put it? Be happy and brilliant? That is legacy enough. That, and knowing that a little piece of us is in every machine for miles around." He kissed my forehead. "As for my mother, we need say nothing. I expect we will be causing all manner of talk, for quite some time."

I liked the sound of that.

Fatigue ousted passion that night, and all we did was sleep in that bed, curled against each other like spoons in a drawer.

***

Shouts of fire and loud rapping on the door woke us. Gideon hastily pulled on some trousers and went to find out what was going on. "There's a fire. Nothing to worry about, the bellhop told me, but they need to evacuate the building, for safety reasons."

I pulled open the door to Elizabeth's room to find her frantically stuffing what remained of her things into her carpet bag. "We don't have time for that, Bessie—come on!"

It was dark and chilly outside, all the hotel's guests standing about in various states of dress. Elizabeth and I followed Gideon as he pressed through the crowd in search of his family. I saw a man with a pocket watch in hand and stopped to ask him for the time. He gave me a dubious look, and I pulled my dressing gown closer about me. "It's twenty minutes past three, miss."

"Thank you, sir."

I hurried to catch up my friends. The women of Gideon's family were also in their night clothes, so I couldn't earn any more disapproval for appearing in mine, but I took Gideon's hand and he shook it free to put his arm about my waist, and that added the missing touch. "Your mother is glaring at us."

"Mmm," he agreed. "Tell me, what do you see?"

I couldn't see anything, even when the big draft horses pulling the water truck cleared people away from the hotel entrance, there was nothing to see except a bit of smoke coming from a single window and I said as much to Gideon.

"Good, I don't know that I could endure having my family at the house."

I chuckled, leaning into his side briefly.

Less than an hour later, the hotel owner himself was announcing that the fire had been limited to one room, but due to the gas lighting and timber construction, evacuation had been done for our safety. The firemen had gone room to room to ensure the building was perfectly safe. Sorry for the terrible inconvenience, free room for the night, and so forth.

As we slowly made our way back inside, the hotel manager called out, "Mr. Lyons! A moment please."

"Charlotte? Would you oblige me? I left my cane in the room."

When we three were within the manager's office, he began to question Gideon until it became clear that the room in which the fire had taken place was his. "Forgive my interruption, gentlemen, but Mr. Lyons didn't have anything to do with the fire. If it was purposefully set, it was meant to, to harm him."

"Then where was he?"

My face reddened. "Erm, my room. We are engaged to marry," I added defensively.

The manager shook his head with impatience. "Please, Miss Backus. This is a hotel, I've heard and seen far larger breaches in propriety than this. Your secret, such as it is, is safe." He rubbed his temples with both hands. "I shall have to involve the constabulary. They will want to talk to you. I'm afraid I can't guarantee their discretion, however."

It was only later that I realized he never imagined I might be lying to protect Gideon. Surely that wasn't because of the gossip about us? We were surely not important enough to set that many tongues wagging!

Elizabeth was pacing when we returned to the room, fully dressed. She whirled on us, "Did you get lost?" I told her what had happened while Gideon excused himself to finish his toilette. I dressed and we finished our packing—we could leave immediately, if I didn't have to spend time with the female Lyons'.

When Gideon had joined us, she said, "Maurice?"

He shrugged. "No way to know for certain. But you were right, staying close to Charlotte does seem safer for me."

Elizabeth and I both blushed, not looking at each other. We both knew that she had not meant quite that close.

I tried to forget that someone, possibly Maurice, would put an entire hotel at risk just to get rid of Gideon Lyons.

I knew I could never pretend to be the type of woman Mrs. Eleanor Lyons would approve of, so I did not try. I behaved only as myself, guiding the women of the Lyons household to shops recommended by Elizabeth and returning to the Collingwood's tea room for a chance to rest our feet and have our purchases sent on to our rooms. I hoped they saw something worthwhile in me, in spite of my unorthodox upbringing, career, and scarred face, if only for Gideon's sake. Then we said goodbye, until they should all descend upon the one hotel in Dorset for the wedding.

25 NICE DAY FOR A WEDDING

THE DAY OF THE wedding dawned a beautiful rosy gold. There had been no more accidents, no attempts on Gideon's life since his return to Dorset, so we supposed Maurice—if Maurice had indeed been the malicious mind behind the attempts—had resigned himself to losing me and Backus Engineering.

It did not surprise me. I was no great beauty and only a man like Gideon could appreciate me for my other qualities—an overweening curiosity, excessive interest in the mechanics of anything, and so forth. Backus Engineering was successful in that we earned a better than average living, but as Gideon had pointed out, I was not and would likely never be on the Vanderbilt guest list. There were many other companies with far higher profit margins and prettier heiresses, if that was how Maurice Westham desired to make his fortune.

Dorset's one hotel was filled with out of town guests, including Gideon's family. He had stayed there with them last night as a hand wave to propriety. I had helped the housekeeper move Gideon's things into my room—our room, how strange that would be! And Elizabeth had moved to his suite. She was part of our household now, and this was the solution we three had worked out, over Elizabeth's protestations. Now, she had privacy if she wished to have her paramour stay with us during one her visits from Paris.

I forced myself to take my time with my bath and toilette, and forced myself again to break my fast with outward calm. That lasted for all of five minutes, between Elizabeth and Hannah's excited exchanges. I ate very little for my stomach was a knot of anxiety I had not expected. I thought the anxiety of a bride came from not knowing what to expect on her wedding night, and I knew exactly what to expect and looked forward eagerly to it, yet I was anxious all the same.

My mother's wedding dress—I was overwhelmed again by Elizabeth's foresight and thoughtfulness—had been turned into a much lighter gown suited for the current fashion and the extra fabric that had comprised the large bustle and train had allowed for two bodices—this sleeved confection suited for the modesty required of a woman on her wedding day and an evening bodice cut so daringly the innocence of the dusty pink was an illusion shattered.

I wished my father was here to see this. I know he'd despaired of me finding a husband, being so masculine in my pursuits and plain in countenance. I wondered if he would have approved of this match. Or maybe he had hoped for it all along, making Gideon his heir. "If you're up there, Papa—if there's an up there to watch from—I hope you're proud," I whispered to my reflection as Elizabeth did my hair.

"He would be, Charlotte. He always wanted you to follow your heart, whether it led you to gears and grease or a man like Gideon Lyons."

Elizabeth's encouraging words pushed aside the obscuring cloud on my anxiety. It all seemed too good to be true. "Too good to be true," I said softly, my fingers twisting in my lap.

"Nonsense. You and Mr. Lyons have traveled a hard road to get here. Too good to be true is a prize unearned. This, you both deserve."

I smiled at her reflection in the mirror. "You know me so well."

She returned the smile, resting her hands lightly in my shoulders. "This is normal. Even for, ahem, experienced brides. You should have seen my mother at her third wedding."

Elizabeth engaged my help to ready herself, which she did not need, maintaining a running discourse of distractingly cheerful small talk. I was settled into the passenger seat of the steam car almost before I realized what was happening.

Being June, the car warmed up quickly, though we pulled the lap blanket across our knees as a matter of course to protect our gowns from the dust of travel. The church seemed full, but someone had kindly left a spot marked just for the car, and I jumped out all nerves and impatience as Elizabeth fussed with the vehicle. "Mr. Lyons certainly keeps this vehicle in efficient condition," she remarked, pulling on the hand brake and walking slowly around it.

"Must you only now pause to admire it?"

She grinned at me, and I realized she was deliberately provoking me. I gave a glare in return that I had little hope she would take as chastisement. Inside the church, now decorated in June flowers collected from local gardens, the pews were full. Suited shoulders, puffy sleeves and feathered hats in a rainbow array, all shifting at the sound of the door opening.

Mr. Montcalm had happily agreed to walk me down the aisle in my father's place, and I was glad of it. He was one of Father's oldest customers, and cheerfully recommended Backus Engineering to all his business peers. He came to us as he needed to upgrade, increase his business and change it to suit the market. I'd known him since I was twelve, due to my constantly being underfoot at the company. I was grateful for the honor he did me.

The organist played a run of keys to collect everyone's attention, then began to play Mendelssohn. My parents might have been married to this very tune, I thought. I stumbled as Mr. Montcalm and I followed behind Elizabeth, even though we were walking in a measured and dignified pace to befit the music. "I don't think I've ever seen you nervous, Miss Backus," he said, his voice little more than whisper.

I wanted to reply, smartly or shakily, but my jaw was tight and my throat dry. I nodded, which I'm not sure he could see, though he chuckled softly and patted my gloved fingers.

As Elizabeth moved aside to stand as my witness, I could see almost every face turned to look at me, except of course Gideon. His head was bent slightly forward, at an angle, as if he were listening for my approach. He probably was, able to judge my passage by the rustle of gown. His hair looked almost tidy, perhaps by his mother's hand. He looked so handsome and something fluttered inside, heart or stomach—nerves. Finally we were there, side by side, and Gideon touched my arm, though if it was for my reassurance or his, I know not. The pastor gave a disapproving look that Gideon was happily unaware of and I ignored.

Reverend Brewer cleared his throat and began to speak, his every word increasing my nervousness. When he asked, in the traditional manner, if anyone knew a just and legal cause why we should not be married, it left me no more or less nervous than any other part, until a familiar voice shattered the rhythms of tradition with a resounding, "Yes!"

Every head in the church turned, and Gideon tensed, his mouth tightening into ferocity.

"Miss Charlotte Backus has a prior engagement to me!" Maurice Westham strode down the aisle amidst gasps of astonishment that turned to horrified silence as he pulled a pistol from his waistcoat. "I do beg your pardon, Rev. Brewer," he said, his calm voice making the pistol all the more frightening. "I had not intended it should ever come to this. It grieves me to kill a man in this sanctuary and then demand a wedding immediately afterwards, but it is hardly my fault." He pointed the pistol at Gideon and his amiable tone grew cold. "As much as I'd like to blame you, Lyons, for not dying the first time I sabotaged the lab boiler, I'm afraid the fault belongs more fairly to Miss Backus."

A cold such as I had never known descended on me at his words. Suspicions I had hesitated to entertain because they were so awful were now confirmed. Maurice had killed my father, and Gideon had been meant to die with him. In the shocked silence, Maurice inclined his head to me, pistol still aimed with steady hand at Gideon. "Or perhaps the person truly at fault is your father—if he hadn't left half his company to Lyons, none of this," he waved his empty hand dramatically, "Would have been necessary."

His eyes gleamed with purpose, so driven that I could barely recognize that, as frightened as I was, what kept me from fainting as many another woman present had already done was not any strength of character I possessed, but an underlying need to understand. Before I could ask for an explanation, Rev. Brewer cleared his throat and said calmly, "Mr. Westham, perhaps you could put that pistol away and we could discuss this—"

"Oh no, kind sir, the time for discussion is long past. I will have what is mine by right, I will be denied no longer."

"By right?" Gideon's voice held an echo of my anger and loss, but I heard no fear in him.

Maurice's expression darkened and, afraid I might lose Gideon forever, I willed myself to move, to put myself in front of Gideon. I meant to yell no, but my voice was caught.

"Charlotte, must you always get in the way? Every time I've tried to get rid of this ghastly cripple, you've gotten in the way. Then when he finally was so kind to put himself where you'd not get in the way, I couldn't find him."

Gideon found my shoulders and pushed past me. "Here I am."

"No, Gideon!" Desperate, I turned to Maurice. "Why are you doing this? For Backus Engineering?"

"You are such a silly woman, Charlotte. I care nothing for your father's company, nor you, nor even that you're whoring around with Lyons. Theodore Backus was in possession of something very valuable, something only he and Mr. Lyons here knew existed. Neither of them seemed able to comprehend just how valuable. The first problem is that it should have been mine. I stole those plans in the first place!"

"Plans—*you* stole them?" Gideon asked, disbelief in his voice.

I blinked in surprise, his words were so unexpected. Plans... stolen. "The Society of Engineers convention in New York, those plans? You..." Another piece of the puzzle was almost in place. "Hiram Clarke," I said recognizing the story. I stared at Maurice. "You're Hiram Clarke?"

He snorted delicately. "I'm not certain how you learned of that name. I've come to like being Maurice Westham, though I expect after this day, I shall need yet another identity. So tedious."

"Dr. Sheldon had no idea you'd changed your name, that's why he thought I'd recognize it."

He bowed sardonically in my direction. "Dr. Sheldon is an idiot. However, I can deal with him later. My plan—"

"The Tesla project," Gideon said wonderingly. "You want the Tesla project."

"Indeed. As a patent lawyer in Bangor, I saw every single patent Dr. Backus filed, and I knew that was my project, my fortune, and my glory. And there was only one way to get it. Kill the good doctor and marry his homely daughter. Boiler explosions are so common, who would question it? And no one did!" He glared at me. "But marrying the ugly daughter, that proved harder than I expected. You do realize, my dear, that your life expectancy after our wedding was always intended to be very short?"

Gideon took a step toward me and Maurice said, "Ah, ah, ah. Mr. Lyons, or I will shoot the lovely Miss Elizabeth. Or perhaps your noble mother. You were ungracious enough to survive the accident, and sadly I could not arrange another so soon after the demise of our Charlotte's beloved father," he said in mock sympathy. "Fortunately, you never told Charlotte about the Tesla project. Unfortunately you inherited half of Backus Engineering. I might have decided that fate had spared you and let you live but for that. I wanted everything that was due me, everything Dr. Backus denied me!"

"You were an errand boy," Gideon pointed out.

"I had a destiny!" His handsome features were distorted by rage, giving glimpse to the ugliness within.

Astonishment replaced much of my fear and as Maurice confessed his sins I grew aware once more that we were not by any means alone. Certain gentlemen in the church had taken it upon themselves to come quietly behind Maurice, but hesitated to do anything so long as his finger remained on the trigger. The doors had been opened, which I also had not noticed until now. Had someone been sent for, or were they quietly escorting people out?

"Maurice," I said quietly. "You've just confessed to a full church—do you really think you can get away with this?"

The hard, unwavering determination in his eye flickered uncertainly, as if he just realized what he'd done. He swung the pistol barrel from Gideon to me, and Reverend Brewer pushed

Gideon to the floor. Maurice snarled and fired at the pastor, missing in his anger, his steady hand no longer steady.

The noise of the shot, loud enough on its own, was amplified by the church's architecture. The bullet had struck the alter, splintering wood and shattering the hand-carved cross on the front. The noise or the sacrilege or both froze everyone, Maurice included, and we stood as useless as statues until Maurice emitted a startled yelp and suddenly fell back. Everyone sprang to life and several men pounced upon Maurice, while I realized with a panic that I couldn't see Gideon. Nor Elizabeth! Where had she gone? Reverend Brewer held me back from the tangle of people, "Let them sort it out, my dear."

And when I would have protested, I saw Elizabeth at the church doors with Dr. Sheldon and two strong orderlies from the asylum. Her eyes were wide as she took in the scene and she covered her mouth with her hands. What could she see from there that I couldn't see? "Gideon? Gideon!" Why didn't he answer?

"Dr. Sheldon! This way," directed a voice that sounded familiar—Mr. Montcalm?

As the muddle of bodies sorted itself out, two men pulled Maurice Westham to his feet. His handsome face was covered in blood and and his nose looked broken, his normally perfect mustache and hair were mussed and marred, and blood had dripped onto his pristine white shirt. As the two orderlies took hold him, one at each arm, Dr. Sheldon administered an injection that took any remaining fight from him. "I can hold him until the constabulary arrives from Bangor," he said, "And I assume charges will be filed?"

"Damn right," said a dear, familiar voice, and I was too happy to notice if there was any reaction to his cursing in church.

"Gideon!"

He pushed himself upright, his hair now properly mussed, his spectacles canted sideways across his face. I shook off Rev.

Brewer's restraining arm and knelt beside him. "It was you pulled him down?"

He nodded. "Then everyone jumped him, and I..." he adjusted his spectacles. "Was in the way."

Andrew Lyons pushed through the crowd and helped Gideon to his feet. "That was very well done, my boy."

Gideon, his face wary at the unanticipated accolade, nodded. I stepped back to allow Gideon some time with his family, too emotionally charged to feel more than a confused sadness for the lack of my own. Elizabeth, seeming aware of my distress, pulled me aside and fussed over my hair and dress until I was conscious enough to say, "Stop! What are you doing?"

She rounded behind me and pointed towards the altar. Mr. Lyons, Gideon, Mr. Montcalm, and Rev. Brewer were in deep conversation as the rest of the assembly remaining in the church buzzed with exclamations and condemnation of the unprecedented excitement. "I believe they are discussing whether or not to continue with the wedding. You should be prepared as I believe Mr. Lyons—your Gideon, that is—will insist."

I was unsure if she merely meant me to be prepared, or if she knew that a decision intimately involving me being made without my presence would pull me fully into the here and now. We'd known each other so long, it was likely both. Annoyed at being left out, I shouldered my way into the circle of discussion. "Excuse me," I said, "does this conversation concern me?"

"Charlotte, there you are, good," said Gideon, a note of relief in his voice. "Tell these gentlemen—no. I would like to know, do you wish to proceed with the wedding or would you prefer to postpone it for a less, hmm, adventuresome day?"

My first impulse was to postpone. My emotions had been wrung out, and I felt like something a good strong drink or two might fix. The men were waiting expectantly for my answer. I drew a steadying breath. "Well," I began slowly. "It has certainly been...

exciting. But it seems like we're all here, and ready. And I certainly..." I stopped. I'd been about to say I was looking forward to my wedding night, and I wondered how my discretion had nearly been lost. "I would certainly be happy to continue," I said, finally. "Gideon? Rev. Brewer? Would that be permissible?"

Gideon held out his hand, and I took it. Suddenly I wanted nothing more than to be held in his arms and this wedding could not be over fast enough. "Rev. Brewer?" Gideon said.

"Could we just pick up from where we left off?" I asked, my voice carrying a small tremble. Gideon squeezed my hand reassuringly, and I squeezed back.

The pastor had no need to give credence to Maurice's objection—he already knew most of the history behind our engagement and the manner in which it had been broken, both in private and at the ball. He considered the engagement to have never existed, given the duress under which it had been made. So he raised his voice as we resumed our places and called everyone's attention, asking them to please be seated. There was a ripple of nervous laughter and then Rev. Brewer completed the ceremony, naming us husband and wife in the eyes of God and the State of Maine. I flung myself into Gideon's arms. "I love you, Gideon Lyons."

"I love you, too. Charlotte Lyons." He bent his neck as if to kiss me and I let it fall on my forehead. I could feel his smile.

"I think we've given them enough to talk about today," I said softly.

"Today," he agreed, releasing me to take my arm.

We walked arm in arm out into the sunshine.

About the Author

Always a voracious reader, I became a writer to write the stories I couldn't find from other writers. I first started reading romance when I ran out of books to read and delved into my mother's stash, from Danielle Steele to Harlequins.

Historical romance seemed problematic to me, in that few stories were set in my favorite time periods, and so very many seemed to equate rape with love. *Imperfect Memories* is my response.

http://sbtales.weebly.com/
https://www.facebook.com/SydneyBee/

If you enjoyed this book, please leave a review!

www.ingramcontent.com/pod-product-compliance
Lightning Source LLC
Chambersburg PA
CBHW07072828O626
47159CB00023B/2860